VICTIM OF THE DEFENSE

Copyright © 2021 by Marianne Woolbert-Maxwell

All rights reserved.

No part of this publication may be reproduced, distributed or transmitted in any form or by any means, including photocopying, recording, or other electronic or mechanical methods, without the prior written permission of the publisher, except in the case of brief quotations embodied in critical reviews and certain other noncommercial uses permitted by copyright law.

Published by: Marianne Woolbert-Maxwell

ISBN: 9798527927276

CHAPTER ONE

Megan O'Reilly could see all the buildings housing the powerful of D.C. gleaming in the light of sunset. It was only five-thirty and red streaks mixed with pale pink and swatches of blue colored the sky.

She leaned back in the soft leather chair behind her desk and looked around her office on the 12th floor of the Tarkington Center. At 55 she was in her prime and ready to ascend to even loftier heights. Ten years ago she'd received the break of a lifetime when she was hired as an associate at the most prestigious firm in D.C.—Tarkington, Wagner, Kreig and DeVoe. One of the founding members, Arthur M. Tarkington, had been confirmed last year as a member of the U.S. Supreme Court. You couldn't get any higher on the legal food chain.

Before taking this job she had worked as a deputy prosecutor specializing in sex offense cases, making a name for herself as a tough prosecutor with the highest conviction rate in the office. Although there had been many guilty verdicts, there were some losses too—those were what haunted her. No matter how long and hard she prepared for a case there always seemed to be something she felt she could have done better. Normally the small oversights didn't make that much difference. Until the Lisa Garrett case, the case that haunted her to this day.

Megan had earned her keep at Tarkington et al. from the moment she was hired. She had handled their smaller cases and worked endless hours, slowly inching her way up the food chain. In addition, she'd donated substantial time to keeping a "presence in the community," representing the firm on various boards and participating in community activities. She'd known that in time it would all pay off and her days would no longer be spent toiling away. And now the time had come.

Someone tapped on her office door. She looked up and saw Craig Tarkington standing in the doorway. Craig Tarkington was a young lawyer who had recently passed the bar and been hired by the firm, not because of his outstanding qualifications but because his grandfather was Supreme Court Justice Arthur Tarkington, founding partner of the firm. Craig Tarkington was tall, broad shouldered, and long limbed. When he sat down it was as if he had to fold himself up to get into the chair. People liked him because he was well spoken and charming. Megan had liked him too when they first met. But he harbored a sense of entitlement that got in the way of any warm feelings she had for him once she got to know him.

What she saw when she looked at him in this moment was the brass ring she had been working towards for years. All new lawyers starting out at the firm were assigned someone higher up to teach them the ropes, usually a seasoned attorney whose next step was becoming partner.

They trained their replacement and then left the fledgling in the nest while they soared to the ethereal realms of the top floor. This was her sign she was on her way to the top—Craig Tarkington. She beamed at him.

"Have a seat," she said, motioning toward one of the leather chairs in front of her desk. Craig lowered himself into the chair and placed his folded hands in his lap.

To date, Megan had spent countless hours showing him the ropes and having him shadow her in court and meetings. Now he was ready to go on his own and so was she—although no one had announced her promotion yet. She knew it was just a matter of time.

Craig looked around her office as if he was studying the layout and all the changes he would make when it was his. Before she could say anything he reached into his jacket pocket, pulled out a robin's-egg-blue envelope, and slid it across the desk. "For you," he said, flashing his perfect capped-tooth smile.

Megan opened the envelope and pulled out the card inside. A $500 gift certificate to Tiffany's. "Oh, thank you so much," she said. "So, do you have any questions for me? Monday will be your first day." She slid open her desk drawer and placed the gift card inside.

Craig wasn't a bad guy, she thought, just full of himself. The real world of law would smooth all his rough edges.

He leaned back in the chair and crossed his long legs. "No, I'm ready," he replied.

They said their goodbyes and Megan stood and watched him leave the office. Once the door closed she turned and looked again through the large wall of windows in front of her desk. Dusk was settling in. Street lights were flickering on and headlights dotted the streets. Life was good.

Now it was 7:30 a.m. on Monday morning two weeks later and she was sitting in the waiting room of the managing partner, Chase Langley's, office. She'd hardly slept all weekend, tossing and turning, running over in her mind what she would say when she accepted the new promotion in front of all the partners in the firm. That's how they did it: All the partners gathered in the boardroom on the 6th floor, they announced and awarded the new partnership, and there were speeches and congratulations all around.

The phone buzzed on the secretary's desk across the room. The young woman took the call, hung up and rose from her chair. "Ms. O'Reilly, Mr. Langley is ready to see you."

Megan followed her to a set of large mahogany doors. The secretary opened one of the doors and motioned for her to enter. Megan looked down at the floor, gathering herself, took a deep breath and entered the room. She looked up and flashed her best and most confident smile.

She felt her breath catch. There was no one there but Chase Langley, seated in a leather chair at the very end of what seemed like the longest table she had ever seen. The room felt huge, hollow, and cavernous.

"Megan, come in, have a seat." Langley pulled out a chair on his left and motioned for her to sit down. He was fifty and had managed the business of the firm for over twenty years. He had a commanding presence and was very exact in how he spoke. "How are you?" he said flashing a frozen smile.

Megan sat down and smoothed out her skirt. Her throat was so dry it felt like there was a clutch of sticks stuck in it. She forced a smile. "Just fine."

A manila folder was on the table in front of him. Megan briefly considered the possibility that the other firm members were coming late. Maybe they had a meeting. Business was business after all. But in her heart she knew that wasn't why they weren't here.

Langley leaned back in the chair and adjusted the half glasses resting on his nose. She could feel his energy shift. "As you know, Megan, times change and people move on. We've been having meetings on where the firm is going—and has to go—to be competitive. Even though we're at the top of the game," he paused and smiled, "you can never rest on your laurels."

Megan looked down at her hands folded in her lap and then back at Langley.

"The bottom line is, we're making some changes to keep competitive and fresh." He paused and took off his glasses and placed them on the table. "You've been a great employee and we appreciate all you've done for the firm."

Here it comes, Megan thought. She took a slow, deep breath. The air between them was filled with awkward silence.

Slowly, Langley opened the file. "The partners have all voted and it appears that we need to downsize." His voice was soft, almost inaudible.

Megan leaned toward him. She felt her stomach tighten. Her heart was thumping in her chest like a piston.

"The firm needs to take a different direction." Langley looked away. "I'm sorry, Megan," he said haltingly. "We need to let you go."

CHAPTER TWO

Megan looked around the coffee shop and snapped open her laptop. Her finger skated across the mouse pad and notes on the discrimination lawsuit appeared on the screen. She scrolled down through the pages.

It had been almost five months since she had been let go from Tarkington, Wagner, Kreig and DeVoe. She had sent out many resumes and heard nothing. It was clear that she wasn't going to be hired by another law firm, at least not one she would want to work for. She had thought about it long and hard and decided that, despite certain risks, a reasonable course of action would be to sue the firm for age discrimination. She'd asked four other women to meet with her: Kate Williams and Christie Charles, both in their mid-fifties, who had been lawyers with the firm for thirty years, and Lisa Remy and Jill Sandefur, paralegals with the same amount of time, both in their early sixties. All of them had been axed in the last four months, after she was.

When they met in Megan's house they'd all said the same thing: They had all been top producers and none of them had ever had any complaints lodged against them or discipline issues; the firm had told them it was downsizing and changing directions; they, also, hadn't been able to get new jobs. Megan had thrown out the idea of suing the firm, and after kicking around the pros and cons for a while, mostly the cons—the difficulty of proving age discrimination, the fact that the firm would fight like bearcats, as Jill said—they had decided to proceed anyway.

By law they had to file a claim with the EEOC and then wait for it to do an investigation, consisting of interviewing all witnesses on both sides and reviewing submitted documentation. After days of work, they had all the relevant materials as well as a sworn affidavit from each of them describing how they had been discriminated against by the firm because of their age. They felt fairly hopeful that the agency would rule in their favor. But the commission had responded by saying they had thoroughly reviewed the matter and found no probable cause to support a claim that the Defendant discriminated against Plaintiffs. The women filed a request for a Review of the Decision, which they could do according to the rules, and shortly thereafter received another letter telling them that their claim was denied. At that point they had felt that they had no other choice but to file suit. The firm had responded with endless reams of paperwork. It seemed that their questions were endless and demanding of detail.

Megan adjusted the computer and settled back in the chair. To be as inconspicuous as possible she had chosen to sit at the back of the coffee shop. She read through a set of questions on the computer screen, making notes on the laptop.

"Excuse me," someone said. Megan looked up. A young woman with shoulder-length blond hair was standing beside her table, looking at her nervously. "I'm sorry to bother you," the young woman said. "Aren't you Megan O'Reilly?" A small smile etched its way across her face.

"Yes, I am," Megan said, extending her hand.

"I thought so. I saw your picture in the paper a long time ago after you won a big case involving a judge. He was accused of a sex crime against one of his staff." The young woman extended her hand. "I'm Lucy Hatfield. May I talk to you?" Her eyes darted around the room. "If it's a bad time I can do it later. I see you're busy."

Megan shook her hand. "Please, have a seat."

"I'm not sure where to begin. I need this to be confidential. I mean in the attorney-client way. I need legal advice. I'm happy to pay you for it." Lucy reached for her purse.

"Don't worry about that now," Megan said. "Let's see if I can even help you."

Lucy set the file she was holding down on the table. Megan could feel her nervousness. Something about her triggered a memory in Megan. She wasn't sure what it was and then it came to her: Lucy Hatfield reminded her of Lisa Garrett. Young and scared. She could still see Lisa on the witness stand being attacked by a criminal defense attorney. The attorney used every tactic he could to make her look like she was the horrible person instead of the victim of a rape.

Lucy sighed. "I was studying for the bar exam with a group of people. One of them –a man—asked me to tutor him. I needed the extra money."

Megan nodded. Here it came: The real reason Lucy Hatfield reminded her of Lisa Garrett.

"Things were okay for a while." She cleared her throat. "One evening he asked me to do the tutoring at his apartment. He said that we needed to meet at his place because a friend was dropping off some law books that belonged to him and he didn't want to leave them sitting in the hallway because they were so expensive."

Megan knew where this was going. She felt something tighten inside her. "Was that concerning to you?"

Lucy nodded. "A little. We had always met at the library. I thought about canceling and asking him to meet at the library the next morning but I didn't."

Megan shifted in her seat. She could feel that Lucy's pain was raw and deep. She felt her own emotions stir, like a sleeping dog waking.

"When I got to his apartment he was okay." Lucy stopped and looked at Megan. "Soon after that he became flirty with me. I brushed it off. We sat down on the couch. I opened the book where we had left off and he flipped the book shut and asked if I would like a drink." She paused. "I told him I didn't drink."

Megan nodded, her heart continuing to sink.

"I could tell he had been drinking before I got there. He wasn't drunk. But I could smell it on him." Lucy let out a sigh. "It just got real bad, real fast."

"He came on to you?" Megan asked.

Lucy nodded. "I told him I wasn't interested and unless he wanted to study I would be leaving. It made him mad. Real mad. Before I knew it he was all over me." Tears trickled down her face. "He threw me on the floor and pinned me down. He raped me."

Lucy was visibly shaking. Megan was shaking inside as well. She'd heard this story many times during her years as a prosecutor and she never got used to it. "Listen, you don't have to go through any more particulars now. I get the picture and I believe you." She placed her hand on Lucy's arm and kept it there until Lucy looked up at her.

"Thank you," she said softly. "I ended up pregnant and had a little girl. She is not quite two years old. The doctors think she might have cystic fibrosis. That's why I need your help. I'd like to sue this guy who raped me for financial help with her medical costs. He has plenty of money."

Lucy told Megan she had gone to the hospital and given a statement to the police the night of the rape. "The police called me a few times afterwards and said they were referring the case to the prosecutor's office for review. That was the last I heard from anyone."

"I know cops drop the ball at times and do political favors, but in this situation I don't know how they could do nothing." Megan shook her head.

"They did all the paperwork and talked to me but in the end they never followed up and I never heard back from the prosecutor's office. I think it's because of who he is."

Megan shrugged. "He was a law student."

"He was a connected law student," Lucy said.

"Regardless, he can't get away with raping a woman." Megan could feel her face flushing. She hadn't been this mad since she had worked in the prosecutor's office handling sexual assault cases. "So who is this asshole? I'll be happy to take him on." She leaned back against the booth and crossed her arms, her gaze fixed on Lucy.

"His name is Craig Tarkington."

CHAPTER THREE

Megan tossed the file bed and cast a glance at the clock. Two a.m. She had been reading Lucy's file and she felt sick. It was worse than she had even imagined. A violent and degrading act had been committed against an innocent woman, by a rich boy who would not be told no. Lucy had tried to fight him but he was too strong. And that rich boy was Craig Tarkington, the very young pup she'd trained to be a practicing lawyer in the firm that had employed her for ten years. *And* his grandfather was a Supreme Court justice.

She threw her legs over the side of the bed. Sleep would not be coming soon. She put on her house slippers and robe, walked over to her balcony, and eased the door open. It was a beautiful, quiet spring night. She lowered herself into a chair on the balcony, closed her eyes, and felt the breeze wash over her.

In all the weeks she had spent training Craig Tarkington at the law firm to take over her job, she would have said he was too careful to do something like this. From her dealings with him, Tarkington was motivated by the desire to make people like him. She had noticed he made a point of giving little gifts to everyone in a position to help him, a gift certificate or maybe just a handwritten note. Just something to add a small final touch to make sure they had a good impression of him. It appeared he was sincere but it also seemed that maybe he wasn't as self assured as he liked to portray. She also knew that he was a self-absorbed rich kid and he had plenty of women who would sleep with him just because of his name. Forcibly attacking a woman, leaving her battered, bruised and bloody, seemed like it wasn't his style. But Megan didn't know him that well. She didn't want to see him in that light. Much to her surprise she'd liked Tarkington—up until now.

Megan supposed there might be a chance that Lucy was lying, although if that was true she would have to be a tremendous actress. But instinctively Megan knew she was telling the truth. Megan had seen this many times and recognized what someone who had been raped looked like. If Megan decided to take on her case and mount a civil suit that would help Lucy get the money she needed to raise her child, she knew she would have to approach the situation carefully. Craig Tarkington, well-connected lawyer, grandson of a Supreme Court justice, accused of raping a woman and getting her pregnant would be explosive front page news if the suit couldn't be settled quietly out of court.

The firm had already been battered by press coverage of the lawsuit against them for wrongful termination. If the civil suit went to trial—and that was a big if, because it would most likely be settled out of court—but if it did go to court, the firm would send their army of lawyers to protect Tarkington and the firm itself, to protect Justice

Tarkington's reputation, and to destroy Lucy. Their public relations division would be in high gear. They would try to discredit Megan and Lucy any way they could.

Megan sat listening to the silence, contemplating what would probably happen if for some reason Tarkington didn't settle and she braved the firm with this case. She pictured it all, the negative publicity, the endless depositions, possible professional ruin for her. But then she remembered Lucy Hatfield.

Megan took a deep breath. She would take this case. It would be hard but she was ready for whatever happened. She had her own reasons for wanting to take it on—reasons she'd been trying to put out of her mind ever since she stopped being a prosecutor and took the job at Tarkington ten years ago.

She went inside, found a pad of paper and a pen, sat down at the small writing desk in her bedroom and began making notes. The best way to approach Lucy's case would be to set up a meeting with Craig Tarkington. It wouldn't be at the office—that was for sure. Despite the age discrimination lawsuit, she thought he would agree to meet. If he didn't, she would be happy to feed him vague tidbits of information that would change his mind.

CHAPTER FOUR

Tarkington had been surprised when she called him. After basic pleasantries she told him she had something she wanted to talk to him about and suggested they meet at Reggie's, a bar and grill on the south side of DC. It wasn't a place where the elite dined, and that was why she suggested it. Tarkington had initially sounded hesitant but agreed to meet.

Megan arrived first and located a booth in the back corner. It was a Tuesday night and the place wasn't very full. She slid into the booth and waited. Before long she saw him come in and waved. Not much had changed. He still looked meticulous: expensive suit, nice tie, good haircut.

"Are you trying to get me killed?" he said sliding into the booth. "This place is a dive."

He laughed and cast a glance around the room.

"Well, it's not the Ritz," Megan said with a smile.

"May I get you a drink while you look at the menu?"

Tarkington looked up at the young waitress.

"Scotch please." He flashed his bright white smile, and then turned his attention to Megan. "So how are you? You know I could lose my job for being seen with you. "He leaned back in the booth and smoothed his tie. At eight p.m. he still looked crisp. Not a wrinkle to be found in his Italian suit.

"I'm fine," Megan said. She took a sip of her Coke. "Things are moving along."

"You know I can't talk about your lawsuit against the firm," Tarkington said.

The waitress drifted up to the table and set his drink down. He smiled at her.

"I'm not here to talk about that," Megan said laughing.

"You know I hate what happened to you and I wish I could help...." His voice trailed off.

Megan looked at him, remembering how he hadn't even glanced in her direction when she passed him while being escorted by security out of the firm after she was fired. Really, she wasn't surprised. Most of the lawyers she knew at the firm were pretty self absorbed. They knew you when you were on top but if anything happened to sully your reputation they distanced themselves from you as if you had a contagious disease. They were all striving to make it to partner and wouldn't let anything or anyone tarnish their efforts to get there.

"How have you been?" Megan asked, trying to make small talk.

"Great." Tarkington flashed his biggest and brightest smile yet. " So what's going on with you? I was surprised to hear from you." He rolled the scotch in his glass and took another sip.

"I have a woman who contacted me." She felt her stomach tighten.

"New business?" Tarkington asked. "That's great." He raised his glass in the air and nodded.

Megan paused. "It's a pretty serious situation," she said. "I wanted to talk to you about it for a variety of reasons. Hopefully something can be resolved."

"What type of case is it? Are you wanting my help? I can't work with you because of the lawsuit but you could refer her to me." Tarkington set his glass down on the table.

" It's a combination of things," Megan said, shifting in her seat. "Part paternity and some potential for a criminal and civil action."

Tarkington waved his hand in the air dismissively. "I don't do that type of law. You know that, Megan. She needs one of those two-bit ham-and-egg attorneys downtown. Not a guy like me."

Megan could tell he had lost all interest in the conversation.

"She says she knows you."

"Has the firm helped her out in other matters?"

Megan shook her head. " She knows you—personally. Her name is Lucy Hatfield."

Craig caught the eye of the waitress and held up his glass. He didn't look at Megan.

" This is a rather sensitive subject and I hope you understand that I'm trying to help a client—and you," Megan said.

Tarkington looked at her. "So far I'm at a loss," he said his expression flat.

Megan could tell he was uncomfortable. She knew him well enough to see that his smooth veneer had a small crack.

"So far, this seems like a waste of my time," he said. The waitress appeared and placed his drink on the table. He grabbed it and took a sip and then reached into his jacket pocket and pulled out his phone to check the time.

"You know, I'm a busy guy, Megan. Not sure where this is heading but it doesn't sound like anything I'm interested in." He leaned back and crossed his arms. "Cut to the chase."

Megan felt anger building inside her. "No problem," she said. She leaned across the table and looked him straight in the eye. "Lucy Hatfield says she was in a study group with you to prepare for the bar exam and one night you raped her." She could see Tarkington's jaw tighten. He broke eye contact with her and looked around the room. "She got pregnant and had a little girl. Your daughter." Megan paused.

Tarkington remained stone faced. A small vein protruded from his forehead. She could feel his anger.

"She needs your help. Your daughter has some medical issues and needs your financial support."

Tarkington slammed his fist down on the table. Megan jumped back. Heads turned and people stared. He leaned in towards Megan. " Listen to me," he said his voice low and cold. "How dare you make such an allegation against me." Quickly, he looked around the room to see if people were still staring. "I can't believe you called me here for this shit."

He ran his hand through his hair. "Is this who you think I am? You have some woman show up on your doorstep and tell you this bullshit and you believe her? Against me?" He pointed at his chest. "You forget who I am."

"Craig, listen."

"No, you listen. I've defended you at the firm. They say you aren't a good lawyer. That's why they fired you. "He paused and stared at her. "But now I see they're right. This proves it." He shook his head in disgust.

"This could be a criminal matter as well," Megan said quickly before his next explosion.

Tarkington leaned in closer to Megan. "You tell your little white trash client that I don't know her and I am sure as hell not the father of her kid." He stabbed his finger into the table as he spoke as if punctuating his words. "She needs to be clear on that. If she continues this extortion bullshit I will take her down." He paused. "And anyone who helps her." His eyes bore into Megan. "I don't know her," he said as if talking to a child. "Got that?"

Megan could see the rage in his eyes. He shot up from the booth and left.

CHAPTER FIVE

"May it please the court," Brockton Mattingly said. At six foot five inches, he towered above those seated in the courtroom. A long-time friend of the Tarkington family, he had been called to represent Craig Tarkington in the matter with Lucy. Brockton Mattingly was a senior lawyer at Devereaux, Winston, Mattingly and Rigaud. The large firm was known in D.C. legal circles for their high-powered attorneys and their political influence. They were among the chief supporters of Justice Tarkington's nomination to the Supreme Court. Brockton Mattingly had been with the firm for over 29 years and was a partner. He was known to be a formidable opponent in the courtroom and very knowledgeable about the law. The fact that he had been hired at this stage of the game—so far all Megan and Lucy had done was file a suit for paternity hoping that that would motivate Tarkington to settle—showed that Tarkington and the firm were taking this seriously. The paternity suit hadn't motivated Tarkington to settle. Megan wasn't surprised.

Megan and Lucy sat back and listened to Mattingly's opening remarks. Megan knew he would be long winded and really say little in the end. She looked at Lucy. She knew Lucy didn't like even being in the same room as Tarkington; this was the first time she had seen him since the rape. "My client objects to the paternity testing for a variety of reasons, Your Honor." Mattingly picked up his notepad and adjusted his half glasses.

Megan and Lucy looked at each other.

"My client does not feel that the agency the plaintiffs have chosen to conduct the testing is appropriate, Your Honor." Mattingly flipped through the pages on his legal pad. "It appears there have been various complaints filed by individuals who have employed this company claiming improper testing procedures and incorrect results." He paused and cleared his throat.

"Ms. O'Reilly?" Judge Kendall said.

"Judge." Megan stood up. "Camden Labs has had some complaints filed against it but they have all been dismissed or resolved. They are still considered one of the best in the field."

Judge Kendall looked back to Mattingly.

"Nevertheless, Judge, my client has concerns. There have been complaints filed and that does say something."

Judge Kendall folded his hands and peered down his nose at Mattingly.

"Mr. Mattingly, are you saying that any company who has a complaint filed against it is suspect and should be immediately ruled out?"

Mattingly shifted from one foot to the other. "No, Judge. I 'm just saying that we must give close scrutiny to any blemish a company may have."

Judge Kendall sighed. "Unless there is something huge here that I'm missing I'm not sure why we're having this discussion. It looks to me like the company has had some issues but they have all been resolved and the company is clear." He scratched his head. "Am I missing something, counsel?"

"You're assessing it correctly, Judge," Megan said, rising from her chair. "The company has a high rating and is respected in the legal community."

"Request to change the paternity testing company denied. What else do you have, Mr. Mattingly? Is that it?"

Mattingly rifled through his paperwork. "Judge, there is one thing that just came to our attention."

Megan felt her heart sink. "There's nothing else that Mr. Mattingly listed for hearing today, Judge."

Judge Kendall let out a sigh. "Well, we're here and this matter needs to get moving. What is it, counsel?"

Mattingly dug through his files and pulled out one sheet of paper.

"We have a technical issue, Judge."

Judge Kendall peered over his glasses at Mattingly.

"By statute, for paternity to be established an action must be commenced before the child's second birthday." Mattingly looked at Megan. "It appears that this action is too late. My research shows me that the child turned two on January 6th of this year. The action was commenced on January 10th. In light of that we ask that the matter be dismissed."

"Judge, this issue isn't scheduled for today and hasn't been mentioned until now." Megan could feel her insides churning.

"We are here, Ms. O' Reilly. Let's see what we can get done," Judge Kendall said. "If you need more time I'll consider that."

Megan could see Tarkington smiling. She grabbed her file and went through the papers, found the paternity petition and checked the filing date and Lauren's birthday. She found the calendar on her phone. The room fell silent. Megan leaned over and said something to Lucy. Lucy nodded.

Tarkington and Brockton smiled. Megan reached into her briefcase and pulled out a small book. She thumbed through it until she found what she was looking for.

Your Honor," she said standing. "I have addressed the issue before the court and in looking at the Rules of Procedure Rule 11 it would appear that we are timely filed with two days to spare. The rules provide that we do not count certain holidays and days recognized as holidays by the court when calculating time frames involving a statute of limitation." Megan went on to explain how she arrived at her calculation. As she finished she cast a glance over at Mattingly and Tarkington. Their smiles were gone.

Judge Kendall looked over at Mattingly. "Mr. Mattingly, the court has considered your requests and the evidence provided. Your requests are denied. Get your client to

Camden Labs in the next ten days for the paternity test. This matter needs to get moving. Court adjourned." Judge Kendall cracked the gavel.

CHAPTER SIX

"Take a look at that," Brockton Mattingly said, tossing a piece of paper in front of Megan.

She reached over and picked it up, studied it, then placed it back on the table.

"Tarkington isn't Dad." A smile etched its way across Mattingly's face.

Two weeks ago the paternity test had come back, establishing Tarkington as Lauren's father. Megan and Lucy had been ready to move on and get a hearing date but when they presented the results to Tarkington's lawyer, he demanded another paternity test—this one done by a company of Tarkington's choosing. Megan wasn't happy but she knew the court would allow the test since Tarkington was willing to pay for it. Megan had been confident the second set of results would be the same.

She looked at Mattingly's test sheet. There it was in black and white: Tarkington wasn't the father. "Not possible," she said pushing the paper across the desk towards Mattingly. "You people probably had this printed up by someone." She leaned over and looked at it again. "I don't recognize the testing company."

Mattingly walked around his desk and sat on the edge. He picked up the paper and held it out in front of her. "*Subject is not the father of the child.*" He dropped the paper back on the desk.

Megan knew that with enough money you could buy someone who would say just about anything you wanted them to—but this was still a shock.

"Maybe your client needs to rethink her position." Mattingly rubbed his hand on his cheek and sighed.

Megan stood up. "I guess we're heading for a third test."

Mattingly laughed. "I don't think so. Tarkington isn't shelling out money to pay for yet another one." He shook his head. "We won't just keep testing until you get the result you want."

"Who said we're asking him to pay?" Megan shot back. Her eyes bore through him.

"Your client doesn't have the money to pay for another test," Mattingly scoffed.

"I'm filing a petition with the court for another test." Megan turned and started for the door.

"We'll object," Mattingly said, raising his voice. "No judge is going to play your game."

Megan turned and looked at him. "The judge isn't going to play *your* game, Mattingly." Before he could say anything she was gone.

Megan filed a petition for a third paternity test and Mattingly shot back with an objection. The judge who would hear this case was Dick Clouse. At 68 he had been on the bench for over forty years and ran his court with an iron fist. Five foot six and balding, brilliant minded but volatile, Judge Clouse had earned the reputation of being highly emotional and easily triggered by attorneys and their questioning of his rulings. Many people said he was not of judicial temperament but the political machine had put him in office. The really good lawyers had learned how to handle him.

At the hearing to request another paternity test, both Megan and Mattingly appeared without their clients and the hearing quickly turned into a storm of anger between the attorneys. Megan questioned the legitimacy of Tarkington's test and Mattingly argued that Tarkington's test was legitimate and it was Megan and Lucy's test that was faulty, both of them talking over each other. Judge Clouse banged his gavel repeatedly, demanding that the arguing stop or they both face contempt. After his last reprimand, Megan went silent and sat down. She could tell the judge was dangling from a very thin rope ready to slam one, if not both, of them with contempt of court.

Once the judge had regained control of the courtroom he slowly and clearly outlined his ruling, speaking in a firm tone as if he were speaking to children. "There will be another test and the parties will split the cost. The court will choose the company to conduct the test and the company will provide sealed results to the court. As part of this ruling, the parties are to submit in writing their objections and concerns regarding the first two paternity tests. The company chosen by the court will examine and critique the first two tests and render an opinion as to their validity and accuracy. This will all be done within sixty days of the court's order."

Before either attorney could say a word the judge marched off the bench.

CHAPTER SEVEN

"Come in," Megan said, opening her front door. Lucy closed her umbrella and came into the foyer. "Go on into the kitchen," Megan said. "I made a pot of tea." She took Lucy's umbrella and hung her coat on a hook in the front closet. It was the middle of February and a cold rain had been falling steadily for all day. "Thanks for stopping by."

In the kitchen Megan poured Lucy a cup of tea. A swirl of steam floated up from the cup.

"I figured I was coming this way so we might as well meet now." Lucy stirred some sugar into the hot drink and sat silently watching the white crystals disappear.

Megan sat down and poured herself a cup. "We have some time before the next paternity hearing. I want to be sure we have all your financial information. I've subpoenaed Tarkington's. Once we have it all I'll figure the child support, assuming he's legally declared Lauren's father." Megan opened the file in front of her. "We'll be asking that he carry insurance on Lauren and pay the cost associated with that." She checked off something on the list in front of her.

Lucy reached over and took a chocolate chip cookie from a plate. "That would be a godsend in and of itself."

It had been a long haul, but after what seemed like endless testing with inconclusive results the doctors at the children's hospital had finally determined that Lauren did in fact have cystic fibrosis. She was in the beginning stage of the disease and the doctors felt hopeful that with the appropriate treatment it could be managed. They were recommending different therapies and medications to help improve Lauren's breathing and hopefully slow down or stop the progression of the disease. Like all medical procedures, the treatments would be costly.

"Do you know how much of Lauren's treatment is currently not covered by government insurance?" Megan asked.

"No, but it's more than I can ever pay." Lucy ran her finger around the rim of the cup.

Megan could see the sadness in her eyes.

"Let's find out how many bills are outstanding. We'll be asking that Tarkington be responsible to pay them."

Lucy nodded.

Megan scribbled something on her legal pad. "He may want to claim the child for tax purposes."

Lucy looked up.

"The court usually awards the exemption to the person who'll get the most benefit from it. He'll get more benefit than you would because he's in a much higher tax bracket. I'm sure he doesn't need whatever money it will save him but he may take the exemption anyway just to spite you, so you don't get it."

Lucy had no income and was not in a position to even look for a job while Lauren was so sick. Because of this she'd had to apply for government assistance, including a few special programs for single mothers. What she received monthly barely met the basics but she got by.

Lucy lifted the cup to her lips, took a sip, gently placed the cup back in the saucer, and looked down at the table.

Megan paused. "What about visitation?"

Lucy's head shot up. "Visitation!"

Megan shrugged and let out a sigh. "He has a legal right to request that if he's declared the legal father."

"Do you think he'll want to see her?" Lucy crossed her arms.

Megan could see her jaw tighten. "No, but he could ask."

Lucy shook her head. "No visitation." She waved her hand in the air. "He doesn't even know her—hasn't even met her."

Megan saw tears welling in Lucy's eyes. "Just be prepared that it may come up." Megan could tell that Lucy was nowhere near ready to even consider this. She could feel the emotion in the air.

Megan closed the file. "Once the paternity is established—and we're pretty sure it will be—and I get all Tarkington's financial information from Mattingly, we can regroup. I know Craig is wealthy beyond our wildest dreams—the Tarkington's have millions if not billions in family money that goes back at least two generations when the great-great grandfather made a bundle with investments. The law firm alone must bring them at least a least million every year. Craig told me when I was training him that he had a good-size trust fund so he's not waiting to inherit. I should get the details when Mattingly responds to the subpoena, unless we settle first and Tarkington gives away all his rights to Lauren."

Lucy said nothing. She folded her napkin and placed it on the table. She picked up her phone and looked at the time. "I've got to run. I have to be back at the hospital at seven to talk to Lauren's doctor." She got up, headed toward the door, gathered her raincoat and umbrella and was gone.

CHAPTER EIGHT

Megan got the call exactly sixty days from the date of Judge Clouse's order for a third paternity test. The results were in and the court was prepared to move forward. A hearing was set for the following Monday, March 8th, at nine a.m. sharp. The parties and their respective counsels were ordered to appear.

Megan and Lucy arrived at the courthouse at eight-thirty am. They had left early, taking no chances they would be late. Mattingly and Tarkington arrived five minutes before nine. Megan could tell it upset Lucy to even be in the same room with Tarkington. Lucy fished her phone out of her purse and began checking emails and surfing the web, her jaw tight and her eyes squinting. Lucy hadn't seen Tarkington since the night he raped her and she had thought she would never see him again. Megan didn't blame her. That's what she would think too.

At nine o'clock sharp Judge Clouse walked onto the bench. Everyone shot up out of their chairs when he entered the courtroom.

"Be seated," he said, motioning for them all to sit down. He cast a glance at both parties. In his hand was a large manila envelope. "Ok, people. Here it is," he said waving the envelope. "And as you can see, it has not been opened."

He turned the envelope over and held it up so everyone could see it was still sealed. "Anyone question that it has not been opened?" He peered over his glasses at the parties and their attorneys.

"No," Megan and Mattingly said in unison.

Judge Clouse ran his hand over the top of the bench searching for something. "Here it is," he muttered, holding a letter opener. He sliced the envelope seal, reached in, and pulled out papers. The room fell silent.

Megan felt bolts of nervous energy daggering her stomach. She cast a glance at Lucy. She was barely breathing. Tarkington was looking down at the table. Mattingly was sitting with his pen poised to write down whatever the judge said, looking off into space as if lost in thought.

Judge Clouse handed the papers to the court reporter and the reporter hurried out of the courtroom. A few moments later she returned with a small stack of papers.

"Very well." Judge Clouse leaned forward and placed his hands on the bench. "The results are in. I have a copy for both counselors and their respective clients." He read his own copy of the paper, peered over the top of his glasses, and looked first at Mattingly, then at Megan. "According to the court's chosen testing company, Mr. Tarkington is 99.9 determined to be the father."

Lucy grabbed Megan's hand and squeezed it. Megan shot a glance at Tarkington. She could see the color drain out of his face.

The judge continued. "The court's chosen company examined the previous tests and believes that the first test, which also established Mr. Tarkington as father, was correctly done, but the second one had procedural and testing defects. The current findings and how they were arrived at are specifically spelled out in the letter sent with the new results. You can read it all in the copies the court has made for you." Judge Clouse laid two small stacks of paper on the edge of the bench. The court reporter stepped down from her seat and took the copies to each lawyer.

"The court will contact you shortly for further hearing on support and other paternity matters." The judge stood and walked off the bench.

Megan and Lucy jumped up and hugged each other.

Tarkington and Mattingly walked silently out of the courtroom.

CHAPTER NINE

"Listen, Chadwick, you've been stalling me for weeks." Megan said angrily. She cast a quick glance at the clock on the wall. She had been home only twenty minutes and had hoped to relax. Instead she was in a fight with Richard Chadwick, the attorney for her old law firm. It had been more than a month that she had been trying to take depositions of the witnesses the firm had listed they would call to testify against her in the wrongful termination case. Chadwick had done everything in his power to block her from taking their statements. Megan knew the game he was playing. The time had come to play hardball. She would take no more of his reasons and excuses why a witness couldn't appear on a date she chose to depose them or why that day wouldn't work for him.

"I'm going to petition the court for an order forcing your witnesses to let me take their depositions. I'm not playing any more games." Megan could feel her blood pressure rising. "Here's the bottom line, Chadwick, subpoenas for the witnesses are going out today with a new deposition date. I'm including another copy of the subpoena requesting they bring any material supporting their testimony. Get your people here on the new date and have them prepared to be deposed or this will get real ugly, real fast."

Megan could hear Chadwick rattling away as she pushed the end call button on the phone.

She leaned back in her chair and closed her eyes. It seemed like their case kept taking one step forward and ten back.

The doorbell rang. She got up and headed to the front door.

"Eric! Just the person I want to see."

"When I got your message I knew it was important."

Eric Covington had an extensive background in police work on both the local and state level and had spent twenty years working for the FBI. Five years ago he had retired and started his own private investigator agency. He was known far and wide as the best in the business. Megan had known him for at least twenty years, since she started out working in the prosecutor's office. They had briefly dated about fifteen years ago but somehow the romance fizzled out. Megan suspected it was her fault; back then she was just too overwhelmed by working on cases day and night to be anyone's girlfriend. Sometimes she caught Eric looking at her a certain way and wondered if he might still have feelings for her. And every now and then she caught herself wondering what it would be like if something happened between them. Neither of them had ever married and he was a good-looking man. But something stopped her from doing anything about it—maybe shyness, maybe the long-standing habit of being single. Also, she worried about ruining their professional relationship. Eric had an uncanny ability to read people and could analyze criminal cases better than anyone.

He followed her into the living room and sat down on the couch.

Megan flopped down in an overstuffed chair.

"I want to hire you."

"Is this about the suit you have against your former law firm? I told you years ago they were assholes." Eric laughed.

"Every time I try to depose these people I get blocked. Richard Chadwick is the firm's attorney and he always has some excuse about why the deposition dates I have won't work with his calendar or the witness is out of town that day." Megan ran her hand through her hair.

Eric smiled. "So, do these witnesses really exist?"

"They're legit. I know them. From what I saw and what my gut is telling me, the firm didn't think this case would go—especially after we lost at the agency level. Losing there was a blow." Megan shook her head. "When I didn't drop the case they had to round up these people for me to depose. "

"So the bottom line is, you called their bluff and they didn't think you would." Eric leaned forward and rested his elbows on his knees.

"Pretty much."

"So you want me to track their witnesses down and see what, if anything, they will say."

Megan smiled and handed him a manila file folder. "Here are all their names and information. I even found photos from the firm office directory."

Eric flipped open the file and scanned the material. He tapped the file on Megan's leg. "Consider it done."

"There's one more matter I need to talk to you about," Megan said. She told him the whole story about Lucy Hatfield, about the rape, about Lucy's daughter Lauren being recently diagnosed with cystic fibrosis and how Lucy had hired her to file suit against Tarkington.

"I want you to do a background check on Lucy and see what comes up. Tarkington's lawyer will be working overtime to find some dirt on her." Megan handed Eric a piece of paper with all of Lucy's information. "I can't take any chances. I'd be surprised if she has anything but I'd rather be safe than sorry."

Eric folded the piece of paper and put it in his jacket pocket. "You and I have been in the business long enough to know you take nothing for granted."

"I'd also like you to do a thorough background check on Tarkington. Has he had any other problems with women? Assaults? Check him out across the board. Who knows what we may find."

"Is Lucy planning to go to the prosecutor and see about bringing criminal charges?"

"I doubt it will come to that. So far we're focusing on establishing his paternity and mounting a civil suit to get financial support for Lucy and Lauren. There are going to be huge medical bills throughout Lauren's life because she has cystic fibrosis. We're just beginning what will probably be a long journey. For now let's see if you can dig up anything on Tarkington and if you find any surprises about Lucy. "Megan felt her stomach tighten. "I want to be sure I've covered every angle.

CHAPTER TEN

"I have spoken with my client about this matter," Brockton Mattingly said, leaning back in his chair.

Megan looked past him at the wall of windows behind his desk. She had been surprised when Mattingly had called and asked for a meeting. Not sure what to expect, she decided she would use this as an information-gathering meeting to see what was up with Tarkington.

"You know that your client..." Mattingly paused. "Well, she is not the most credible person." He smiled.

Megan looked him straight in the eye. "No, I did not know that. From all I see, she's a very credible person."

"Well, we have information that she has done this before—to rich guys."

Megan pulled her legal pad out of her briefcase and set it down on his desk. Could what he was saying be true? She decided he was probably blowing smoke to rattle her. Still, she felt glad she had asked Eric to look into Lucy's background. She clicked her pen and held it poised above the pad of paper. "If Lucy did this to someone else, who are these people? Name and full contact information."

Mattingly shifted in his chair. "I'm just saying she's not clean. In the event of litigation it may not be pretty. Tarkington is only her latest."

"I don't believe that for one minute, Mattingly. Tell me who they are and I will depose them."

Mattingly waved his hand. "Listen, I'm not here to show you all my cards. I'm here to be the voice of reason so this matter can get resolved and without dirtying the water. The point of this is to make you aware that Hatfield is not who you think she is."

Megan felt her insides churn and her face getting warm. She put the pen down on the table.

"Well, Tarkington will not let his name and reputation be sullied by someone like Hatfield. And we owe it to Justice Tarkington not to let his name be dragged through the mud."

Megan leaned forward. "Someone like Hatfield was raped by your Ivy League boy and now has a daughter who is lucky to be alive. She has some medical issues that will be quite expensive to treat and no good health insurance."

"This is going nowhere fast," Mattingly said angrily.

"My client and I will fight to the bitter end to get Tarkington to step up and be a dad," Megan said. "This poor little girl needs help and he has the money to give it to her." She leaned in and placed her hands on the edge of his desk. "The bottom line is, your client isn't a saint and we can prove that quite easily. Why did you ask me to come here today? Unless you have something important to say you're wasting my time." Megan got up and started putting her legal pad and file folder in her briefcase.

Mattingly took a deep breath. "I called you here to discuss a proposed settlement that could benefit all of us and avoid a blood bath."

Megan stopped putting things in her briefcase.

"My client is willing to give your client fifty thousand dollars in full settlement of any claim she may have against him in this matter and he will sign away all his rights to the child. In exchange your client will sign a confidentiality agreement and state that the rape never occurred and she made a false report and Tarkington will waive any rights he has to sue her for defamation of his character and this little debacle will go away." Mattingly smiled and leaned back in his chair.

"Fifty thousand?"

"That's right. Immediately."

"Do you know how much medical expense this little girl has and will have in the future?" She avoided looking at Mattingly and went back to putting things in her briefcase. "Fifty thousand wouldn't even scratch the surface."

"It's fifty thousand she doesn't have now and it's gratis without a big court battle that could hang your client out to dry—not to mention sully her reputation when the truth comes out."

"Your client is the one who needs to worry about the truth coming out."

Mattingly leaned back in the chair, folded his arms behind his head, and smiled. "Take the offer to your client. She needs to understand how high the stakes are and what she has to lose. We have a lot on her. It will be a long and bloody battle. And Justice Tarkington will be watching."

Megan remembered why she didn't like Mattingly. She got up from the chair and headed toward the door.

"Megan."

She stopped, turned and looked at him.

"Let her know that if she wants this to go to court that we'll take no prisoners."

CHAPTER ELEVEN

"You've got to be kidding." Lucy leaned back in the booth and took a sip of her iced tea. She made a face. "Fifty thousand?"

Fifty thousand dollars wouldn't begin to touch Lauren's medical bills, those that already existed and those that would continue to rack up. The diagnosis of cystic fibrosis had come only after a battery of tests and hospitalizations. What at first had appeared to be a serious respiratory infection that would not clear up turned into gastrointestinal problems and significant weight loss. It was clear that Lauren had something major going on. Once the formal diagnosis was made the doctors started treatment. Medical science had made great strides in treating the disease but on-going treatment was costly. Lauren's condition had stabilized and she and Lucy were now living a more normal life. But she could get a lot sicker at any time.

"My thoughts exactly," Megan said. She pushed the manila file to the side of the table. She had known what Lucy's answer would be—and she agreed.

"That asshole has millions of dollars and wants to toss a pittance to his daughter and be free?" Lucy said.

Megan nodded. She had seen it before and Tarkington didn't surprise her.

The women sat in silence for several moments.

"What's next?" Lucy said softly.

"Well, we can make a counter offer."

Lucy stopped eating and looked at Megan. "Like what? It seems pretty obvious that we're nowhere near the same page as Tarkington." She shook her head.

Megan pushed the food around on her plate and cast a glance at the dining room. The Maadi was a Mediterranean restaurant popular with the locals and there wasn't a seat to be had anywhere. "Keep in mind we've just started negotiations. We don't even have to negotiate. We can just take it before the court." Megan paused and leaned forward. "You do have the upper hand. Where are you at on bringing a criminal rape charge?"

Lucy said nothing.

"You hold the trump card, Lucy. Tarkington can't risk that you'll go to the prosecutor. Let's put it this way. If Tarkington doesn't do right by you and Lauren, he risks you requesting criminal charges be filed against him." She could see Lucy's expression brighten. "It's called leverage. Tarkington is between a rock and a hard place. But if we bring it to court at this point—if you file charges now—you might lose your chance of negotiating a big out-of-court settlement. If Tarkington goes on trial for rape the gloves will be off and they won't be interested in settling. So better try to settle now and get the money, since that's what you really need."

"I hate to see him get away with what he did to me. But Lauren's medical expenses…." Lucy paused. "Not to mention future expenses. In any case, $50,000 is ridiculous. That won't even cover the medical bills we've already incurred."

"They've come up some." It was a week later and Megan was sitting on the couch in Lucy's apartment. Lucy's face showed no emotion. Megan handed her a piece of paper. 'They're offering $150,000."

"$150,000?" Lucy looked at Megan.

"It's better than fifty but still...."

Lucy sighed and laid the paper down on the coffee table.

Megan popped the tab on her can of Coke. "They want to pay that and have you sign a confidentiality agreement. If you accept the offer you'll agree to tell no one that you had sex with Tarkington or that he fathered your child—so there will be no chance of filing criminal charges for the rape. And Tarkington will give up legal rights to Lauren." Tarkington had been threatening that if Lucy didn't settle this matter that he would insist on visitation and joint custody.

"So we'll be rid of Tarkington."

Megan nodded. "It's your call."

Lucy leaned back against the couch. Megan could see the emotion welling up inside her.

"His lawyer acted like I was breaking the bank getting this amount." Megan rolled her eyes. She picked up the file from the coffee table. "Is cutting a deal and getting a decent amount of money enough to make a difference with Lauren your priority? Even if it means letting Tarkington totally off the hook?" Megan tapped the end of the file on the coffee table and studied Lucy's face.

"I suppose so. Lauren is the priority." Lucy grimaced. "But I'm not exactly happy letting Tarkington get away with what he did to me. He ruined my life. Not because I have Lauren, I'd never want to not have her, but because of how I felt about myself after the rape. How I still feel about myself. I'd love to see him go to prison."

"That avenue is still open. But like we see here, with any agreement you take Mattingly and Tarkington will demand that the agreement say you won't press charges. Are you sure you're alright with that?"

Lucy swallowed hard. Megan could see her struggling with the decision.

"If I don't press charges he'll be a rapist at large, who knows who else he'll harm. And he'll end up with a great life with all that money and prestige and I'll have nothing. $150,000 is nothing to Tarkington." Megan saw tears well in Lucy's eyes. Lucy looked down at the coffee table.

"We don't have to make a decision now," Megan said. "We'll continue to try to negotiate a settlement for Lauren and see where that goes. And we can lay the foundation to file criminal charges in case you decide you want to do that at some point. Any time you're even considering filing criminal charges, the first step is approaching the prosecutor's office to determine whether you have a case. It takes them a while to look into it. So if you want to keep your options open, let's contact the prosecutor's office and fill out a report. You need to do it. The prosecutor will review it and possibly ask us to meet with him."

Lucy glanced down at the floor, and then looked up. As someone with a law degree herself, this wasn't brand new information to her. Still, Megan could see she hadn't thought of approaching the prosecutor's office at this point.

"Yes, let's do that," Lucy said after a long moment. "We need to keep our options open.

CHAPTER TWELVE

Chief prosecutor Steve Windfield's office was in the government center in downtown D.C. Megan and Lucy rode the elevator to the 13th floor, got out, and walked down a long sterile hallway filled with government offices. It was a Thursday afternoon in the middle of May. Megan had received a call yesterday from the chief prosecutor's secretary requesting that she and Lucy come in and talk to him about the report Lucy had filed three weeks ago, stating that Tarkington had raped her.

The prosecutor's office was at the very end of the hallway. They sat in the reception area for fifteen minutes, then a tall blond secretary ushered them into Steve Windfield's office.

"Good to see you, Megan," Windfield said, reaching out to shake her hand. At fifty-seven he was still fit and trim with only a smattering of gray hair at his temples.

Megan had known him for years. When she was right out of law school she had started out as a deputy prosecutor. Steve Windfield was working in the prosecutor's office as another young attorney getting experience trying cases. After ten years as a deputy prosecutor, he decided to run in the election for main prosecutor and won. Tough and no nonsense, he had gained a good reputation.

Megan motioned toward Lucy. "This is Lucy Hatfield."

Windfield reached over and shook her hand. "Please, have a seat."

The office was cold and nondescript with government-issued furniture. Nothing like the luxury private attorneys in big firms were used to.

Windfield walked around behind his gray steel desk and sat down. The chair squeaked. "I've reviewed all your paperwork and have some questions." He reached into his jacket and extracted a pair of glasses. He flicked them open and perched them on his nose.

"Your position, Ms. Hatfield, is that there was no romantic relationship between you and Mr. Tarkington is that correct?"

"That is correct."

"Anyone who can verify that besides you?

Lucy cleared her throat. "Excuse me?"

"Is there anyone else who knows that your relationship was all professional?" Windfield stared at her.

Megan could see Lucy getting nervous.

She shot a glance at Megan.

Windfield continued to look at her waiting for an answer.

"We were part of a study group that met three evenings a week." she paused. "We all got to be friends. I imagine some of them could verify that there was no romantic relationship between us."

"Anyone else?"

"I have friends who have known me for years that I see regularly. They could verify that I wasn't involved with

Tarkington." Lucy paused. "My best friend Katie Robinson can tell you she never heard me say a word about being involved with Tarkington. As a matter of fact, she knew about a guy I was dating at the time. If anyone would know I was involved with Tarkington it would be her."

"Do you need a list of potential witnesses to verify that?" Megan asked.

"Yes," Windfield said. "These cases usually boil down to the perpetrator saying it was consensual and the victim saying it was rape. Would your client be willing to take a lie detector test if need be?"

Megan looked at Lucy.

Lucy nodded.

"Yes, if need be."

Windfield scribbled something on his legal pad. "Any problem with us doing a background investigation on you?" He shot a glance at Lucy.

"My client is willing to do whatever it takes to get this matter moving." She looked at Lucy.

Lucy nodded and looked Windfield in the eye. "Whatever needs to be done I am 100 percent on board."

"You know how brutal a criminal prosecution like this can be. The victim becomes the victim of the defense attorney." Windfield paused. "We have to be sure that the victim is telling the truth and can hold up under scrutiny." He ripped off a sheet of paper from his legal pad and handed it to Megan. "Here are the names of some polygraph experts we use. I'd like to have her done." He looked at Lucy. "Just business. Hope you understand."

Lucy nodded.

"Please get me a complete list of all the people who can verify that you and Tarkington were not involved romantically and include their contact information." Windfield leaned over his desk and shook their hands. "I'll be in touch."

Megan and Lucy got up, left Windfield's office, and headed down the hall toward the elevator. When the doors were closed Lucy looked at Megan. Megan could see the dismay on her face.

"Don't let any of that upset you. We both know he's just doing his job. He doesn't want to have a witness who has something in their background that could destroy the witness's credibility and sink the prosecution's case."

The elevator doors eased open and Megan and Lucy found their way out of the building.

"Do you think this is really a good idea?" Lucy said once they got to the sidewalk.

Megan stopped and looked at her. "Yes. Don't forget this is all Plan B anyway, in case Tarkington doesn't come through with a decent settlement. It almost certainly won't come to a trial."

CHAPTER THIRTEEN

"Let's start with the discrimination case," Eric said.

Megan was sitting in the worn leather chair across from his desk. He had everything he needed in his small office: One medium-sized room with a desk, computer, printer, a couple of client chairs, and some file cabinets.

The age discrimination suit had been filed two months ago. Recently the firm's attorney, Richard Chadwick, had sent Megan a list of witnesses he claimed would testify that the firm had fired her and the other women because of performance, not age. The so-called witnesses were support staff and some attorneys. Looking at the list, Megan did not believe that the people listed would testify against her. She had asked Eric to track down all these so-called witnesses and see if he could talk to them.

One of the witnesses had disappeared, Eric told her now, another said she didn't know a thing about being a witness against Megan and would have no part of it. She'd told him she had recently left the firm and was working at a new place across town, and that she didn't think two of the other so-called witnesses would testify against Megan either. Only one woman, Kathy Demarco, who was reportedly gunning for a promotion at the firm, had refused to talk to him.

"Let's switch gears," Megan said. "What did you find out about Lucy?"

"Your client is spotless. Not even a parking ticket," Eric said and tossed a file on the table.

Megan reached over and opened the file.

"I interviewed people, employers—a whole background check—and she passed with flying colors."

"I'm not surprised." Megan flipped through the papers.

"I put asterisks by the people who said they knew her and were part of the study group with Tarkington. They all said they never saw her out socially with him. I also talked to her best friend, Kate Robinson. She said there was no way Lucy ever dated Craig Tarkington. They could have been having a secret romance but it seems unlikely. According to these folks, Tarkington exclusively dated socialites. Lucy was also going out with another guy. I'll keep digging to see what else I can find."

Eric leaned back in his chair. "The only thing I could find on Lucy that seemed strange to me was that she didn't take the bar exam and pass until four years after graduating."

Megan stopped and looked at him. "Four years?"

Eric nodded.

"What did she do for employment during that time?"

"From what I could tell a variety of things." Eric opened the file. "Let's see... She had a retail job, worked at a resort in Reno, she was a paralegal for a while."

Megan sat up. "Are you serious? Let me see that." She took the file and scanned the notes. She shook her head. "I can't believe this. Why? The only legal job she had was that paralegal work for some small firm."

"I checked with all these folks and they gave her a good reference. Who knows, Megan, maybe she just wanted a break after law school before she committed full time to the legal grind."

Megan closed the file and set it on the desk. "I need to talk to her about this."

Eric paused. "I have one other thing. It's some news on Tarkington." Eric told her that he had done a complete background check including Tarkington's undergraduate college, teachers, and law school friends. "I checked out every resource on him. For the most part there was nothing earth shattering. Most people I talked to painted him as a rich boy who never had any responsibility. Likeable enough, just very self absorbed."

Megan felt a wave of disappointment wash over her.

"But then I spoke with some of his undergraduate friends." Eric smiled. "It seems our boy Tarkington was quite the ladies man and didn't like being told no." Eric flipped open the file. "According to some people I interviewed, he got into trouble with a couple of women. Both of them were not romantically involved with him but just friends. That is, until Tarkington decided to take the relationship to another level."

Megan leaned forward and rested her elbows on the desk.

"According to my sources, both these women made claims that he raped them. Similar facts to Lucy's situation.

Daddy and Grandpa made the unfortunate incidents go away. I understand that both women received extensive counseling to help them try to get over it and then dropped out of school and moved away."

"Where are they now?" She felt her heart thumping in anticipation.

"One's in California and the other's in New Mexico."

CHAPTER FOURTEEN

Megan sat on the couch, placed the file folder on the coffee table, and looked around the room. Lucy's apartment wasn't very big but it was all she probably needed. Two bedrooms and one bath with a small balcony. The location was close to the hospital and the neighborhood was safe.

Lucy sat down in the chair across from her. "The doctors said today that Lauren is continuing to improve." Lauren had been in the hospital with a flare-up.

Megan could see the relief in Lucy's expression. It had been a long, tiring haul for her and Megan was glad things seemed to be on the upswing.

"I wanted us to meet and go over a few things." Megan picked up the file and flipped it open.

"Tarkington's attorney keeps threatening that they know something about you." Megan looked at Lucy and studied her expression. "He keeps blowing off that they have the goods on you and will use them. Any idea what they could possibly be referring to?"

Lucy shifted in her chair. "No idea," she said, shaking her head. "They give any clues as to what it is?"

"They paint a picture of you as a woman who hunts down men with money and makes false allegations trying to get money out of them."

Lucy laughed. "Really?"

Megan smiled. "That's the story. They claim that Tarkington was only the latest in a string of them and the biggest fish. Please don't take this the wrong way, but I need to know if there is anything in the past that could come back to haunt us." Megan could see Lucy's expression darken.

"You're asking if I have extorted money from men?"

"No, I'm just asking if there are any skeletons, so to speak, that I need to know about. Any relationships I need to know about."

"Like what? Former lovers that could cause me problems?"

"That has been known to happen in this world." Megan sighed. "Any relationship that could be construed as…" She paused.

"Where I set a guy up for money?" Lucy said curtly.

"Anything."

Lucy leaned back in the chair. Megan could see she was not happy about this line of questioning. They sat in silence for several minutes.

"The worst thing I can think of was a married man I dated. I was young and stupid. It went on for a few years until I had finally had enough. I regret that relationship more than I can say."

Megan poised her pen on the legal pad. "Anything at all about that situation they could use against you?"

Lucy shook her head. "Nothing more than a very poor choice on my part."

Megan picked up the file folder and looked through it.

"I noticed in the background check I had done that you didn't start looking for a job in law until four years after graduating law school. Any reason why you waited that long?" She flipped through her notes. "It looks like you had jobs in other fields but not law except for a stint as a paralegal. Why?" Megan looked directly at Lucy.

For a couple of moments Lucy said nothing. "After I did the internship during my last year of law school with that firm in DC, I didn't know if I wanted to commit to being a lawyer." She ran her hand over the arm of the chair. "The day in day out practice of law was so stressful and ….." she trailed off.

"And what?"

"I just wanted to be sure this was for me. That's all."

Megan said nothing for several moments. "I saw that you did take the bar exam after graduating."

Lucy nodded. "I failed."

"After that you decided to make sure this was for you? Didn't you know that when you took the bar?"

"After I didn't pass I took it as a sign that maybe I needed to slow down and look around. Decide if this was really for me."

"At what point in all that did you start tutoring Tarkington?"

"I met him in a study group I attended to get ready to take the bar again after being out of law school for four years. I needed to brush up on everything so I would have the best chance to pass the exam that time."

Megan scribbled down something on her legal pad.

"And Tarkington was in this study group getting ready for the bar?"

Lucy nodded. "It was a pretty big group, and Tarkington approached me after one of the meetings and asked me if I'd help him one on one. I had quit my last job a few months earlier so I could focus on getting ready for the bar."

Megan sighed. "So an affair with a married man and you failed the bar exam. Those are the worst things you have in your background?"

Lucy looked away. "Yes."

Megan leaned back in the chair. She tapped her pen on the legal pad. Lucy seemed to be telling her the truth but something didn't feel quite right. Something was niggling at her but she didn't know what. She decided to let it go for now.

CHAPTER FIFTEEN

"I'm not sure what I think of your client," Steve Windfield said.

He took a seat behind his desk and Megan closed his office door and sat across from him. It didn't comfort Megan to hear him utter those words. He had been a prosecutor for years and knew how to assess a case. When he'd called two days ago wanting to have a private meeting with her, Megan had felt her stomach drop.

"What's the problem?" She rested her hands in her lap and took a slow breath.

Windfield leaned back in his chair and folded his arms behind his head. He sat for several moments thinking. "Well, for the most part Lucy's polygraph went fine." He paused.

Megan was hanging onto his every word. "And..." Megan prompted, leaning forward in her chair.

"There's one area of the test that had some funky results." Windfield leaned forward and started rifling through the file on his desk.

Megan watched as he thumbed through the sheets of paper. In a short period of time the file had grown from virtually nothing to being at least two inches thick. A result of all the paperwork she and Lucy had submitted as well as the investigations by the prosecutor's office.

Windfield stopped, opened his desk drawer, and took out a pair of glasses. "Better use these," he said flicking them open and perching them on his nose. "Now let's see."

Megan reached down and pulled out a pen and legal pad from her briefcase. She wanted to have notes on whatever he was about to say.

"Right here," Windfield said, pointing to a place on the paper. "The test results of the subject Lucy Hatfield appear to indicate that her responses to the majority of the questions were truthful." Windfield looked up at Megan. Her breath was shallow and she could feel her heart beating.

Windfield looked back at the paper and moved his head from side to side as he read silently.

"Here it is," he said. "The test subject showed some unsettledness and potential lack of truthfulness regarding questions concerning her career and schooling. Results showed inconsistency, confusion and potential avoidance." Windfield looked up. "So what is the story here? Is she hiding something?" He put the paper down. "The test is not saying she is out and out lying. But…"

Megan shifted in her chair. "What I understand is that she had an affair with a married man while she was in law school. She was really embarrassed when she told me about it. It's something she's very sensitive about and regrets a lot. I think that's probably what's showing up in the polygraph."

Windfield rubbed his hand on his chin and said nothing. Megan could see he was digesting what she had said.

"I saw in her file that she waited four years to retake the bar after she graduated law school and failed the first time. Why wait so long?" He raised his eyebrows. "Doesn't that seem strange to you?"

Megan ran a hand over her pants smoothing out a crease. "I understand from Lucy that after the affair ended and she completed an internship with a local D.C. law firm she wasn't sure she even wanted to be a lawyer."

Windfield picked up a pen and slowly tapped it on the file. Megan knew how he thought. He left no stone unturned and this snag in an otherwise clean polygraph didn't please him. "The office has done a very thorough background investigation on her." He paused. "Do you have any concerns about her?" His eyes locked on Megan.

"Eric Covington did a background check for me as well and he brought up the same concerns you have."

Windfield folded his hands and rested them on the desk.

"I made a point of talking to Lucy about this."

Windfield nodded slowly. "So you think she's telling the truth."

"The internship wasn't a good experience and I know the whole situation with the married guy was very upsetting. I have no proof she's telling me the truth but I don't have any that she's not telling me the truth either. My instinct is to trust her."

Windfield sighed and scratched his head. "I just wonder..." He looked at Megan. "I've tried too many cases. I just have a weird feeling." He paused. "Oh, hell. I can't say Lucy is lying when there's no real evidence to support it. "

Megan stood up and extended her hand. "Let me know if you need anything else."

"Will do." Windfield walked Megan to the door. "We'll be reviewing the case and considering whether to file the charges in the next few weeks."

Megan hoped it wouldn't come to that—that Tarkington would come through with a decent settlement that Lucy could feel good about accepting. That would be better for Lucy and also for herself—she had no desire to go through the familiar exhaustion, mess, and anxiety of an inevitably brutal rape trial, not to mention all the drama that would come up around the fact that the rapist was the grandson of a Supreme Court justice. The age discrimination law suit was going to be ugly enough.

She waited for the elevator and when it arrived she slipped inside and pushed the button for the lobby. The doors eased shut. She leaned against the wall and closed her eyes. There was something else nagging at her. Truth be known, she had the same feeling Windfield did.

CHAPTER SIXTEEN

Mattingly slapped the manila file down in front of Megan and flipped it open.

"Here it is," he said sitting down in the chair. "I put tabs where she needs to sign." Tarkington had gone up to $250,000 and Lucy had decided to settle.

Megan's eyes scanned the words. *Confidential Settlement Agreement.* Slowly, she flipped through the pages.

"The bottom line is, there are four major settlement points." Mattingly held up a finger. "One, Lucy agrees to drop all allegations against Tarkington and never to pursue criminal charges." He raised another finger. "Two, she agrees not to speak to anyone about this settlement *ever*." Another finger. "Three, she accepts in full settlement $250,000. She waives any claims she may have now or in the future against Tarkington, including any for Lauren. Lucy will never mention Tarkington has anything to do with Lauren in any shape or form. She's not his kid. She will dismiss the paternity action with prejudice so that it can never be filed again." Another finger. "Four, Tarkington will agree not to pursue any and all claims he has against Lucy regarding her fitness to parent Lauren and custody. He will not speak about Lucy or Lauren now or ever to anyone. He is giving up all legal rights to Lauren."

Megan looked up. "You have an affidavit in here that you want Lucy to sign saying that the allegation of rape she has made against Tarkington is false?"

Mattingly nodded. "That's right. The charges haven't been filed so she's not in a position of making a false statement or committing perjury." He leaned back in the chair and placed his hands behind his head. "There is no way that Tarkington is going to shell out a chunk of money unless she signs this. "

Megan looked back down and continued to read. She felt sick.

"How does she want the money?" Mattingly asked. "Cash, bank transfer?

Cashier's check? "

Megan shook her head. "I don't know. I'll have to discuss it with her."

"How soon will you have it signed?" Mattingly tipped forward in the chair.

Megan let out a small sigh. "I don't know."

"This blue light special does have an expiration date, you know." Mattingly laughed.

"Give me a week."

"I will note it on the calendar, counselor." Mattingly extended his hand.

Megan just looked at him. She picked up the file and put it in her briefcase.

"I'll be in touch."

CHAPTER SEVENTEEN

Megan stopped for coffee and to decompress after leaving Mattingly's office. She just didn't feel right about this—any of it. Even though she was relieved to be avoiding a trial for Lucy's sake, it just seemed wrong to let Tarkington off the hook. It was Lucy's choice and all she could do would be to advise her. She spent a couple of hours drinking coffee and going over the agreement. Mattingly hadn't missed anything. It was airtight. After mulling it all over she called Lucy and set up a time to meet that evening at Lucy's apartment.

When she arrived Lucy was cleaning up the kitchen. She let Megan in and told her to have a seat in the living room while she finished up and washed her hands. When she came in and sat down Megan gave her the Confidential Settlement Agreement to read. The room fell silent as Lucy flipped through the agreement. "How many pages is this?"

"Too many, with all the legal mumbo jumbo. The main points have post-it note arrows sticking out."

Lucy looked at the designated spots. "Pretty much covers it all, doesn't it."

Megan nodded. "Once you sign it, it's all over. Tarkington is off the hook across the board. For Lauren and for being made accountable for raping you."

Lucy stopped reading. "I don't know what else to do," she said softly. Megan saw tears well in her eyes. Lucy looked back down and continued reading. "Do you want me to sign it tonight?"

"No. You need to take a few days to really think about this." She sighed and leaned back in the chair. "Give this some real serious thought, Lucy. Don't rush into it. I told Mattingly we would get back with him in a week."

Lucy held the agreement in her hands and just looked at it. "I know it's a huge decision. I appreciate all you've done for me." She looked up at Megan and smiled.

Megan felt a catch in her throat. She stood up and gathered her coat and briefcase. "It's getting late and I still have a lot to do at home."

Lucy started to get up and Megan motioned for her to stay seated. "I'll let myself out." She headed for the door.

"Thank you, Megan," Lucy said softly. Megan turned and smiled. Lucy looked like a lost little girl. The decision Lucy was making was life altering for her, for Lauren, and for all women who found themselves the victim of an assault.

CHAPTER EIGHTEEN

"Can you believe the number of people in the lobby? It's Monday at the Prosecutor's office." Steve Windfield cast a glance back at Megan. When Windfield set out to go somewhere he did it with purpose. Megan was hustling to keep up with him.

"I'm amazed by how crowded your lobby is today," she said, a little short of breath.

Steve Windfield's office was located on the 13th floor of the county building. Three other floors housed the rest of the prosecutors and their staff. Steve Windfield's floor alone was usually a beehive of activity but today it seemed busier than usual.

Windfield shook his head. " People are all mad and wanting to file complaints. Must have been a rough weekend. Maybe a full moon." He laughed.

"I appreciate you taking the time to see me." Megan followed him into his office.

"Shut the door if you don't mind," Windfield said. "Usually, if they see my door closed people leave me alone."

Megan eased the door shut and went over and sat down in one of the chairs in front of Windfield's desk. There were boxes of files everywhere and stacks sat all over his desk. Megan set her briefcase down on the floor.

Windfield sat behind his desk. "It's never ending," he said with a sigh. "Just finished a trial. Monday we start another one."

Megan understood from her own years as a prosecutor. It was a never-ending grind of trial work. Exhausting. One of the happiest days of her career was when she left the job. She'd learned a lot but she couldn't imagine being a career prosecutor like Windfield. The love of trial—it just had to be in your blood.

"Want some coffee?" Windfield swiveled his chair toward the coffee maker sitting on a small metal stand in the corner. "I can brew up a batch. It'll only take a few minutes."

Megan looked at the coffee pot. It was dry as a bone and looked like it could use a good cleaning. "That's ok. I'm fine." She moved a small stack of files in front of her on Windfield's desk to the side so she wouldn't feel like she was talking over a hedge. Windfield reached over, picked them up and placed them on the floor by his chair.

"Glad you stopped by. I was just getting ready to call you." Windfield leaned back in the chair and propped his legs on the desk. "We're ready to roll. The charges against Tarkington are ready to be filed and we plan to ask for a high bond." He ran his hand through his hair and laughed. "Hell, this is a win win for us. We'll nail pretty boy Tarkington for Lucy and I'll get a ton of publicity just in time for my reelection campaign." He flashed a big smile.

Megan could see that he was all fired up and flying high at the prospect of front page news. He seemed to have forgotten for the moment how hard it was to win a rape trial. She shifted in her chair. She wasn't looking forward to this. "That's what I want to talk to you about." She took a deep breath.

"The media will have a field day with this," Windfield crowed.

Megan nodded. "We've had some new developments I need to talk to you about."

Windfield stopped and looked at her.

"I met with Tarkington's attorney the other day. I think they're really worried."

"I bet they are," Windfield said with a grin.

Megan paused, gathering her words.

"I'd like to have Lucy come in and see me again," Windfield nattered on. "I have a few questions for her. Nothing to be worried about. Just trial prep." The chair squeaked as he leaned back.

"Mattingly has made an offer on Tarkington's behalf. And…"

Windfield cut her off. "Tell him too late." He laughed and waved his hand. "These guys think they can call the shots, they get a client who has committed a crime and they think they can throw some money at the victim and that's all it takes. Poof! It's all gone." He snapped his fingers and shook his head.

Megan gathered herself to deliver the news. "Lucy is a great person who has been through a lot." She could see Windfield getting ready to say something. She raised her hand. "Let me finish please." Windfield's expression darkened. "Lucy's little girl has cystic fibrosis. She's been diagnosed recently. Lucy will have to be trained in how to care for her while Lauren continues to recover." She folded her hands in her lap and cast a glance out the window. She could feel Windfield's gaze locked on her.

"The offer Tarkington made... I'd like to see her get more but..." She paused. "She's decided to take it. She doesn't want to press charges."

Windfield snapped forward in his chair and slapped his palms on the desk.

Megan jumped.

"She wants to drop the charges?" His face turned bright red. "You're kidding me?"

Megan was taken aback. She had never seen him mad like this. She shook her head. "We've given this a lot of thought and consideration and..."

He cut her off. "You have given this a lot of thought?" Windfield shot up out of his chair.

"Listen, Steve," Megan raised her own voice.

"No, *you* listen to me." Windfield started pacing behind his desk. He whirled around and looked at her. "You see all those people out there?" He stabbed his finger toward the lobby. "They're all here wanting us to do something. File charges. Help them. Most of them we can't help. But I decided to try to do something for Lucy. We can help her. And you're telling me she's backing down?" He stopped.

Megan could see a vein protruding at his temple. His fists were clenched by his side. She knew the prosecutor's office didn't like people who wanted to bring charges and then backed out, but this response was more than she could have anticipated.

"It's about Lucy and what's best for her and Lauren," Megan managed to say.

"Lucy was raped," Windfield yelled. "What don't you get about that?" His eyes bore through her. "She has a case. A case that could help her and help other women come forward."

"Steve, it's her decision," Megan said exasperated. "She's not going to press charges. She's not happy about it but she can't." Megan shrugged. "And you know as well as I do that it's hard to win these cases and the trials are brutal for the victim. I don't know what else to say. This settlement is what she wants. I'm sorry but that's where we're at." She gathered her briefcase, stood up, and started heading for the door.

"You forget, Megan," Windfield said in a clear low voice behind her. "It's not up to the victim to press charges. The prosecutor has the power. "

Megan turned and looked at him. "Without a victim you don't have a case." She started to open the door.

"I have a victim, Megan, and her name is Lucy Hatfield. I'm not going to drop the charges. In case you forget, I have a sworn statement in writing, signed by her, saying he raped her, along with a detailed video of her describing what happened. Both were done under oath and under the penalties of perjury. I can prosecute her for false reporting and perjury if she refuses to go to court."

Megan said nothing. She gathered her briefcase and left. She knew what he was saying was true. He could force Lucy to go forward—and it was pretty clear that he was going to do that.

In the elevator Megan closed her eyes and rested the back of her head against the cold silver wall.

CHAPTER NINETEEN

"Here it is," Lucy said, laying the manila file down in front of Megan. "All copies are signed." She sat down on Megan's couch.

Megan felt her stomach tighten. She looked at the envelope lying on the coffee table.

"I'm glad you called about it," Lucy said. "I've had it ready for a few days but have been so busy with Lauren I lost track of time. We're still within the week time frame Tarkington's lawyer gave us to respond, aren't we?"

Megan nodded. They had a couple of days to go before the deadline. Lucy called her this morning and said she was dropping off the agreement today at one. Megan hadn't been able to bring herself to tell Lucy what had happened at her meeting with the prosecutor. It wasn't like her to stick her head in the sand but in this case she just couldn't face Lucy's reaction when she found out. So she'd said nothing and just kept hoping Windfield would change his mind or the whole thing would otherwise somehow magically go away. Windfield hadn't changed his mind, the whole thing hadn't just gone away, and now she had no choice but to tell Lucy charges against Tarkington would be filed soon.

Megan picked up her mug of coffee and took a sip.

"When will all this be finalized?" Lucy asked. Megan glanced at her and looked across the room. "Getting this over with will be a huge relief," Lucy went on cheerfully. "Thank you for everything you've done."

Megan let out a small sigh. "Lucy," she said.

Lucy's phone started ringing. "Sorry." She looked at the number on the screen. "It's Lauren's specialist."

Megan nodded. "Go ahead. No problem."

Lucy got up and walked into the other room. Megan could hear her quietly talking to the doctor's office.

"Okay, now, where were we?" Lucy said, coming back into the room.

Megan shifted in the chair. "I want to talk to you about something."

Megan saw concern wash over Lucy's face. Slowly, Lucy lowered herself down into a chair.

"I thought we needed to let the prosecutor know that we had a deal with Tarkington and you didn't want to press charges—before you signed the agreement and we gave it to Mattingly."

"I bet he's happy he has one less case to mess with." Lucy crossed her legs and leaned back.

"Well, we have a problem." Megan picked up the file from the table.

Lucy's smile disappeared. "What?"

Megan cleared her throat. Where to begin and how to tell her. This was one of the areas in the practice of law she hated—telling a client bad news.

"He didn't take it well," she said her words fast and clipped.

Lucy cocked her head. "He didn't take it well?" Megan could see she didn't understand.

"No, he took it pretty badly, as a matter of fact."

Lucy laughed. "I can't believe that." She shook her head. "I guess he'll have to die mad or get over it."

"I wish it were that easy." Megan tapped the edge of the file folder on the table. "Windfield doesn't want to drop the charges."

Lucy sat up. "They aren't even filed."

"Well no, but they're ready to be." Megan felt her stomach tighten.

"Then he can just not file them," Lucy said disdainfully.

"To make a long story short"—Megan paused—"Windfield will not let the charges go. He plans to file them. And soon."

Lucy shot up off the couch. "What do you mean? He can't file charges if I don't want him to." She circled the coffee table and stood in front of Megan. "I'm not pursuing the criminal stuff. I *can't*." Her eyes were cold and her jaw was tight. "It's not happening," she said. Pure panic had set in. She looked like a deer in the headlights.

"Lucy, sit down." Megan motioned to the chair beside her.

Lucy flopped down in the chair and turned and looked at her.

"Windfield will not let the charges go. He's filing." Megan kept her voice calm and even.

"Well, good luck to him," Lucy said with sarcasm. "He can't file them without a witness and *I* am the witness." She smiled as if she had scored a big point.

Megan shook her head. "The prosecutor has the last say, Lucy. You must've learned that in law school." She sighed and laid the folder down on the table. "I never thought this would happen when we filed the paperwork. I'm not sure what's gotten into Windfield, but I don't think he's going to bend on this. He says he has an affidavit you gave under the penalties of perjury as well as a video statement you gave under oath. That's all he needs." She paused and took a breath. Her heart was thumping so hard in her chest she felt like it would explode. "He says if you try and back out he'll prosecute you for false informing and perjury." Megan could see that Lucy was teetering on the edge. Her hands were shaking and tears were welling in her eyes.

She pointed at Megan. "It's not happening. I am not filing charges and he can't make me. That asshole. He can't do it. I'll lose everything. I am not going to trial! Do you understand that?" She stared at Megan. "You thought we should investigate filing charges against Tarkington. It was *your* idea and this is your fault. So now *you* fix it."

"There's nothing we can do." Megan's words were soft and slow. She looked at Lucy. "He can force you to press the charges. And it looks like he will."

Lucy sat down on the couch, rested her head in her hands, and began to cry. Moving slowly, Megan went over and sat beside her. She reached out and touched Lucy on the shoulder. "Lucy, you can't sign the agreement with

Tarkington," she said in a soothing voice. "If you do, we'll have even more problems. I have no doubt that Tarkington and his lawyer would come after you for violating the agreement and who knows what else."

Megan sat for several moments rubbing Lucy's back. "We can't do the agreement, Lucy. And we can't stop a trial. Come on," she said quietly. "You can do this for you and all the other women who have been assaulted and are afraid to come forward. Do it for Lauren, show her what a strong woman is."

"I won't even have a daughter by the time Tarkington and his attorney get done with me. Megan, I don't think I can hold up. I have all this and Lauren's illness too." She rested her head on her folded arms. "It's just too much."

Megan took her by the shoulders. "Look at me."

Lucy slowly lifted her head.

"We'll get through this and it will be alright. I'll be by your side every step of the way. I promise."

CHAPTER TWENTY

At nine a.m., three days after Megan's disastrous meeting with Lucy and exactly eight days after Mattingly had given her the settlement agreement, her phone rang. She groaned when she saw the caller ID. She had learned from years in the practice of law that when you don't know what to do, you stall. She'd been employing that method in the last two days since she didn't have a clue what to do. She didn't want to tell Mattingly that Lucy couldn't sign and have him unleash the dogs. Lucy didn't need that. After much thought, she'd decided to do nothing and pray that somehow it all went away. Foolish as it might seem, sometimes the worst cases did just that. She'd hoped it would happen in this case.

It didn't.

"Good morning, sunshine," Mattingly said. "Another fun-filled week in the practice of law?" He laughed.

"Good morning," Megan said, trying not to sound as sick as she felt hearing his voice.

"Thought I would check in with you and see when you'll have the signed agreement back to me. I can send my assistant over to pick it up if that helps."

Megan heard his chair creak.

"Sorry. It's been really busy." She paused. The line fell silent for several seconds. "Brockton, I talked to Lucy and I've also talked to the prosecutor, Steve Windfield."

Silence.

"Lucy was prepared to sign and willing to. However."

"However, what?" Mattingly said curtly.

Megan felt like a freight train was headed down the tracks straight toward her.

"The meeting with Windfield didn't go well. He doesn't want to...,"

Mattingly cut her off. "I know him. What's the issue? What say does he think he has in this agreement? Such a prima donna." Mattingly laughed.

"He won't drop the criminal charges."

"Oh bullshit, Megan. They aren't even filed yet. What's there to drop?"

"At the start of all this Lucy and I met with Windfield and talked about filing criminal charges. He reviewed the case and interviewed Lucy. He feels that he has a case and he's going to pursue it. He made that very clear."

She could hear Mattingly clearing his throat. "Listen," he said clearly, in a cold voice Megan had never heard him use this tone so far, even though he'd said some nasty threatening things. "The only thing he's interested in is getting re-elected and the primary is next year. He wants a front page story on how great he is as a prosecutor. You need to make it clear to him that Tarkington isn't the case that will keep him on the throne."

Megan picked up a pen and tapped it on the desk. She could feel tension rising in her.

"I talked to him at length the other day. He's not going to drop it. Period. Lucy is willing to sign the agreement but she can't. She's not the one causing the problem."

"Lucy *is* the one causing the problem," Mattingly said, his voice filled with anger. "She's the one that started all this shit and she can stop it—and you can help her."

Megan felt her jaw tighten and her head begin to ache. "You know how the prosecutor's office works. They can bring charges even if the victim doesn't want to. Lucy could be prosecuted for perjury and false reporting if she goes against him."

"You know, Megan, you and your client need to get something real clear." Mattingly paused. "We're done playing games with both of you. The prosecutor and his threats are *your* problems. They aren't ours. If I don't have the signed agreement in my hands by four p.m. today, all gloves are off. Understand?"

Before Megan could say a word the line went dead.

CHAPTER TWENTY ONE

Megan collapsed on the couch. She was exhausted. She had spent whole chunks of the day talking to Lucy on the phone trying to calm her down. After hours discussing the whole nightmare, Megan felt she had answered every question Lucy had about the criminal matter, why she had no choice but to go forward, and what their strategy should be now. When she wasn't talking to Lucy she'd worried about the trial herself and had gone over and over in her mind what Mattingly had said: It was going to be ugly.

Now she just wanted to relax and zone out watching some mindless TV. Wrapped in her favorite robe and fuzzy socks she picked up the remote and turned on the TV. She clicked through an endless array of stations, spending a few moments on each trying to decide what, if anything was worth watching. Nothing was. Finally she gave up. "Oh well," she muttered to herself. She looked at the clock on the wall. It was getting late.

She leaned back on the couch and pulled her robe tight. It was the second week of April. She had barely remembered to file a tax extension yesterday with all the tension around Lucy, Windfield, and Mattingly. The house felt chilly. She stared at the TV screen trying to keep her eyes open.

All of a sudden the screen changed. In big bold letters the words BREAKING NEWS appeared. She sat up and leaned forward. A newswoman with a microphone in her hand, wearing a jacket with the letters of the TV station emblazoned on the front, was standing outside the county jail. She was on point waiting for her cue to begin speaking. The studio anchor introduced her and said she was reporting on a major development. On cue, the woman started to speak.

"Thank you, John. Tonight one of DC's most prominent young attorneys, the grandson of Supreme Court Justice Arthur Tarkington, was arrested on one count of rape and one count of criminal confinement. Craig Tarkington, age 32, was taken into custody this evening at around nine p.m. at his home."

A mug shot of Craig Tarkington flashed on the screen.

"Oh my god." Megan groaned.

"Craig Tarkington has been practicing at the family firm Tarkington, Wagner Kreig, and DeVoe, for nine months. The firm was founded by his grandfather, Supreme Court Justice Tarkington, in the early 1970s."

The screen cut away from the reporter to show footage of the police taking Tarkington into custody. Tarkington had his head down and was handcuffed with his hands behind his back. A blitzkrieg of camera lights and flashes made it hard to see his face. Reporters were crawling everywhere, yelling questions and crowding in trying to get a sound bite. Megan watched as the police ushered him to the waiting police car and one of the officers pushed Tarkington's head down, lowered him into the back seat, and slammed the door. A flood of reporters rushed up, yelling questions and taking photos and video. She could see Tarkington turn his head away from them.

This was the beginning of the nightmare that would become the trial—it was suddenly a reality, not just a possibility—and she felt sick to her stomach, even a bit guilty because she had set this whole mess in motion by talking Lucy into filing the charges when Lucy had doubts about doing it. But some other part of her felt thrilled to see a rapist, a rich young man who ordinarily would get away with anything, held accountable.

The screen cut back to the reporter.

"The alleged victim in this matter is Lucy Hatfield, a fellow law student who was part of a bar exam study group Craig Tarkington was a member of. The probable cause affidavit states that Tarkington confined her and raped her in his apartment. Hatfield was studying with Tarkington for the D.C bar exam at the time of the alleged incident. Craig Tarkington is being taken to the county lockup. I understand his bond is high. He is expected to bond out. We'll continue to keep you up to date on this as we learn more. Back to you."

"Holy shit," Megan said out loud. She grabbed the phone and dialed Lucy's number. The phone rang and rang. Finally voicemail kicked in. Megan felt her chest tighten. She had to be sure Lucy knew before she was ambushed by the media.

She jumped up, rushed to her bedroom, threw on a sweatshirt and yoga pants, and ran to the front door while she was still trying to get her shoes on.

When she arrived at Lucy's apartment building there was a sea of men and women holding microphones surrounding the entrance. Megan threaded her way through the wall of reporters, pushing people aside until she got to the front door. A big burly police officer was standing at the entrance. Megan heard him talking on his radio, calling for other officers to come and assist. The officer turned. "Megan, what are you doing here?"

She looked at him and felt hope surge through her. "George!" George McKinley had done security for a lot of the firm's parties and community events and over the years he and Megan had become friends.

"I've got to get in the building. I need to see Lucy," she told him.

McKinley looked confused. "You want in there?" he said, jabbing his thumb toward the building. "*Everybody* wants in there."

"I'm her attorney." Megan could see McKinley's expression change. He motioned her to come forward and opened the door to let her in.

"That's her attorney," someone yelled out. The crush of people started pushing toward Megan, yelling questions. McKinley grabbed Megan by the arm, shoved her inside, and pulled the door shut behind her.

Megan ran to the elevator as fast as she could. She punched the button for the 7th floor and slowly the elevator doors slid shut. She leaned back against the wall, her heart pounding in her chest like a piston.

Lucy was a wreck. In addition to everything else, Lauren had come down with a cold a couple of days earlier. It had turned into pneumonia and Lucy had taken her to the emergency room early yesterday morning and spent all day, all night, and all day today in the hospital with her. She had just come home to change her clothes and take a shower when the news broke. Megan could see the strain in her face.

"I barely got in the door when the reporters started showing up and calling." Lucy turned, walked over to the window, and looked down at the large crowd. "I can't believe this."

Megan sat on the couch and cast a glance at the clock. It was after midnight.

"Arthur Tarkington is a Supreme Court justice," Megan said. "This is big news. Even bigger than I thought it would be."

Lucy sat in the chair across from Megan and looked her straight in the eye. Megan could sense a difference in her. Something had shifted. She could tell Lucy was still upset, but despite all the chaos she seemed to have changed now that the charges had been filed and Craig Tarkington had been arrested. There was a resolve about her that Megan hadn't seen before.

"I can't say I'm not terrified," Lucy said. "But somehow when I saw him in handcuffs on the news I felt sort of glad he's being forced to face what he did, even though I know it's going to be awful for me in court. And having your help… well, that makes a big difference."

"And I'll be with you to the very end."

The women sat in silence for several moments.

Lucy shook her head. "I don't like Windfield. There's just something about him. I felt it the first time I met him." Lucy got up and went into the kitchen. She came back with two cans of Le Croix and placed them on the coffee table.

"He's a top notch prosecutor. One of the best." Megan picked up a can and popped the tab.

"Maybe, but there's something. I just can't put my finger on it." Lucy leaned back in the chair, ran her hands through her hair and let out a sigh. "I don't want to deal with Windfield. He'd be representing me during the trial, right?"

Megan's expression changed to concern. "Yes. There's no choice on that. He's the prosecutor for the case."

"I don't feel good about it." Lucy stared across the room and Megan could see she was deep in thought. Lucy got up and walked over to the window. The crowd of reporters was still down there. She stood silently looking out at the inky blackness and the people in front of the building. "I think a woman needs to be involved in prosecuting Tarkington. A woman needs to be the one to take him down." She turned and looked at Megan.

"It might be a good move in front of the jury to have a woman involved," Megan agreed. "Windfield has some women prosecutors who work for him. Maybe he would consider having one of them be co-counsel with him."

Lucy looked at Megan. "I don't know them. I want you to be co-counsel."

Megan felt her breath catch. "I'm not a prosecutor, Lucy."

"But you were." Lucy looked straight at her.

Megan nodded. "That was more than ten years ago. I quit."

"I know Windfield is up for reelection. I'm not going to be made a sacrificial lamb for anyone's reelection campaign. If I'm going to go out on a limb and do this trial I want to nail the bastard." She paused. "I know that you'll see to it that everything is done to win—and protect me. I'm not sure Windfield will. And besides, I really feel like a woman needs to play a big part in this case. I don't want it to be some woman I don't know and trust."

Megan didn't know what to say. People didn't get to pick and choose their prosecutors or how the case would be handled. She leaned forward, rested her elbows on her knees, and steepled her fingers.

Lucy sat down and picked up her can of Le Croix. "Megan, I've seen how political the legal system can be. I've seen women get shredded by defense lawyers. Humiliated—regretting they ever came forward in the first place."

Megan looked at her. She knew Lucy was right. Too many times the victim of a rape was attacked and treated like the criminal.

Lucy shifted in her chair. "I'm trying to be strong through all this. I need someone I trust and know will be there fighting for me. Otherwise… I just can't do it. *I won't.* I don't know how to get out of this nightmare. But I will."

Megan sighed. "Lucy, we've been over this before. There's no way to get out of this. If you don't cooperate you're facing criminal charges. The only way out is through."

"I'm not going to fight this battle alone. The only way I can get through all this is if someone I trust has my back. I can't handle Lauren and…" Lucy paused.

Megan saw a single tear trail down her face. Lucy wiped it away with the back of her hand.

The room was so quiet Megan could hear Lucy breathing.

Lucy leaned forward in her chair. "Will you help me, Megan?"

CHAPTER TWENTY TWO

Megan looked around the room. Jackson Bar and Grill was packed. It looked more like a Friday night than five o'clock on a Tuesday. She glanced at the door just in time to see Steve Windfield walk in. Always the consummate politician, he immediately saw someone he knew and struck up a back-slapping conversation. The primary was more than a year away and he still worked his way toward the bar pressing flesh and politicking, already campaigning. Megan waved at him. He nodded and slowly threaded his way to where she was seated.

"Have you been here long?" he asked, sliding into the booth.

Megan shook her head. "I just got here. Glad I came when I did. The bus must have unloaded outside. It's been an endless stream of people since I sat down."

Windfield caught the eye of a waitress and mouthed the words "Scotch and water on the rocks." He looked down at Megan's drink. "Do you need anything?"

"I'm fine, thanks."

Megan looked around the room. "Wasn't that Fred Johnson you were talking to when you came in?" Megan nodded in the direction of a short bald man seated at the bar.

Windfield nodded. "I heard he wants to run for county assessor. He's been calling me wanting some advice on how to handle his campaign." Windfield leaned back in the booth and looked at Megan. "How did I get so lucky to be invited by you for a drink, Ms. O"Reilly?"

Megan watched as the waitress set down the scotch and water. Windfield picked it up and the ice cubes clinked against the glass.

"I need to talk to you."

Windfield rolled his eyes. "Everyone needs to talk to me," he said laughing. "The office wasn't good enough to meet with me? Hell, I thought you were going to ask me to run off to Paris or something." He took a sip. "You're buying, right?" A smile appeared on his face.

"Yes," Megan said, feigning exasperation. She reached over and took a handful of peanuts in the shell out of a small silver bucket in the center of the table.

Steve leaned forward. "Can you believe the publicity this Tarkington case is getting? My phone hasn't stopped ringing. I've had calls from all over the country. Everyone's all excited because the grandfather's a Supreme Court justice." He paused and looked around the room. "Some Me-Too group called and left a voicemail about making sure women are taken seriously and that I don't sell out." He shrugged. "Even USA Today called wanting an interview."

Megan could see he was thrilled with all the attention, thrilled to be involved in something involving a Supreme Court justice even though he was on the other side, and he had forgotten for the moment how brutal rape trials could be and how hard they were to win.

"I want to talk to you about Lucy," she said as she took a sip of Perrier.

"What about her?" Windfield dumped some peanuts onto the table and cracked one open.

"The other night, right after you filed the charges, Lucy and I had a long talk. She's really uncomfortable with doing this."

Windfield's expression changed. He jerked forward and slapped his hands on the table. "She's not wanting to drop it all again, is she?" He shook his head. "That ain't happening. You need to help her get *real* clear on that, Megan."

Megan shook her head. She picked up a peanut and cracked it open. "No. She understands your position." She could see Windfield's expression brighten. "She's just very uncomfortable. She hasn't been through anything like this before and she's terrified. She knows what a circus it will be, how Tarkington's lawyers will turn it into a witch hunt with her in the role of witch."

Windfield raised his glass and caught the waitress's eye. "Most people haven't been through something like this before." He crossed his arms. "I want her to understand that she is not to talk to anyone or do any interviews without my prior knowledge and approval."

Megan brushed some of the peanut shells off the table and into another small bucket. "She won't. Believe me, this is tearing her up."

The waitress appeared and placed a fresh drink in front of Windfield.

"She feels like it would be a good idea, and it would make her more comfortable, if a woman prosecutor could be co-counsel."

"Since when did Lucy become a trial strategist?" Windfield cast a glance across the room.

"With a case like this and with all the recent media attention on women being assaulted, I don't think having a woman as co-counsel would be a bad idea."

Windfield didn't say a word. Megan could see the wheels turning in his head. "I think a man going after another man for assaulting a woman is more powerful," he said.

"Speaking as a woman, I'd rather see a woman take down a man like Tarkington." Megan could see Windfield was losing interest. "I think women on the jury, as well as women in general, would really respond to a woman prosecutor." Megan leaned back in the booth and cast a glance at her phone laying on the seat beside her. They had been talking for a little over twenty minutes and it felt like hours. She could tell that Windfield wasn't buying the idea.

"Where is this all going, Megan?" Windfield asked with an air of impatience. "Cut to the chase."

"Lucy wants me to be co-counsel."

She had given Lucy's idea a lot of thought. After all, she did have a background in prosecuting sex offense cases and had been very successful doing so; she'd had the highest conviction rate in the prosecutor's office. From her years of experience she also knew that a victim needed someone to have their back throughout the whole process. Someone who believed in them and would help them through one of the toughest experiences of their lives. After much thought she'd come to the conclusion that, for Lucy, she was this person. Still, everything in her rebelled against going to court to prosecute a rape trial. The very thought of it had been keeping her awake at night. Finally she'd decided it was the right thing to do no matter what her personal feelings were. There might even be something she could learn from it.

She raised her glass and took a sip.

Windfield looked stunned. "What?"

"She said she knows I'll have her back and that's important to her."

"And I won't?" Windfield shot back.

"It's different. No disrespect to you." Megan paused and gathered her thoughts. "Look, you need Lucy to cooperate and be a good witness. To do that you need to help her with this whole process."

"And I need to hire another prosecutor to do that? One who's not on the payroll now? Wouldn't the county council love me? I have floors full of prosecutors already on the payroll but I want special funding to hire another one?" He looked incredulous.

"Who has the experience I do of trying sexual assault cases?" Megan shifted into her lawyer mode. Windfield said nothing. She leaned in toward him. "You know my work ethic and skill. Didn't you tell me I was the best prosecutor you ever had?"

Windfield looked away.

"This is a case that's receiving national attention. You need to handle it with that in mind. Women need to be taken seriously. They want to be respected. What better way than to have a woman play a key role in the prosecution? And don't you think women would love to see you show confidence in women by bringing a super-qualified woman on board to help convict Tarkington?" She paused. "I think nothing would make women voters happier than to see a woman like me nail a guy like Tarkington. It would be a smart choice."

For several moments Windfield sat lost in thought. "I wonder if there would be a conflict because you've worked at the firm. Hell, you even have a lawsuit against them in progress."

For a moment Megan thought all bets were off. She felt a stab of relief at the thought of telling Lucy she'd tried her best with Windfield but there was no way he was going to let her prosecute the trial. Then he rubbed his face and let out a sigh. "Oh well. Maybe there's some way we can make that work in our favor." Slowly, he picked up his glass, drank the last of the scotch, and looked at Megan. "You're hired."

CHAPTER TWENTY THREE

Megan watched Eric Covington lay a picture on the table. He had called earlier in the day and wanted to meet. They chose Ricardo's, a casual steakhouse on the outskirts of D.C. It had great food and was off the beaten path.

Megan glanced at the picture. The photo showed a young woman with auburn hair, fair skin and bright blue eyes smiling into the camera. After weeks of searching, Eric had managed to locate a good lead on her, one of Tarkington's assault victims. Katie Menifee had been a friend of Tarkington's and served on the student government board with him in college. From what Eric could uncover, she had suddenly dropped out of school and moved. With much elbow grease and a series of bad leads, Eric had discovered her in a small town in New Mexico.

"Truth or Consequences, New Mexico," Megan said with a laugh. "How appropriate."

Eric smiled, and Megan felt a spark pass between them. Once again she found herself wondering briefly how Eric felt about her. It had been years since she had dated and she suddenly found herself wondering if she might be almost ready for that again.

"Yeah, what a name, right? It really is a town of around six thousand people. It's a nice place—and far from the east coast and the Tarkington's." Eric took his knife and cut into his huge steak sandwich. Ricardo's was known for great food and huge servings.

"Do you believe she's there?"

Eric nodded. "She's teaching at a small school outside of town. High school literature."

"What's your game plan?" Megan took a sip of her iced tea. "You heard about another possible victim too, didn't you?"

Eric wiped his mouth with his napkin. "I want to do some more research into the other victim and see if I can locate her. I would like to go see them both at the same time if possible."

"Any information on the other woman?'

Eric shook his head. "Some leads but nothing concrete yet. Last information I received was that she was in Oregon."

Megan looked around the room. Ricardo's was beginning to fill up with the early dinner crowd.

Eric cleared his throat. "Did you talk to Lucy about her polygraph results? Not retaking the bar exam for so long after she failed it the first time?"

Megan told Eric about her meeting with Lucy, how Lucy said she wasn't sure she wanted to be a lawyer and it took her four years to figure it out. "It makes sense to me," she said. "These jobs are no picnic." She told Eric that the worst thing Lucy confessed to was an affair with a married man.

"Did she tell you his name?" Eric stopped eating and stared at Megan.

Megan shook her head. "It was some guy she knew when she was in law school. I don't know anything else. She played it down as a bad mistake on her part."

Eric was silent for a moment, lost in thought.

Megan could see the wheels turning. "Did you find something?"

"In my poking around I received some information from a woman who went to law school with Lucy. They had been friends. She knew a little about Lucy's personal life. For the most part she said Lucy kept to herself." He paused and took a sip of his drink.

Megan leaned over. "And?"

"She said that she knew Lucy had had an affair with a guy who had a government job. He was an older guy. Brilliant computer type. He was the person who took care of all the computer programming for the D.C. licensing agencies. She said he helped write the testing software and maintained the computers." Eric leaned back in the booth. "He was the IT man who took care of all that."

Megan took a bite of her salad. "Does he still work there?"

Eric shook his head. "From what this woman knew he left the job. She didn't know why. Maybe he just wanted to move on."

Megan crossed her arms." I know agencies pay real well for people who do that type of work. I've heard that people would kill to have that job. Really great money and great benefits."

Eric pushed his plate to the side. "He worked there for quite some time. I think eight years or so. He was the guy to go to. At the time he left the Federal courts were using him too. Sounded like he had a really bright future. A lot to lose by leaving. But he may have been vested in his retirement or very close."

Megan reached into her purse and took out a piece of paper and a pen. "What's his name?"

Eric flipped open his notebook. "Edward Thompson."

"Let's look into Mr. Thompson."

Megan looked up at the bright blue sky. It was a beautiful day in May, a perfect day for a walk in Rock Creek Park. She glanced down at her phone, it was two p.m. Eric should be here any moment, she thought as she sat down on a bench. Just as she was walking out the door, Eric had called and wanted to talk. She'd invited him to meet her here.

"Sorry I'm a little late," Eric said, hurrying toward her. His face was red and he was short of breath. "I got held up on a phone call."

Megan got up from the bench. "No problem. I just got here myself."

Eric came up beside where she stood and they started down the main walking path. It snaked around the edge of the park and covered the most scenic areas.

"I wanted to get with you and tell you the update." Eric reached into his jacket pocket and pulled out a tin box of mints. "Want one?"

Megan reached over and took a mint. Eric popped one in his mouth and placed the small box back in his pocket.

"I've confirmed the address of Tarkington's victim who lives in New Mexico, "Eric said. He was holding a small spiral-ringed notebook that he opened and scanned. "Alexis Steiner. 6278 Rose Court, Truth or Consequences, New Mexico. I confirmed she's still employed at the school I found in my research and this address is where she lives. "

Megan nodded. "Have you spoken to her?"

"Not yet. I want to talk to you about something first."

Megan picked up her pace and cast a glance in his direction. "About what?"

"I've been thinking about how to approach her."

Megan looked at him. For several seconds he said nothing. "And…," she prompted him.

"I wondered if you might go with me to see her."

Megan said nothing. She kept walking and glanced down at her Fit Bit. She'd walked 1,229 steps so far today.

Eric stepped up his pace. "I wondered how she might respond to a guy showing up on her doorstep asking her about this nightmare she thought she had left behind. I've had other women who've been through traumatic events not want to talk to me. In the past I've even had to hire a woman agent to interview women."

Megan looked over at him. "Why aren't you using that agent for this case then?"

Eric shrugged. "I thought about it. But I decided it might be good for you to do it. You can see the woman and get a feel for her firsthand."

Megan nodded. She remembered other cases where she had relied solely on a witness's statement and hadn't met the witness face to face. She'd learned that wasn't always a good practice. The person might give a good statement but when you met them face to face they weren't credible at all.

"The stakes are pretty high in this case," Eric said. "I feel like you may need to see and hear what she has to say in person."

Megan slowed down. She was getting hot. "I can't say I disagree. When do you plan to go see the woman in New Mexico?"

"In the next couple of weeks. If you can fit that into your schedule."

"I'll check the calendar when I get home, but I think it will work."

CHAPTER TWENTY FOUR

"You take the lead," Eric said, nodding. Megan knocked on the door. The house where Alexis Steiner lived was a small bungalow on the outskirts of Truth or Consequences, about 150 miles south of Albuquerque. From the looks of it the house was old and in need of some repair. Eric's investigation had revealed that Alexis lived alone, wasn't married, and had no children. Megan shifted her weight to the other leg and waited. It was six p.m., and from what they had learned about Alexis's schedule she should be home. Megan knocked again.

Then she heard a car behind her, turned, and saw a small dark brown jeep pull into the driveway.

A tall thin woman with curly auburn hair, probably in her late twenties or early thirties, stepped out of the Jeep and glanced at them cautiously.

"That's her." Eric nodded at Megan. "Looks just like the picture I have."

Alexis retrieved a plastic sack of groceries from the front seat and came over to where they were standing. She set the bag of groceries down and fished around in her purse. After a second she pulled out a ring of keys.

"Can I help you?"

Megan extended her hand. "I'm Megan O'Reilly and this is Eric Covington. We're from the D.C. area. I'm an attorney and Eric is a private investigator."

Megan could see concern and confusion appear in Alexis's face.

"Who are you looking for?"

"Alexis Steiner. That's you, isn't it?"

Alexis said nothing. She jabbed a key into the front door lock and turned it. She pushed the door open a little way and set the bag of groceries down inside the foyer. Then she turned back and faced them. "Well, I'm Alexis Steiner. You seem to know me but I've never heard of you. No offense, but do you have any ID?"

Eric reached in his back pocket and pulled out his wallet, flipped it open, extracted his PI license, and handed it to Alexis. She studied the photo and then handed it back to Eric.

"You know, anyone can have those printed up," she said. She cast a quick glance around as if checking to see if there were any neighbors nearby in case there were any problems.

"You're welcome to call the state licensing agency if you'd like," Megan said. She gave Alexis her bar identification card. "And you're welcome to confirm my identity with the bar."

Alexis studied the card and then handed it back to Megan.

"At the moment, the bigger question I have is why you're here. What do you want?"

Megan could see she was leery of them. Megan couldn't blame her much in this day and age. May we come in and talk to you?"

Alexis stood for a moment and said nothing. "I suppose." She pushed the door open and Megan and Eric followed her inside to the kitchen. She placed the bag of groceries on the counter, turned, and faced them.

"Come on into the living room." She motioned them to follow her.

The living room decor consisted of a tan leather couch and two matching chairs. Alexis sat on the couch. Eric and Megan each took a chair across from her. Between them was a coffee table with magazines scattered on top.

Alexis stared at them. "So why are you here?"

Megan cleared her throat. "We came to talk to you about someone you used to know. I have a client now who's in the same situation you were put in years ago."

Alexis looked at Megan blankly. "I have no idea what this could have to do with me—or who you think I know. I'm really lost."

"We came to talk to you about Craig Tarkington."

Alexis's expression darkened. She crossed her arms and leaned back against the couch.

For several moments the room was silent. Megan could see Alexis wasn't going to volunteer anything.

"Here's why we're wanting to talk with you." Megan rested her elbows on her knees and outlined Lucy's situation, how Tarkington had raped her and she was pressing charges. She told Alexis that Eric had learned from his investigation that several years ago she had been attacked by Tarkington as well. "We came to see you because we wanted to see if you would be willing to help in Lucy's case. We also wanted to know if you're interested in suing or pressing charges against Tarkington and making him accountable for what he did to you."

Alexis said nothing. She looked down at the couch and ran her hand over the soft leather.

Megan cast a quick glance at Eric. He was sitting quietly with his hands folded in his lap. She continued. "Lucy is going forward with her prosecution of him. The charges have already been filed." Megan paused and leaned back in the chair. "We wanted to meet you and see if you would be willing to come forward as well."

Megan felt a wall of ice form around Alexis. Eric shifted uncomfortably in his chair. Megan knew he was sensing the same thing. This wasn't good. Megan opened her legal pad and extracted a pen from her purse. "May we ask you a few questions?"

Alexis leaned forward and looked at the coffee table. She rearranged some of the magazines. Megan could see that her mind was racing. After a few moments Alexis stood up. "I'm not sure what your information is or if it's even correct." She walked to the front door, opened it, and cut a glance at Megan and Eric who were still seated.

Megan felt her stomach tighten. "Men like Tarkington need to be stopped," she persisted. "We thought you might be able to help. We won't take much of your time."

"I'm not interested." Alexis looked pointedly at them.

Megan and Eric got up and crossed the room. They stepped through the door and onto the porch. Before they could say anything the door shut behind them.

CHAPTER TWENTY FIVE

Megan eased the car up the small gravel drive and pulled to a stop. Kat's Katfish House, the sign said in shiny red neon. "You have got to be kidding," she said to herself out loud. Earlier in the day when Windfield called and wanted to meet he had suggested they go somewhere off the beaten path—she'd had no clue how off the beaten path he meant. He'd picked this place and set the time. Six p.m. She cast a glance at her phone—she was five minutes early.

The restaurant appeared to be an old trailer that had been rehabbed. Fish netting, shells and life preservers dangled from hooks and poles on the outside. A deck had been added on for outdoor dining. Megan cast a glance around, wondering what would be the attraction to eating outside. There was nothing to see. The restaurant was situated on a nondescript piece of ground with nothing but scrub brush even close to it. The last sign of life was about a mile down the road and that was a gas station.

She pushed the door open and heard bells jingle. She looked up and saw a string of them dangling from the ceiling next to the door. A line of stools with red plastic coverings dotted the length of the counter which ran parallel to the booths lining the wall. Windfield was seated in the last booth. "Hey," he said waving his arm. Megan looked around. The place was empty. She walked back to where Windfield was sitting and slid into the seat across from him.

Windfield slid a menu over to her. It consisted of a piece of paper encased in a page protector.

Megan picked it up. "You sure do know how to show a lady a good time."

A waitress wearing torn jeans and a t-shirt with Kat's Katfish House emblazoned on the front drifted over and took their orders.

"So what's all the mystery?" Megan picked up her briefcase and placed it on the seat.

"No mystery," Windfield said. He was grasping a glass of beer with one hand and was drumming the fingers of his other hand on the vinyl table top.

Megan could tell there was something up.

After a few moments he cleared his throat. "We've had a little development in Lucy's case." He took a swallow of his drink. "This thing is a hot potato. My phone has been ringing off the wall. I wanted us to meet at a place where the press wouldn't find us." He nodded toward the empty tables.

"Well, this just might be the place," Megan replied laughing. She could see that he loved all the attention the press was giving him but she knew him well enough to see that he was also troubled by something.

"So what is it?" Megan leaned back in the booth and rested her hands on the table.

Windfield reached into his jacket pocket and pulled out a folded piece of paper and pushed it toward her. "Tarkington's lawyer wants to have you disqualified as special prosecutor."

Megan was taken aback. She grabbed the paper and glanced at it. *Petition to Disqualify Special Prosecutor*. She tossed it down on the table.

"They're saying you know too much about Tarkington because you worked with him at the law firm.

"You've got to be kidding me," she said, shaking her head. "Mattingly thinks I know personal things about Tarkington and that will make it a conflict for me to prosecute the case against him?"

Windfield nodded. The waitress appeared and placed two heaping baskets of catfish sandwiches, french fries, slaw and hushpuppies in front of them.

Megan pushed hers aside. "I know nothing about Tarkington—at least nothing I learned as a result of training him at the firm. Everything I know I learned from Lucy."

"Of course they're going to say this, Megan." Windfield took a big bite of his catfish sandwich. He picked up his napkin and wiped his mouth. "They're going to try and play any card they can."

"I did nothing but train him. Plain and simple."

"No personal friendship, right?" Windfield winked at her and laughed.

Megan glared at him.

"I had to ask that." He paused. "Is there anything at all you feel you learned about Tarkington while training him that you could use against him now?"

Megan shook her head. "Nothing."

For several moments they sat eating in silence.

"I just wanted to tell you this had developed and get you prepared." Windfield poked his fork into the cup of coleslaw.

"Prepared for what?"

"The hearing to disqualify you."

Her expression darkened.

"No worries, I'll be representing you." Windfield looked up and smiled.

Megan hadn't even thought about a hearing. She felt her stomach tighten. "Is there a date set?"

Windfield nodded. "A week from today—nine a.m."

"What? "Megan was stunned. "The hearing is that soon?"

Windfield leaned in and rested his hands on the table. "I'm not worried about you. You'll be fine. This is just a bunch of bullshit by Tarkington and his lawyer." He paused. "I'm more concerned about what a media circus this will be and wanted to prepare you. It's already been incredible. It might have been anyway, but having the accused be the grandson of a conservative Supreme Court justice is driving the media wild. Everywhere I turn there's some reporter shoving a mike in my face. They're going to have a heyday with this hearing." Windfield picked up his beer and drained the last of it.

Megan nodded. She couldn't believe how fast this was all happening,

"I'm sure Tarkington and his lawyer will want to have the press there in full force so they portray what victims Tarkington and his grandfather are. They'll want to try this case in the media. And of course, they will be taking a big shot at you." Windfield shifted in his seat. "Tarkington and his lawyer will want to attack you any way they can."

Megan could feel anger rising in her. She knew how the defense game was played. The defendant was always the poor victim and the prosecutor was always the bad guy who had wrongfully accused him.

"I filed a motion with the court asking that the hearing be closed to the public to keep the press out." Windfield wadded up his paper napkin and tossed it onto the plate.

Megan looked at him. "Has the court ruled yet?"

Windfield looked down at the table. "It was denied."

CHAPTER TWENTY SIX

The morning was a fiasco, with the press crawling everywhere. Hoping to help Megan avoid the crush of reporters Windfield arranged for the police department to pick Megan up in a transport van with tinted windows. The van pulled up at Megan's house at barely seven a.m., two hours before the hearing, and took her to the judge's private courthouse entrance. But the press was already there. Camera men were busy setting up and TV reporters were huddled together talking. Megan couldn't believe that they were all out in full force this early. She scrunched down in her seat in case anyone could see her through the tinted windows. The whole experience was off the charts and she didn't see it calming down. As a matter of fact, it was just warming up.

Ever since the meeting with Windfield she'd been trying to figure out why Mattingly and Tarkington wanted her off the case so badly. The trial would go forward anyway, but why did they want her out? Could it just be due to the fact that she had been a special prosecutor in the Judge Booth trial several years ago and they knew she would be a better prosecutor than anyone Windfield had on staff? After all, she had received high accolades for being the person who didn't hesitate to take on such a sensitive high profile case against a man who had been revered in the eyes of the public and legal world as a fine jurist and man of impeccable character. Or could it be something else? Did they know something she didn't know?

At nine a.m. sharp the hearing started and Mattingly called Tarkington to the stand. Dressed in a conservative gray suit and tie, Tarkington recounted how he met Megan and described their relationship. She was stunned by some of his answers. According to him, he'd divulged personal information to her and they had become friends. He also testified that he had talked to her about some business matters and had hired her to represent him in them. He said that she had not been paid yet but they had agreed on the rate and on what she would be doing.

Windfield did a brief but thorough cross examination and Tarkington didn't budge from his story.

Mattingly next called Megan to the stand. She testified that she did not agree with what Tarkington had just said. She told the Court that she was not his attorney and that they had never had a discussion about Tarkington hiring her to represent him. She knew nothing about this business venture he'd testified about.

"You and Mr. Tarkington had an employment contract did you not?" Mattingly rubbed his chin.

Megan shook her head. "No we did not."

Seeing that he was not making the headway he had hoped Mattingly changed his tactics. "Ms. O'Reilly, isn't it a fact that your relationship with my client was at least partly more of a friendship?"

"No," Megan said emphatically. "I trained him to work at the law firm. Period. We had no personal relationship."

"No meetings outside of work? Nothing romantic, of course." Mattingly shook his head. "You claim you didn't learn anything personal about Craig while training him?"

"Nothing."

"Nothing." Mattingly arched his eyebrows.

"Nothing," Megan said firmly.

Mattingly looked at the floor and then slowly began to pace back and forth in front of her. After several seconds he spoke. "What about business? Isn't it a fact that right before you left the firm you agreed to represent him in a brand new business venture he was starting?"

"I have no clue what you're talking about."

"You heard him testify, didn't you?" Mattingly stared at her for several moments.

Megan held his gaze.

"You're saying that my client isn't telling the truth? He's lying."

The whole courtroom was silent. Megan cast a glance at the reporters sitting in the gallery. Their eyes were fixed on her.

"I'm saying that we had no business or personal relationship outside of the office. I never discussed or agreed to represent him in any business venture."

Mattingly walked up to the witness stand and stopped directly in front of her. He was so close Megan wanted to push back the chair in the witness box but she didn't. She knew he was trying to intimidate her. "So, he's lying." He paused. "He's a liar. That's what you're saying, Ms. O'Reilly. Isn't it."

Megan knew exactly what his game was. People didn't like it when a witness claimed another person was a liar—even if it was true it didn't sit well.

Megan sat quietly and gathered her words. "I'm saying, Mr. Mattingly, that I have never been Craig Tarkington's attorney. I learned nothing about him while I was training him to work in the office."

Mattingly walked back to his seat, turned, and looked at her.

"You were fired from the firm, were you not?"

Megan felt a dagger of white hot anger cut through her.

Windfield shot up from his chair. "Objection, Your Honor! Mr. Mattingly is assuming facts not in evidence."

"Poor performance, I believe." Mattingly smiled.

"Again, he's arguing with the witness," Windfield said.

"This is cross examination and I have the right to—" Mattingly said loudly, talking over Windfield.

Judge Crawford slammed the gavel down.

Megan jumped.

"Order in the court!" the judge yelled.

Megan cast a glance at Mattingly and Windfield. They both looked like two little boys who had been scolded and were being sent to the principal's office.

"Counsel, I highly suggest you both listen to me carefully," Judge Crawford yelled, banging his gavel on the bench. He peered down at them. "We have already had enough drama in this case this morning with the media, and the Court is not tolerating anymore." He looked at the clock on the wall. "This hearing was set for one hour and we've already exceeded that. I suggest we move this matter along. I have other hearings." He tossed the gavel down, let out a sigh of exasperation, and looked at Windfield sternly. "Objection overruled. Continue, Mr. Mattingly," he said curtly.

"You've been unemployed now for several months."

Megan said nothing. "Being hired by a guy like Craig Tarkington would pay well and help you out financially, wouldn't it?"

"I don't know. I was never hired by him," Megan answered calmly.

"So how have you been getting by since you were fired? I imagine you have the same lifestyle, just not the income?"

Windfield was on his feet again. "Judge, this is not appropriate questioning. Mr. Mattingly is...."

"I'm allowing it, counsel," the Judge said, interrupting him. "Proceed, Mr. Mattingly."

"Do I need to repeat the question, Ms. O'Reilly?"

"No." She paused. "I have my own resources and private clients—and Craig Tarkington isn't one of them." She cast a glance over at Tarkington. He was looking down, taking notes.

Judge Crawford rubbed his face and let out a sigh. "Counsel, the Court is clear on what the testimony is. I understand the parties' respective positions."

Megan could tell Judge Crawford was at the end of his rope. She'd never practiced in front of him but she'd heard the stories. According to other lawyers who knew him, he allowed people to testify only for so long and then he was done. If he felt he didn't need any more information he would shut down a hearing. This behavior was often criticized by lawyers and it often put them in a difficult position with clients who wanted the Court to hear more testimony.

"Mr. Mattingly, the Court does have a question."

Everyone looked at Judge Crawford then at Mattingly.

"Does anyone have a copy of this employment contract between Mr. Tarkington and Ms. O'Reilly I have heard about?"

"Yes sir we do. It clearly shows what Ms. O'Reilly and Mr. Tarkington agreed to"

Tarkington picked his briefcase up off the floor, snapped it open, and pulled out a file folder. He flipped the folder open and began rifling through the contents. After a few moments he stopped, extracted a sheet of paper, and gave it to Mattingly. Mattingly looked at it. "May we approach the bench, Your Honor?"

Judge Crawford nodded. Mattingly handed him the paper.

"Have you seen this, Mr. Windfield?" Judge Crawford asked.

Megan felt her chest tighten. She had no clue what was going on but she didn't feel good about it.

The Judge handed the paper to Windfield who quickly read it.

"May I show this to my client?"

Judge Crawford nodded.

Windfield walked over to the witness stand and handed the paper to Megan. It was an employment contract between her and Tarkington.

Megan couldn't believe it. "I've never seen this," she said, shaking her head. "Never." Windfield was reading the document over her shoulder. She took her finger and pointed to the bottom of the page and looked at him.

Windfield took the paper and walked back to the bench. "This document is not signed by Ms. O'Reilly, just by Mr. Tarkington." He put the paper on the bench.

Judge Crawford looked at Mattingly. "Is there a signed copy?"

Mattingly hurried over to Tarkington and whispered to him, then returned to the bench.

"My client indicates that he does not have the signed copy. Ms. O'Reilly should have it."

Megan couldn't believe what she was hearing. She cut a glance at Tarkington. He looked away.

"My client has never seen this document before," Windfield said angrily. "She certainly doesn't have a copy of it."

The room fell silent.

Everyone watched as Judge Crawford scribbled something on a legal pad.

"Very well then." He put the pen down, leaned forward, and folded his hands. "The Court, having heard and considered the evidence, finds that the defense has failed to show cause as to why Ms. O'Reilly should be removed as the special prosecutor in this matter. The Court finds no conflict. Record is closed." Judge Crawford got up and walked off the bench.

Megan looked at Windfield. She was stunned. She knew that Mattingly and Tarkington would come at her tooth and claw but fabricating evidence? She sat for a few seconds just trying to take in what had happened.

"The disciplinary commission might have a different opinion." Mattingly said looking at Megan. "Lawyers lose their licenses for doing things like you've done." He snapped his briefcase shut and headed for the large double door with Tarkington following. Before they could get there the door flew open and the press came rushing into the courtroom, yelling questions and demanding interviews.

CHAPTER TWENTY SEVEN

Megan looked in the rearview mirror. The car was still behind her. She had first noticed it when she pulled out of the parking lot of Alonzo's Café. A sleek black BMW sedan with tinted windows. It had stayed behind her for the last several miles. She kept an eye on it and on the road. The drive home took around a half hour and the roads were curvy and not very populated at this time of night. Her phone started ringing. She looked at the screen on the dashboard. *Blocked number.* She pushed the Decline button.

She speeded up and the car behind her followed. She decided to take the back way home and turned onto Alhambra Road. The sedan turned too. Megan felt a nervous energy course through her body. Her phone started ringing again. Still *Blocked number.*

She looked in the rearview mirror. The car was close but she couldn't make out the driver. It was dark out and the windows were tinted. She pressed her foot to the accelerator. Her house was only a mile away. She grabbed her phone and pressed a preset button.

"What is your emergency?" a voice said.

"This is Megan O'Reilly. I want security to meet me at my house. I've been followed for miles by someone driving a black BMW sedan. No matter where I turn it follows me and I'm concerned." She looked in the rearview mirror. The car was still there. It was at times like this that Megan was grateful to have a private security firm monitoring her neighborhood. It cost the residents extra each month but it was well worth it. She gave the operator her address. "I'm about five minutes from my driveway."

"An officer will be waiting."

As Megan hung up she saw a flash of light in the rearview mirror. Whoever was in the car behind her was flashing their lights at her. She ignored them and drove on. She wound her way up her driveway and stopped. There was a security guard waiting for her by her front door. The sedan pulled up behind her and stopped as well.

The guard walked over to the driver's side of the car. Megan heard the whir of the window being lowered.

"Good evening, officer," a deep voice said. "I'm sorry to have startled Ms. O'Reilly. She knows me."

Megan recognized the voice but couldn't place it. She got out of her car and went over to where the officer was standing.

"Justice Tarkington," she said in disbelief.

"I'm sorry to have frightened you." The Supreme Court justice went on to explain that he was having dinner at the same restaurant and had seen Megan. She had left a little ahead of him and he had tried, but couldn't get her attention. By the time he got to the parking lot she was in her car getting ready to pull out. "I tried to call you a couple of times but got your voicemail," he said smiling.

The officer gaped at Justice Tarkington, and then looked at Megan. "Do you know him?"

Megan nodded. "Thank you. I'm sorry to have called you for nothing."

"Not a problem," the officer said, looking with wide eyes at Justice Tarkington, who was still sitting in his car. "Have a good evening." Megan saw the shocked expression on his face as he drove away.

Justice Tarkington got out of the car. "Good to see you, Megan." He extended his hand.

Megan was at a loss for words. Except once, at a Christmas party at the firm right after she had started working there, she hadn't seen Justice Tarkington since she had clerked for him right out of law school. Even when she clerked for him, she didn't have much direct contact. His personal secretary usually gave her instructions about what Judge Tarkington needed researched and proofed the briefs she wrote. He was always polite but kept a distance. And that had been when he was only a federal judge. She was stunned at the sight of him now, a Supreme Court justice, standing in her driveway.

"Do you have a few moments to talk?" he asked.

"Yes."

Megan unlocked her front door and invited him in. "Would you like some coffee?"

"No, I'm fine, thank you. I won't take much of your time."

Megan motioned toward the living room. "Make yourself comfortable." She sat down in one of two leather chairs and Justice Tarkington sat across from her on the couch. A large square coffee table was between them. On top were newspapers with Craig Tarkington's trial coverage.

Justice Tarkington leaned back and crossed his legs. "Megan, I want you to know that I had nothing to do with your getting fired from the firm." He shook his head. "I had no clue that had happened until after the fact."

Megan said nothing. She was still stunned that he was sitting in her living room. Justice Arthur M. Tarkington, Supreme Court justice, founder of the top law firm in D.C., not to mention the real reason she even got a job at the firm. Being his law clerk had opened a door to a world she probably wouldn't have been privy to otherwise.

"I've wanted to tell you that for sometime."

Megan shifted in her chair. "It was a big shock to me," she said.

Justice Tarkington nodded. The room fell silent. Megan felt awkward and uncomfortable.

"Although I'm on the bench and not practicing law anymore, I try to keep tabs on the firm. I don't agree with what happened to you and I want to make it right."

Megan blinked. She had no clue where this was going.

"Let me cut to the chase. I would like to offer you full reinstatement to your position with full back pay. I'm happy to suggest the firm make you a senior partner as well."

She couldn't believe what she was hearing. If what he was offering happened she would be set for life.

"I don't know what to say." Her mind was racing trying to make sense of it all. She leaned forward and placed her elbows on her knees. "Who all knows you are doing this?"

"No one, but they'll go along with me." He smiled.

Of course they would. When Supreme Court Justice Tarkington spoke they all listened and jumped just as high as he wanted. Maybe she would too. In the legal world he was practically God.

"I want the firm back the way it used to be before all this nonsense." He waved his hand in the air. "The firm has made a poor choice getting rid of you. I'm also concerned about…" his voice trailed off.

"Craig," Megan said, filling in the blank. She could see Justice Tarkington's expression darken.

He let out a sigh. "That grandson of mine may be a lot of things but he isn't a rapist." He folded his hands and looked at the floor. "I'd like to ask you to consider stepping down as special prosecutor in the criminal matter and coming back to work for the firm."

"The case can still go forward without me, sir." Megan looked at the deep lines etched in his face. He had aged a lot since she saw him at that Christmas party ten years ago.

"Yes, it can. But it doesn't have to go forward with you being a part of it." He glanced at her and then averted his eyes.

"There were other people who were wrongfully fired besides me. " Megan could see his expression change

"If you accept my offer I will suggest they all be rehired with full reinstatement just like what I have offered you."

He stood up and picked up his coat. "You think about it and let me know. If you're interested I'd like to get this matter resolved and get you back to work in the next couple of weeks. That should give you time to let Mr. Windfield know you're leaving the prosecution team. Good to see you, Megan. I look forward to hearing from you." He reached into his coat pocket and pulled out a business card. On the back he had written a phone number. "Here's my private cell." He pressed the card into her hand and left.

Megan shut the door behind him and leaned against it. What had just happened? Old Man Tarkington was willing to give her everything plus partner status. Of course he was upset about the charges against his grandson, and he might even want to get rid of the lawsuit against the firm. But why didn't he want her involved in prosecuting Craig?

Megan collapsed on her couch. She clicked on the TV but couldn't concentrate on anything. She kept coming back to the same question over and over: What was it about her in particular that made him want to get rid of her? Try as she might she couldn't think of anything.

CHAPTER TWENTY EIGHT

Megan looked around the room. Windfield had given her an office on the same floor as his and only a few doors down. She was back in the prosecutor's office, this time not as a pup out of law school handling small-time cases but as a special prosecutor handling a high-profile case.

She leaned back in the leather chair, turned Justice Tarkington's business card over in her hand, and looked at the phone number written on the back of it. She sat for several moments thinking about what Justice Tarkington had said to her.

It had been two days since he followed her home and offered her reinstatement as a partner in the firm. It still didn't seem real. Nothing seemed real anymore. Since taking on Lucy's case a month ago, she'd felt like she was on a roller coaster. One moment she felt she was the right person to champion Lucy's cause and the next she wondered if she had lost her touch in handling criminal cases. The last case she had tried, more than ten years ago, had been Lisa Garrett. To this day she was haunted by that loss. Now that she was special prosecutor the stakes were higher than ever. She had absolutely no privacy with the press always lurking around.

Every time she turned around it seemed like some reporter was trying to get a comment from her or a TV station wanted an interview. Earlier in the week, when she left her house to go to work she was met in her driveway by a reporter for one of the local news stations.

And since accepting the position her days had been crazy busy preparing the case and her nights had been mostly sleepless as she tossed and turned going over it in her head. At the office she had gone over the police reports and put together a list of possible attacks the defense might make on Lucy. If the evidence was tight enough, the only real attack the defense could make would be on Lucy's credibility. She had gone over the night of the rape with Lucy several times making sure her testimony was solid—and it was. She'd had what seemed like endless meetings with Windfield.

Megan had given Justice Tarkington's offer a lot of thought in the last two days. She hadn't mentioned the offer to any of the other women who'd filed suit with her. She wanted to be clear about what she wanted to do before she brought it up to them.

She put the card back in her purse. People at the prosecutor's office pretty much respected each other's privacy, but she couldn't take a chance that someone might see she had Justice Tarkington's card with his cell phone number written on the back.

She picked up Lucy's file and opened it. The trial date had not been set but she knew from previous experience that you never had enough time to prepare. There was always so much to do. Someone knocked on her office door. Steve Windfield opened it and stuck his head in.

"Have a moment?"

"Sure." Megan shut the file and laid it on the side of her desk.

Windfield came in followed by a woman who appeared to be in her late fifties. She had shoulder-length auburn hair and was wearing a tan jacket and slacks.

"Megan, this is Carol McGuire, the head of the victim's advocate program. She's assigned to Lucy's case."

Megan extended her hand. "Nice to meet you."

Carol smiled. "I've heard a lot of good things about you."

Windfield motioned for Carol to have a seat. "I wanted you to meet. We call Carol in to work on our really big cases. She has a lot of experience and does an excellent job." Megan knew how it worked, a victim advocate's role was to help the victim understand what was going on and feel comfortable during the trial process. Victim advocates had no real power and when Megan was a defense lawyer she felt like they got in the way more than helped anything. But now that she was in the prosecutor's role she was glad for any help she could get for Lucy.

Windfield smiled and headed out the door. "See you both later."

"Can I get you anything?" Megan looked around the office. She didn't have coffee, tea, or anything to offer. Some offices had individual coffee makers but hers didn't.

"I'm fine." Carol placed her briefcase on the floor.

"Have you met Lucy yet?" Megan asked.

Carol shook her head. "No. I wanted to talk to you first."

Megan found that strange. Usually the victim advocate made contact with the victim before they met with the prosecutor assigned to their case.

Carol's expression turned serious. "I really admire you for taking this case on."

Megan smiled. "I'm here to help people and Lucy is a great person who has had a terrible thing happen to her."

Carol nodded. "You worked at Tarkington, Wagner, Krieg and DeVoe, didn't you?"

"Yes," Megan felt something wasn't right but she couldn't pinpoint it. Do I know you?"

"No, we've never met." Carol placed her hands in her lap. "I just thought you might have heard of me."

Megan shook her head. "I'm sorry. I don't understand."

"The inner circle of that firm knows me very well."

"I wasn't part of the inner circle."

She saw Carol's expression change. "So you don't know of me."

Megan leaned forward. "I have no idea what you're talking about."

"You don't realize what you've done. There's been an allegation of abuse against one of the big shots who work there. We've been trying to nail him for a long time."

Megan felt her breath catch. "Who are you talking about?"

"Rick Harwood. Do you know him?"

Megan nodded. Rick Harwood was a senior partner held in high esteem by the firm and the legal community.

"Several years ago he beat his wife and she ended up in a shelter for battered women. She was lucky to be alive." Carol shook her head. "We did our damndest to get him prosecuted. Between the powers that be at the firm and his wife refusing to prosecute we couldn't do anything."

Megan was stunned.

"My sources say that his wife is still with him and the abuse continues." Carol tapped her hand on the arm of the chair. "I expect he'll end up killing her."

"And how does that not come to light?" Megan asked incredulously.

"That firm is very powerful and they protect their own. They will allow nothing to sully their polished public image. And they're pretty good at making things go away." Carol made quotation marks in the air.

Megan knew Rick Harwood's wife Melissa. She didn't seem like the type to put up with that. Of course, Megan knew from years of practicing law that appearances could be deceiving. Cases of spousal abuse were always more complicated than they looked on the surface. But was Carol suggesting the firm was somehow keeping Melissa from coming forward? Megan didn't doubt that the firm was deeply invested in keeping their lawyers looking lily white. She knew the firm did whatever it took to win a case. But this was the first time she'd ever considered the lengths to which it would go.

Carol smoothed out a crease in her slacks. "The prosecutor's office asked me to talk to Melissa Harwood when she was in the shelter and I tried to gently encourage her to press charges. For a while I checked in with her every now and then but then she stopped taking my calls. I heard through the grapevine that the firm isn't happy I'm on Lucy Hatfield's case." She paused and looked at Megan. "I've also heard they're shitting bricks because you're prosecuting Lucy's case."

She paused and thought for a moment. "Rick Harwood's wife said she was afraid to go forward with pressing charges partly because she didn't have confidence in the prosecutor's office. If you win this case that could change. I think that might be one reason the firm is set on you backing down. Not only are they afraid you'll find a way to win the case against Tarkington, they're afraid it will bring Rick Harwood's crimes to light. And that will be the last straw in sullying the firm's reputation."

Carol stood up and picked up her briefcase. "I'm really glad to meet you. I'll set up a time to see Lucy. I have her contact information." She extended her hand. "I'm happy to see there's someone who isn't afraid to stand up to the firm. And isn't afraid to make a Supreme Court justice's grandson pay for what he's done. " She shrugged on her coat. "Hell, Old Man Tarkington may even intervene and try to save his grandson. Nothing would surprise me at this point. Here's my card." Carol dropped the card on the desk.

Megan looked at it and nodded. She didn't know what to say. She was stunned.

"Talk to you later." Before Megan could say anything Carol was gone.

CHAPTER TWENTY NINE

Megan leaned back in the chair. It was almost ten p.m. and she was ready to turn in for the night. The day after Carol's visit she'd gotten a notice the trial date had been set for October 15th. That was roughly five months away. She knew better than to fall into the trap of thinking she had lots of time to prepare. Time would fly by.

Since Carol McGuire had come to her office she'd been wondering what lengths the firm would go to keep her off the case or even to keep the trial from happening. If the firm could get her out of the picture it might be able to manipulate whatever prosecutor took her place. She'd be surprised if Windfield backed down but the election was coming up and the firm could potentially kick a lot of money to his reelection campaign to bribe him to drop the charges. Windfield appeared to be on board one hundred percent; however, when it came to politics and money she'd seen stranger things than a case going by the wayside.

Megan closed her laptop and put it into her briefcase. Her phone rang just as she started to get up. She cast a glance at the screen and a bolt of nervous energy daggered through her. Reluctantly, she pressed Answer.

"Good evening, Megan. This is Justice Tarkington. I hope it's not too late to call. I lost track of time today."

"Hello, sir. No, it's not too late." Megan wished she had let the call go to voicemail but she needed to get this conversation over with.

"I just wanted to check in with you and see when we can expect you back at the firm." The Justice's voice brimmed with confidence.

Megan paused and chose her words carefully. "I've given your offer a lot of thought."

"I'm making things right," Justice Tarkington said. "This should never have happened to begin with."

Megan cleared her throat. "I agree. But things have changed in my life and I've moved on. I appreciate it very much, but I can't accept the offer to come back to the firm. "She could feel Justice Tarkington's energy shift. "I'd be interested in a financial settlement for the wrongful dismissal lawsuit—one that would include all of the women …"

The distinguished old man cut her off. "That's not what we talked about."

Megan could hear him exhale. She could tell he was not happy.

"This is the opportunity of a lifetime for you, Megan. If you accept we can talk about the other women involved, but it's all or nothing. There's no staying on as a prosecutor and also resolving your case against the firm."

He paused. "You won't win your age discrimination suit." His voice was bold and mocking.

"With all due respect, sir, I thought you said you wanted to make things right and that this should never have happened to begin with."

"That's just my personal opinion…" His voice trailed off. "I suggest you rethink your position. You'd be foolish to turn down my offer. Very foolish. You're a smart woman, Megan. You know that there are ethical issues with your remaining as special prosecutor in Craig's case. You could be facing charges with the disciplinary commission. I don't think you want to risk losing your law license."

Megan could tell it was taking everything the Justice had to keep his composure and not explode.

"I don't believe I have anything to worry about with the commission or losing my license, sir. The Court ruled that I had no conflict. I've given your offer a lot of thought and I can't accept. I would like to talk about a settlement that…"

The line went dead.

CHAPTER THIRTY

The alarm clock blared and Megan jumped. She reached out from under the blanket and felt around on the nightstand, trying to find the off button. She cracked open her eyes. It was nine a.m. She had quit working on Lucy's case and gone to bed around five. It seemed like she had just fallen asleep. She leveraged herself up on her elbow and turned the alarm off, then collapsed back onto the bed and stared at the ceiling. She was bone tired—both physically and emotionally.

After a few moments she swung her legs over the edge of the bed and put on her house slippers. The room felt cold even though it was the end of June. She got up, slipped on her robe, and wrapped it around her. As she headed for the bathroom her phone rang.

"Have you seen the morning news?"

It was Steve Windfield.

"Good morning to you too, Steve."

Windfield ignored her. "Have you seen the news?" His voice was full of impatience.

"No I haven't. Why?"

"Mattingly is on the news talking about how the firm you used to work for fired you."

Megan sat down on the edge of the bed.

"They've filed a suit against you for slander saying that you've fabricated stories against the firm that have damaged their reputation. Mattingly was being interviewed and he was blowing off about how the firm had to let you go and they have witnesses who will say you've set out to damage the firms' reputation." Windfield paused. "Mattingly said they can prove substantial damage and that you're attacking them from *all* angles."

"He means prosecuting Tarkington?" Megan said with a sigh of exasperation.

"Wrongfully," Windfield added. "According to Mattingly, Tarkington is just a victim of your vicious attack. You were fired from the firm and all of a sudden here you are as a special prosecutor going after a member of your former employer and the grandson of the founder. Mattingly said that they had tried to resolve the issue with you—just to make a good faith effort—and you refused and then started this campaign to prosecute Tarkington."

Megan felt sick. "Old Man Tarkington," she said softly.

"What about Justice Tarkington?" Windfield said.

Megan hadn't told anyone about her encounter with the Supreme Court justice. "He followed me home a while back and wanted to talk."

"He did what!" Megan could hear the shock in Windfield's voice. "Why didn't you tell me?"

Megan recounted what happened, adding that the justice had called her a couple of days ago to see if she was taking his offer.

"I told him no and before I could finish my sentence he hung up." She let out a sigh.

"They're going to do an all out attack on your credibility. Saying that you're taking on this case simply to gore the bull, so to speak. They're going to use the press to make us look bad. They've already started doing it."

A huge knot of tension balled in Megan's stomach. "They can attack me, but the law and the facts are still the same," she said angrily.

"And who decides the outcome of this case?" Windfield paused.

"The jury...."

"They're trying to hurt your credibility with the public, Megan. We'll have to be very careful in picking the jury to make sure this hasn't made them prejudiced against you."

Megan lay back down on the bed and stared at the ceiling. "I hate this."

"We'll have a press conference and address it all. Damage control. I fear this may just be the first of their tactics. Just wanted to give you a heads up before you turned on the TV or saw it in the paper."

Megan thanked Windfield and hung up. She knew how the game was played. Juries could be funny. If they had an ax to grind with a prosecutor it could come back to hurt the victim with a finding of not guilty or guilty of a much lesser charge. The prosecutor represented the law, and people would hold her to a high ethical standard. She'd seen it before in other cases. If she wasn't credible it could hurt Lucy's case.

She closed her eyes. She hadn't even made it to the bathroom yet and the day had turned into an emergency. Her phone started ringing again. She groaned and glanced at the screen. It was Eric Covington. "God, now what," she muttered. She picked up the phone and pressed the answer button. "Please tell me you have good news."

"Good morning to you, sunshine," Eric said with a laugh. "Having a tough morning?"

Megan told him about her conversation with Windfield.

Eric wasn't surprised. He'd been in police work for years before becoming a PI and knew how the system worked. "You must have them running scared and they're pulling out all the stops."

Megan could hear him take a sip of a drink. She'd known him for years and she knew he always started his day with a strong cup of black coffee. "Please tell me you have some good news," she said again.

The line went silent.

"Well," Megan said with an air of hesitancy.

"I just located Tarkington's second victim."

'What!" Megan hoisted herself up on her elbow. She felt her mood brighten. This could be just what she needed to get a conviction. Her heart was in her throat. "What did you find out?"

For several seconds the line was silent. "I'm sorry to add to your problems, Megan." Eric paused. "She's dead. She died in a car crash two years ago."

CHAPTER THIRTY ONE

"I have no further questions," Brockton Mattingly said and flipped his file folder shut.

Megan glanced at Lucy. She was white as a sheet.

"I want your client to sign the deposition after she reads it." Mattingly snapped the cap back on his pen. He had spent the best part of four and a half hours grilling Lucy on every aspect of her life. His questions were probing and varied—and at times some questions seemed to have absolutely no bearing on the case. He'd asked her everything from where she had grown up to questions about whether she had been a member of any sororities in college.

Mattingly told the court reporter to make two copies of the deposition, got up from the table, and began stuffing his briefcase with legal pads and files. He pressed shut his briefcase and turned to Megan. "Did you get the message from the court?"

Megan shook her head. "No clue what you're referring to," she said curtly. Since he had filed the lawsuit against her on behalf of the firm she trusted him even less than she had before and preferred to have as little interaction with him as possible.

Mattingly rested his hands on top of his briefcase. "The big criminal case that was scheduled to go to trial two weeks before our case got settled. The court wants to move our trial up earlier."

Megan felt like she had been kicked in the gut. She needed all the time she could get to prepare and pull this rabbit out of the hat. Now the situation was even worse. She did her best not to show her feelings; she knew Mattingly would love to see her show any sign of distress. Mattingly had defended enough rape cases to know that without any corroborating witnesses to support Lucy's allegations against Tarkington, he had at least a fifty-fifty chance of winning.

"Did the court officially move up our trial date?" she asked.

"Sure did." Mattingly smiled. "I'm sure you'll be getting notice." He spoke briefly to the court reporter about another case he had set for deposition and then turned and walked out the door.

The court reporter started gathering her materials and files. "No hurry," she said. "We don't have another deposition set for a couple of hours. You're welcome to use the room until then."

Megan smiled and thanked her. She'd always used this company for all her cases. They did great work and were good people.

Lucy leaned back in the chair and sighed. Megan could see her hands were trembling. Even though Lucy was an attorney, she had never practiced criminal law or been a victim in a case. This was an experience no one could adequately describe or prepare someone for. Megan reached over and touched Lucy on the arm. "You did a great job."

Lucy shook her head. "That was awful. I've never felt so….. degraded." Megan could see emotion welling up in her. Lucy raised her hand and quickly wiped away a tear that was starting to trickle down her cheek. "I feel like I'm the criminal who's on trial." She picked up her purse and searched for a tissue.

Megan understood. She had tried a lot of cases in her career and had seen many victims of a crime become yet another victim—the victim of the defense attorney. Once a victim came forward they were a target and the defense attorney did everything they could to tear their credibility apart and destroy their story. Especially in rape trials. Sadly, many times the victim came away more damaged by the legal system than they had been when they first came forward and asked for help.

Megan had done her best to protect Lucy throughout the deposition. She'd repeatedly objected to how aggressive Mattingly was being towards her. He asked his questions in a loud rude manner and tried to encroach on Lucy's personal space in any way he could. Megan knew that he was trying to intimidate her. The whole four and a half hours was a constant battle. Megan was exhausted.

"I can't believe he asked me about getting sued for non-payment of a credit card back in college." Lucy's face was riddled with confusion. "What does that have to do with me being raped?"

"He's doing a fishing expedition," Megan said. She reached over and took a hard candy from the small crystal dish in the center of the table. The candy was the best part of taking depositions. The court reporters always provided something. It helped with the boredom of the lawyers' endless questions.

Lucy shook her head. "But a small claims suit on a credit card? Years ago? And how did he know that I and my college roommates had been evicted?"

"Obviously they've done a big background investigation on you. Lawyers use whatever they can to attack a plaintiff or a witness's credibility."

Lucy sighed. "I know. This is what I've been dreading all along. All the digging around in my personal life looking for something to use to attack me in court. I thought I was prepared for it, but I wasn't. I didn't appreciate Mattingly asking me personal details about the guys I dated. Did they have criminal records? Were any of them married? Did they do drugs—and did I do them? Not to mention wanting to know when I became sexually involved with them and how that came about. The way he questioned me about them seemed to imply that I was either a money grubber or prostitute." She leaned back in the chair and looked at the crumpled tissue in her hands. "I feel like I've been raped again—but in a different way." She looked at Megan. "It was brutal. His questions sounded like I'm hiding something or...."

"That's the game, Lucy." Megan sighed.

Lucy nodded. The room fell silent. "I'm beginning to see why women don't want to come forward." Lucy said, casting a glance at Megan.

"This is just practice for the trial. Now you have an idea of how Mattingly will be." Megan started putting files in her briefcase. She didn't feel good about how the whole deposition had gone. Mattingly knew how to keep Lucy upset and how to make her look bad. He was a master at pushing people's buttons. At one point Megan, could feel Lucy getting ready to burst into tears and called for a break. She knew if Mattingly thought he had gotten to Lucy he would take that as a huge victory and intensify the attack.

Lucy shook her head and looked down at the table. Megan could see that her hands were still trembling when she picked up her glass of water and took a sip.

"One thing he didn't ask you about was the married guy you had the affair with—the IT genius." Megan could feel Lucy's energy shift. "In light of the extensive background investigation they've obviously done I'm kind of surprised they didn't ask about him."

Lucy said nothing.

Megan snapped shut her briefcase and set it on the table. She looked Lucy straight in the eye. "Was there anything significant that happened with him we need to be aware of? Tarkington and Mattingly are leaving no stone unturned and if there's something they'll find it."

Lucy reached down and picked up her purse off the floor. Suddenly, she let out a small gasp and placed her hand on her stomach.

"Are you alright?"

Lucy pushed her chair away from the table. "If we're done I need to go home. My doctor thinks I have an ulcer." She looked at Megan. "Imagine that. Me, an ulcer, after everything that happened this year."

The last couple of times Megan had seen Lucy she'd noticed Lucy didn't look well. She was pale and seemed emotionally spent. Megan knew the trial would be stressful but she was concerned about what a toll it already was taking on her. Megan got up from the table. "What can I do to help you?"

"Nothing. I appreciate your asking though. I just need to go home and take my medicine and relax."

"Let me know if you need anything. It's going to be alright."

Lucy smiled and Megan watched her walk out the door. Megan stayed in the room a few minutes longer, collecting her thoughts. How would Lucy hold up under the full pressure of a trial? she wondered. Mattingly had been hard on her today but the stress of actually going through a trial was a whole different thing. This deposition paled in comparison. If Mattingly tore her apart on cross examination it could be disastrous. And if Lucy couldn't hold up under all the pressure, not only Mattingly attacking her from every angle and prying into all aspects of her life, but the press snooping around and dogging her every step, there would be no case and the worst nightmare would come true: Another powerful man who'd committed a violent sexual assault on a woman would walk free.

CHAPTER THIRTY TWO

Steve Windfield tossed one newspaper after another down on the desk in front of Megan. "Look at this." He pointed to the array of media from all over the country.

"Endless press coverage of this case. It's the Justice Tarkington factor combined with Me Too. You'd think all that Me Too stuff would have died down by now."

Megan leaned forward and looked at it all.

"Hell," Windfield went on, "I even got a call from some women in Texas who've formed a support group for men who are wrongfully accused. She chewed on me for about twenty minutes, telling me how awful it was. I would allow a prosecution to go forward with you as prosecutor and no other witnesses supporting Lucy's claim." He rubbed his forehead, flopped down in the chair, reached into his top desk drawer, and pulled out a bottle of aspirin. He shook out two, popped them into his mouth, and washed them down with a swig of Coke. He tilted back in his chair. He looked weary, without a trace of the enthusiasm he'd shown when he took on the case and then forced Lucy to go through with it when she tried to back out. Back then he was positively aglow with excitement about the media attention the trial would bring and how much it would help his chances of getting reelected as prosecutor. Now he just seemed annoyed that he even had to deal with Megan on the case.

"Maybe I didn't think this through," he said. "Tarkington and Mattingly are working the media from every angle with the idea that you have an ax to grind with the firm and that's why you're helping prosecute Tarkington. I'm stunned that people are buying into that silliness. I'm not sure this has been a good idea. I worry about getting an impartial jury." He ran a hand through his hair.

"Are you saying you want to fire me?" It sure sounded like that to her. She felt her insides tighten. Part of her liked the idea of being fired. That would be one way to get out of this circus, to not have to deal with the discomfort that rose up in her whenever she thought about trying another rape case. But the other part of her felt furious that Windfield might be entertaining the possibility of getting another prosecutor to handle this case.

Windfield shook his head. "No, no, no," he said waving his hands. "However, I do think we need to do some damage control. I scheduled a press conference for tomorrow at two. So far we haven't responded to anything that Mattingly has put out to the press about you—all this vendetta bullshit."

Megan noticed that Windfield, who typically had nerves of steel, seemed rattled.

"I didn't think all their media propaganda would get much play . . . but I was wrong. " He paused. " We have to address these allegations to protect your credibility as prosecutor."

Megan let out a sigh of exasperation. "Look, Steve, I have no problem stepping down if that's what it takes. I want Lucy to win and I'll do whatever it takes for her to have the best chance." She shook her head. "I'm tired of living in this fishbowl. I went out to get my newspaper the other day and some TV guy jumped out of a car and shoved a mike in my face and started asking questions." She leaned back in her chair. "I won't miss this craziness at all. Everywhere I go there's someone in my face."

Windfield rested his hands on the desk. "You can't get out," he said softly.

"I can't?"

"If you get out now, then Mattingly and the media will have an even bigger field day. They'll claim you got out because you were acting in bad faith toward Tarkington and it came to light." Windfield leaned back in the chair and rubbed his eyes. "Oh, I can see it now. "

"They have *no* proof that I have any bad intentions toward Tarkington," Megan said angrily.

"We know that. But Mattingly's trying this case in the media and hoping to make it really hard for us to get a jury that will be impartial. Hell, I got a call from a friend of mine in Oregon. He knew all about this case. He's a prosecutor out there and he called to tell me we need to do some damage control. He said the more we don't respond the more the public sees us as hiding something."

Megan crossed her arms. "Oh, please." She was so angry she could hear her heart pounding in her ears. "So we have to get down in the mud with Mattingly and Tarkington."

Windfield said nothing.

"I'm here to help a victim of a crime. That's it." Megan stared at Windfield. She could see he was thinking and getting ready to say something.

"Look, I think we need to have the public see you." He tapped his finger on the desk. "The public evidently needs to hear from the prosecutor's office."

"What are you saying?" Megan said impatiently.

"You need to be at the press conference tomorrow. I'll address the press and then you should speak. Let the public see you and hear what you have to say."

"I'm not playing games with Mattingly and the press."

Windfield pointed his finger at her. "We need to do damage control, Megan. We have *no* choice. Otherwise, it'll be almost impossible to get a good jury that isn't against the victim from the start."

Megan was taken aback by his anger. She could tell he was really worried about where Lucy's case was headed.

"We have to fix it now. The press conference is set for tomorrow at two p.m. in the auditorium on the main floor of this building. I expect you to be there."

CHAPTER THIRTY THREE

Megan was seated on the stage behind the podium. She couldn't believe the number of people who had come to hear what the prosecutor's office had to say about the Tarkington case. From the looks of it there were around 1500 people crammed into the small auditorium on the first floor of the government building. Members of the media and members of the public were elbow to elbow waiting to hear the latest news. Windfield was right. People wanted to know what was really going on. Mattingly had done a great job of stirring up the public and making Tarkington look like the victim. In the audience were groups supporting Tarkington as well as supporters of Lucy.

Megan sat back and listened to Windfield address the crowd. He explained where the case was at as far as trial preparation and told the crowd that all safeguards were being taken to assure that Tarkington received a fair and impartial trial. He said that it was a prosecutor's duty to uphold the law and he took that duty very seriously, that Tarkington would receive no special treatment as the grandson of a Supreme Court justice and would be tried just like any other defendant, with the same protection the law gave to everyone accused.

"At this time I would like to introduce the special prosecutor handling this matter, Megan O'Reilly." Windfield turned and motioned for Megan to come forward. Camera flashes exploded all around the auditorium and reporters started yelling questions as she started toward the podium.

Windfield stepped back to the microphone and raised his hand. "Please, Ms. O'Reilly would like to speak and then afterwards she may take some questions." He cast a glance around at the sea of faces. The roar of voices subsided.

Megan could feel herself shaking inside. She looked out at the crowd. Some of the faces looked welcoming—some didn't. Megan grasped the podium and held on as tightly as she could. She felt as if her legs were going to give out. From years of trying cases in front of juries she knew how to appear completely calm even when her insides were churning. "Good afternoon. I'm Megan O'Reilly, special prosecutor for the Craig Tarkington case." She could hear a murmur of discontent threading through the crowd. "I wanted to introduce myself and let you meet me and understand my role in this case." She cast a glance down at the notes she had made about the points she wanted to cover.

She started off by telling the crowd about her legal training and her career, noting that she had been a deputy prosecutor in the sex crimes division for over fifteen years before she came to work at the Tarkington firm slightly more than ten years ago. "While I was a sex crimes prosecutor at the prosecutor's office I had the highest conviction rate to date."

A soft round of applause broke out.

"I am proud to say that I was the prosecutor who obtained the conviction against Judge Booth—proving that no one is above the law." The Booth case had been a front page trial that got national attention. "Judge Booth, a highly esteemed judge in D.C., retired amidst allegations of sexual assault against a member of his staff."

"You didn't happen to work for Judge Booth and get fired, did you?' a reporter yelled.

A light sprinkling of laughter broke out.

Megan ignored the comment. She described her spotless career at the Tarkington firm and explained that Lucy Hatfield had requested that she take the role of special prosecutor in the case against Craig Tarkington. She told the crowd how she had initially refused.

"Doesn't Windfield have seven floors of prosecutors?" another reporter yelled.

Megan looked towards the area where the voice had come from. "Mr. Windfield has a team of wonderful prosecutors. However, with my extensive background and experience Lucy Hatfield and then Mr. Windfield felt confident that I would be the best fit for this case." She cleared her throat, picked up the small glass of water sitting on the podium, and took a sip.

Jeff Hawkins, a well-known reporter for The New York Times, stood up. Megan instantly recognized him. She felt her heart thumping in her chest. Jeff Hawkins covered the biggest stories and asked the toughest and most probing questions. He was tall with graying black hair and sharp features. Many people who had been subject to his questioning felt like he was Satan in human form.

"It seems interesting; Ms. O'Reilly, that you get fired and now you are prosecuting the grandson of the firm you've sued for wrongful termination. Mr. Windfield is a fine prosecutor with quite a few highly trained attorneys on staff who could handle this case. Why you then?" He cocked his head and looked at Megan.

Megan looked right at him, and then quickly looked around the room. She could tell that the other reporters were chomping at the bit to pounce on her. They were letting Hawkins lead the way.

Steve Windfield got up and walked to the podium. "I can answer that question for you, Mr. Hawkins. And I am probably the best one to answer it since I'm the one who hired Megan as special prosecutor in this case."

Megan stood silently, grateful to have Windfield at the podium with her. It wasn't true that he had pursued her to be special prosecutor—she had requested it herself, because Lucy was so desperate to have her take the job. But she was grateful to Steve now for just saying he had hired her instead of going into all that.

"Megan O'Reilly is the highest trained sex crimes prosecutor in the D.C. area. You can check that out with the legal education division of the bar association. She also has the highest conviction rate." Windfield nodded in the direction of Hawkins and sat back down.

Hawkins waved his hand as if to completely dismiss Windfield's comments. "Ms O'Reilly, I am asking you this question, once again: Why are *you* agreeing to handle this case? I'm not interested in why Windfield wanted you to come on board, I get that. What I don't get is why you would agree to come back and prosecute one case—that case being against the grandson of a Supreme Court justice and the founder of the firm you were fired from and have sued for wrongful termination. Can you honestly say you don't have an ulterior motive?"

Megan stepped back up to the podium. She thanked Windfield and turned to look at Hawkins. She took hold of the podium and stood for several seconds collecting her thoughts. She hadn't wanted to take on this trial but another part of her did want to, and for basically the same reasons. For years as a prosecutor she had championed the cause of women who had been victims of violent sexual attacks. She was known to leave no stone unturned and fought for the victim with every bit of her ability. If something didn't go as she had hoped during trial—for example, a witness for the prosecution didn't come across well before the jury—she'd felt flashes of frustration and anger. She prepared a case until it was air tight.

Over the years, reporters and other people had asked her where her intense passion came from and why she seemed to take any loss or problem in a case so personally. In the past she had given a variety of plausible reasons. At least, she thought they were plausible. But today with Jeff Hawkins asking the question she knew she would have to give the real reason, as hard as that was going to be, as much as everything inside her was screaming at her not to.

She looked around the room and then at Hawkins. She took a deep breath. "I am a survivor of a rape."

A wave of hushed voices washed across the room.

Megan felt emotion welling up inside her. In all the years since the attack she had never come out and said those words.

"I'm one of those women who was too afraid to come forward." She inhaled, trying to push down the volcano of emotion erupting inside. The last thing she wanted to do was cry.

"I am one of those women who was afraid to stand up. I was a young woman in college with a wonderful future ahead of me—until this happened. It devastated me and cut me to the very core of my being." She paused. "The man who raped me was prominent in the community and held a very powerful position. He was much older than I was. I was young and scared. Really scared. I didn't have any support and he made it very clear I had better not say a word. "She looked out at rows of people hanging on to her every word and felt her hands tremble. "I spent years carrying the shame of it all. I chose to prosecute sex crimes to help heal, not only other women, but myself. To see that justice was served for those women who are brave enough to come forward and make men accountable." She looked down at the podium.

"I've prosecuted hundreds of cases. As many of you know, it's not always easy to get a guilty verdict in rape cases. I won more trials than other prosecutors, but I couldn't win every one. Every time I lost I felt more terrible than I can say. But there was one loss in particular that has haunted me." She shook her head and quickly wiped away a tear trickling down her face. She inhaled deeply, gathering her strength. "State versus Baker. Twelve years ago." She looked down at the podium. "The victim, Lisa Garrett, was a young woman who was brutally attacked, an attack so vicious that it left her suicidal and hospitalized with extensive injuries. Lisa was a young mother raising a two-year-old child all alone. The father was nowhere to be found. He had made it clear he wanted nothing to do with Lisa's little girl." Megan paused. She breathed in deeply and exhaled trying to calm herself. The mere thought of that case upset her.

"Lisa worked nights at a convenience store trying to make ends meet. It was at this store that she met the man who raped her, an all-star athlete from a Big Ten university." She swallowed. "It was my fault we lost the case. If I had done my job properly I would have found some background evidence on the defendant that I believe with all my heart would have insured a guilty verdict." She stopped and looked out at the crowd. "You see, in my opinion . . . I didn't do my research thoroughly. I was a prosecutor who had experienced great success and believed I could rest on my laurels." She shook her head. "If I had done my research properly I would have learned that there was another victim who had been raped by the guy who raped Lisa. I didn't find out about her until after the verdict. After Lisa Garrett's life had been destroyed."

Hearing these words spoken out loud was even harder than she had ever imagined they would be.

Lisa had gone steadily downhill after the not guilty verdict. She had gotten so depressed she couldn't get out of bed, and then started drinking heavily, lost her job and then her little girl. She had hung herself a year after the trial. Megan didn't tell the reporters any of that. What she had told the reporters was painful

"I let Lisa down," she said simply, looking at the crowd. "And after that I quit prosecuting."

Windfield walked up beside her, touched her gently on the shoulder, and handed her a glass of water. She thanked him and took a sip. She held the glass for a few moments, and then set it down on the podium.

"Lisa Garrett and her family never blamed me." She shook her head. "They should have." She glanced at the crowd and wiped at the tears slipping down her cheek. "So to answer your question, Mr. Hawkins, I have no ill will against Craig Tarkington or his family's law firm. I am doing this for Lucy, Lisa, and myself. For all the women whose lives have been torn apart by sexual violence. I wasn't as brave as Lucy is and Lisa was. I was too afraid to come forward to say my truth and try to keep the man who raped me from raping someone else."

Megan stood for a moment looking out at the crowd.

"I've been a coward in another way since I lost Lisa Garrett's case too. I've been afraid to face my failure with Lisa and go back to court to bring other rapists to justice. So, to repeat: This case is about Lucy, Lisa, me, and every woman who has been a victim. Every woman I help also helps heal me as a woman and as a lawyer."

The room was completely silent.

"And what if you lose again, Ms. O'Reilly," Jeff Hawkins asked.

Megan looked straight at him. "I won't."

CHAPTER THIRTY FOUR

Megan rubbed her eyes and looked at the clock. It was 4 a.m. and she was still wide awake. No matter how hard she tried she couldn't go to sleep. Her mind continued to churn through all the things she needed to do to prepare for Tarkington's trial. Finally she gave in at around 4:30 and got up. Three cups of coffee and half of a very large danish later, she was still stuck. What was bothering her was the fact that the whole case still came down to credibility contest between Lucy and Tarkington. Who would the jury believe?

The Lisa Garrett trial came back to her for the hundredth time since she tried to go to sleep last night. The jury had returned a verdict after only a couple of hours of deliberation—not guilty. She remembered Lisa's family bursting into tears when the jury foreman announced the verdict. She could still see Lisa's face—ashen and awash with complete disbelief. Megan herself had felt more devastated than she ever had in the courtroom. Now she would be back in the courtroom fighting to help another woman who had been sexually assaulted. She had to convince all twelve members of the jury that Tarkington was guilty. Right now, 45 days from the trial date, she had nothing but the rape kit and Lucy's testimony.

On the other hand, since the press conference the public had changed its perception of the prosecutor's office. She had received emails from women all over the country telling her how much they respected her for what she'd admitted at the press conference and for taking Lucy's case. She'd also received numerous requests for interviews from newspapers and TV shows. Overnight she, and the Washington, D.C. prosecutor's office along with her, had gone from having a questionable motive to being the champion of women everywhere. Windfield loved it and of course Mattingly and Tarkington didn't. Since the press conference they had both laid low, no doubt licking their wounds.

In some ways all the media attention had just increased the pressure on her. She tapped her pen on the desk. She had the complete burden to prove the allegations against Tarkington beyond a reasonable doubt—and that was no small measure.

She rubbed her temples. Her head was beginning to ache and her neck and shoulders felt so tight they hurt when she moved even slightly. She remembered again why she'd quit prosecuting rape cases. There was way too much stress involved in preparing and trying a case and the stakes were too high—all that on top of her own personal history made it almost unbearable at times.

She leaned back in the chair and looked out the window into the inky blackness. Daylight was still an hour away. The dark stillness made things seem worse to her. She thought about the woman she and Eric had talked to in New Mexico. That woman had made it very clear she wanted nothing to do with the case. And the other potential witness had been killed in a car accident. All she had was Lucy. And what if that wasn't enough? She felt her stomach tighten.

She grabbed a notepad and wrote down everything Lucy had told her about the rape. Lucy had said that it happened at his apartment. What time of day was it? She made a note to find out. Lucy had gone to help tutor him for the final law school exam. He asked her to meet him at his apartment and not their usual place at the library. Lucy had hesitated but agreed. Megan looked up from her notes. Eric Covington popped into her mind. She wrote a note to herself to call him. There were several things she wanted to talk with him about. She tapped the pen on the pad. Her mind continued churning through everything she remembered about the case. She couldn't recall the name of the apartment building Tarkington lived in. She made a note to find that out. She got up from the table and headed to the kitchen, taking her notes with her.

She put on a pot of coffee, grabbed a bowl, some milk, and a box of Cheerios and sat at the kitchen table. There had to be more to Lucy's case. Some way to help support what Lucy was saying about what had happened. Some piece of evidence. She needed to talk to Lucy again and make sure nothing had been missed.

CHAPTER THIRTY FIVE

The conference room at the prosecutor's office was bare and impersonal. It had one long rectangular table in the center lined with six chairs—three on each side—and rows of bookcases holding law books along the back wall. Most, if not all, of the law books were now available online and these were largely a decorative addition. A large artificial tree stood in one corner next to a small table holding a Keurig coffee maker. Next to that was a free-standing water cooler.

Megan had chosen to meet Lucy here instead of in her office because it was quieter on this end of the hall. Lately there seemed to be constant noise and activity outside her office and too many interruptions, too many people popping in, too many "only take a second" questions.

Megan took a seat at the conference table and opened the file. It seemed like the file of State vs. Tarkington had taken on a life of its own. What had once been a relatively small file was now bulging with papers. The other night when she couldn't sleep she had extracted each document, read it, and put it back in the file in its proper place.

Megan heard the door open and looked up. "Lucy, come in."

Lucy took off her jacket, rested it over the back of a chair, and looked at the clock on the wall. "I'm a little late. Sorry."

"No problem. I'm just reviewing your ever-growing file." Megan gestured toward the paperwork strewn across the tabletop and the bulging file lying on the table looking like a beached whale.

Lucy glanced at the lake of paper. "I saw Windfield when I came off the elevator. He said that you were deep into trial preparation."

Megan leaned back in the chair and rubbed her eyes. "I need to go over all this with you." She sighed and tipped the chair back to an upright position. "I want to ask you about some things."

Confusion washed over Lucy's face. "Is there a problem?" she asked.

Megan shook her head. "No. I just want to make sure the case is as tight as it can be. Just being cautious." As she said the words Lisa Garrett popped into her mind and she felt her stomach tighten. "I've made some notes." She picked up the legal pad. "The day of the rape, what time did you go to Tarkington's apartment to tutor him?"

Lucy's expression darkened. Megan could tell that just hearing Tarkington's name upset her. Every time she talked to Lucy about the attack Lucy emotionally shut down. She always recounted the nightmare in a matter-of-fact way as if she was trying to control her feelings. Megan wondered how she would do at trial. She didn't want Lucy to be an emotional wreck that a jury might write off as an unstable woman, but she also didn't want her to appear cold and indifferent, which could make the jury question her truthfulness or not like her. Megan knew how juries could be. You never knew what they might do, and sometimes they would take a dislike to a victim.

Megan knew she had to have Lucy tell her story the way she had originally told it to Megan and then to Windfield, in a truthful and sincere way.

"It was around nine p.m. I wanted to go to his place earlier but he said he couldn't. He had a meeting or something." Lucy looked down at the table.

Megan scribbled some notes. "Where exactly was his apartment? You said he lived off campus." She'd found the name and location of Tarkington's building in the file but she wanted to hear where he lived at the time of the rape from Lucy.

"It was on Menlo Avenue. The apartment building there by the park. The Lakeworth."

"Pretty fancy place. What floor did he live on? "

Megan saw a flash of frustration in Lucy's eyes.

"Why does that matter?"

Megan put down the pen. She had barely started questioning Lucy and Lucy was already upset. "Everything matters. You know that. Something that may seem trivial can lead to evidence that helps the case."

Of course Lucy knew that every detail mattered when it came to trial preparation—she was essentially a lawyer herself, had a law degree and had been a legal assistant. But it was a familiar joke in the law business that lawyers made the worst clients and witnesses. They violated all the rules they set for clients and forgot what was involved in preparing a case.

Lucy sighed. "The 12th floor."

Megan asked her whether she had seen anyone the night she was there. Lucy told her she had seen no one. She said that when she got there Tarkington was waiting on her. He said he had gotten out of his meeting early. She didn't know where he had been or what his meeting was about.

Megan started going through what Lucy had told her about the attack itself, what Tarkington had done to her. She stopped when she saw Lucy trembling. She could tell it was taking everything Lucy had to keep herself pulled together and that her frozen emotions were breaking free. Lucy began to cry, first tears and then sobs, as if she was reliving the whole nightmare.

Megan got up, got a box of tissues sitting on a table in the corner, and set them in front of Lucy.

Lucy stopped crying, grabbed a fistful of tissues, and wiped her face. "This whole thing is killing me," she said. "The closer it gets to trial the worse I feel. My doctor gave me sleeping pills. I've never taken sleeping pills in my life." She looked down at the table. The women sat in silence for several moments.

Then Megan touched Lucy's arm. "I'm sorry to put you through all this. We just have to be prepared." She picked up her legal pad and scanned her notes. "You went directly to the hospital after the attack, right?"

Lucy nodded "Yes."

Megan rifled through the file until she found the paperwork from the hospital. It showed that Lucy had reported what had happened that night to the hospital staff, describing it just as she did today—word for word. Her story was solid. That would help some when Lucy was testifying. Unless Mattingly found some way to make Lucy look like she was lying, which he would no doubt try to do. Megan wondered what he could say to take apart Lucy's story. Knowing Mattingly, he would probably try and make it all sound like it was Lucy's idea to meet Tarkington at his place and that she was interested in him romantically.

Megan knew Tarkington's DNA would be in the rape kit but nobody would know it was his without him agreeing to give a sample. He wouldn't give a sample, for the obvious reasons. Even legally that would be inadmissible in court since it would be incriminating himself. "The clothing you had on that night was kept by the hospital and is part of the rape kit," she said, thinking out loud. "Do you have anything of Tarkington's? A book? Notes? Anything that he would have touched?"

Lucy thought for several moments and then shook her head. "I'm pretty sure I don't."

Megan wrote something down on her legal pad.

"After you left the hospital what happened?"

Lucy looked at the crumpled tissue in her hands. She told Megan she had gone home. She received a call from the Sheriff's Department the next day. The department had obtained the rape kit from the hospital and wanted to talk to her. She told Megan she had gone and met with the main detective who handled sexual assault cases and gave him a statement.

"When I said it was Craig Tarkington I felt like he lost interest. He told me he would be back in touch. I never heard another word."

Megan stopped writing. "Unbelievable. A woman gets attacked and they let the guy get away with it if he comes from a well-known family, a family with a member who is a Supreme Court justice. I thought things had gotten better with the MeToo era but I guess all that still lives on in D.C. "Megan scribbled something on the legal pad. "Did you try to follow up?"

"I did. I contacted the department two weeks after I filed the report and they said they were still processing it and if they had any questions or needed more information they'd be in touch. When I called them two weeks later they said the same thing. I called two more times and received the same story. After that I gave up and started thinking about who else I could contact for help. When I saw you in the coffee shop that day I recognized you as the prosecutor in the Judge Booth case and decided to try to talk to you."

Lucy gave her a long serious look.

Once again Megan thought of Lisa Garrett and felt a twinge of anxiety. She pushed the outcome of Lisa's trial out of her mind.

"Is there anything you can recall that you haven't told me or the police about the attack? Anything at all." Megan studied Lucy's face hoping there was something else. Anything that might help the case or lead to more evidence against Tarkington.

Lucy shook her head. "There's nothing else. That's it."

Megan heard the door open, turned around, and saw Windfield.

"Remember we have a meeting in five minutes," he said. He nodded at Lucy. "Good seeing you. Things are on track and looking good." Before Lucy could respond he was gone.

Lucy smiled, got up and gathered her coat. "I hope this helped. If I can think of anything else I'll let you know." She smiled apologetically as if she should have given Megan better information.

Megan thanked her and told her she'd be in touch. Once Lucy was gone Megan collapsed in the chair and sighed. "Nothing seems to help this case."

CHAPTER THIRTY SIX

Megan's eyes flew open and she shot straight up in the bed. She grabbed her robe, threw it on, and hurried down the stairs to her study. She looked at the clock. It was seven-forty a.m. She had spent another restless night tossing and turning, searching for something—anything—that could help bolster Lucy's testimony. She had finally dozed off at around four a.m. But now she had it: the solution to the problem of the DNA. It had come to her when she was making the transition from sleeping to waking a few minutes ago. The gift certificate. Tarkington had given her a gift certificate from Tiffany's to thank her for training him for his new job at the law firm. That would have his DNA on it that could be compared to the DNA in the rape kit to prove it was him that raped Lucy.

Megan jumped up, pulled on her robe and headed downstairs to her office.

She pulled open her center desk drawer and rifled through the contents. She felt certain she had kept the used certificate and envelope. She didn't see it. She yanked open each of the remaining drawers and searched their contents. She let out a sigh of exasperation. "Nothing." Her mind raced trying to think of anywhere else she could have put the certificate. She could think of anywhere else.

She sat down at her desk, opened her laptop and watched the screen came alive. She looked up the inmate list for the D.C. jail. Once she found it she scrolled down through the intake records that were completed when Tarkington was booked after he was charged with the rape. The jail staff always completed the intake immediately when prisoners were booked into the jail. Shortly after Tarkington's was completed he had bailed out

"There," she muttered and pressed a key.

'D.C. Police Department Intake Procedure List for Inmate Craig Tarkington.'

Nervously, she scrolled through the pages. She knew the procedure. After arrest, an inmate's personal items were taken from him, inventoried and placed in secure storage until the case was over. Then they conducted a physical examination. She continued scanning the page. 'Inventory of clothing, personal items....' She scrolled down farther. 'Body exam for infectious diseases...' The more she read the more nervous she became. "There!" she slapped her hand down on the desk. "Yes! There it is!"

'Defendant Craig Tarkington was given a DNA mouth swab test and the results will be provided to the DNA Central Repository for inclusion in the National Registry.'

She leaned back in her chair. "I knew it!" She grabbed her phone and tapped in a number.

"Hello," Eric Covington answered groggily.

"Hey Eric, it's Megan. Wake up, sunshine."

Eric groaned. "Isn't it a little early, Megan?"

Megan laughed. "It's never too early to nail a criminal like Craig Tarkington!"

"I'm lost, what's happened. Fill me in."

"I was laying in bed the other morning thinking about this case. All of a sudden I remembered that Tarkington had given me a gift certificate to thank me for training him for his new job at the firm. "She gently slapped her palm against her forehead. " I thought that would solve our problem of not having Tarkington's DNA since he had handled it and his DNA would be on the envelope."

Megan could tell he was hanging on her every word.

"I had used the gift certificate and put it in my desk. I 'm thinking there was a tiny amount still left on it. Maybe five dollars."

Megan leaned back and ran her hand through her hair. "I searched through the whole desk and couldn't find it."

Eric sighed.

"Then I remembered some case law that allows police agencies to take a DNA sample from criminal defendants who are charged with serious felonies. They place the DNA in a repository that everybody in the U.S. has access to. This can help other victims find perpetrators."

"Wasn't there a big to-do about that?" Eric said. "Lots of people thought that by taking a mouth swab for DNA you were forcing a defendant to give evidence against himself—like testifying against himself. I remember there were all sorts of protests and court hearings about how that would violate a person's constitutional right against self-incrimination." Megan could hear Eric yawn. "Last I knew people were still fighting about whether it should be allowed."

"The Supreme Court ruled a few months ago that police agencies could take DNA mouth swabs and it was not a violation of a defendant's right not to testify against himself,"

Megan said. "I looked on the sheriff department's website. They did a mouth swab on Tarkington. Now we have his DNA to compare to what's in the rape kit for Lucy." Megan felt more alive than she had in days.

She could feel Eric's energy change too. "This could destroy the defense. Mattingly will throw a fit and do everything he can to block the admission of the swab test."

"Tough for him. He doesn't have a say in it. All any defense attorney can do is try to attack the procedure that was used to collect the DNA or try to show that the testing on it wasn't done properly."

"This is huge! I'm surprised you didn't think of this before."

"I know," Megan said. "But the ruling is really new. I haven't seen any precedents for it although there probably have been some."

"What do you want me to do?" Eric said. Megan could feel his excitement.

"I'm going to call the sheriff's department and ask them to pull their results from Tarkington's intake swab test and the report on the DNA in Lucy's rape kit. If you can, run by the department and pick them up."

"No problem."

"I'd also like to have you snoop around at the building Tarkington lived in when the rape occurred," Megan continued. "He still lives there. "It's that apartment building on the east side of town called The Lakeworth. He lives on the twelfth floor. Who knows, maybe someone saw Lucy that night when she came in or left."

"Will do."

Megan could hear a bed squeak. Eric was getting up. For a moment she pictured him in a t-shirt and boxers and felt herself blushing, even though she was all alone in her house and Eric couldn't possibly know what she was thinking. And there was really nothing to be embarrassed about. They had briefly dated back in the 80s but the timing wasn't right. They both were going different directions building their careers. Still at times, she wondered if they would have had a future together if the timing had been different.

"How soon do you need all this done and for me to get you the info on the DNA testing results?" Eric asked, clueless.

"No big hurry. It will take at least three days for the police department to compile all the info I want," she said. "At least I hope it's that quick. " From experience she knew that the police department was overworked and understaffed. "I'll call and give them permission to give it all to you when it's ready."

"I'll go to the Lakeworth apartments today and see what I can come up with."

Megan thanked him and hung up. Things were on an upswing. Now it was just putting the case together.

CHAPTER THIRTY SEVEN

Megan's phone buzzed on the coffee table. She looked down and saw Eric's number flashing on the screen. It had been over a week since she'd asked him to pick up the reports on the results of Tarkington's intake swab and the hospital's findings on the rape kit exam, which the hospital had shipped to the police department for review and to be made part of the possible prosecutions file.

Megan touched the Answer button, leaned back against the couch, and cast a glance out the window. It was August 5th and the trial date was September 30th. Megan felt hot just looking outside, or maybe it was the thought of the trial getting closer every day that made her sweat.

"Have you picked up the DNA and rape kit results yet?" she asked Eric.

"No, I haven't. The last time I called the police department they still didn't have them ready. I have to run by the jail on another matter. I can check on them while I'm there."

Megan thanked him. "I'll call and let the jail know you'll be by today."

"I went by The Lakeworth," Eric said. "Nice place. I'm sure those apartments cost a pretty penny. I forgot how the other half lives." Eric laughed.

"Only the best for Tarkington," Megan said. In the background she could hear the soft sound of Billy Joel singing 'I love you just the way you are' on the sound system in Eric's car.

"I cased the whole place. Quiet, much to my surprise. The people I did see were older couples—obviously with money. They made it clear that they were about their own business. I was lucky if I got brief eye contact. To tell you the truth, I'm kind of surprised that place doesn't have a doorman."

"How did you get in?"

"I walked in behind a guy who lived there. He acted like he knew me and held the door." Eric explained how he had gone around the building, visiting several floors and looking around.

"So it was a dead end?"

"Far from it."

Megan sat up.

"I noticed while walking around that there are security cameras everywhere. I finally found the security guy in an office on the second floor—he wasn't happy that I'd managed to get in. We talked for a while. Bottom line is, the cameras run 24/7 and they keep the videos for a few years. Three, I think."

Megan felt new energy shooting through her. "Then they would have footage from the day of the rape." Her mind raced with the possibilities this new discovery could have.

"We could see Tarkington get home, Lucy go in a while later and then come out in rough shape."

"That's right," Eric said. "While I was there the security guard replayed the videos taken that morning and found the one with me entering the building. It wasn't the best video I've seen but it was clear enough to tell it was me coming through the door."

Megan jumped up and began to pace the room. "Incredible work, Eric! What does the security guy need from us to turn over the video for the day of the rape? A subpoena?"

"Yeah. He said if you get him a subpoena with the dates you want to view and what floor you want the video from he can pull the files and email the videos to you."

"The videos have the date and time on them when they were taken?"

"Sure do."

Megan ran over to her laptop, flipped it open, pulled up a subpoena form, and filled it out while Eric gave her the info on the security guard. Then she emailed a copy to the guard as well as one to the clerk of courts. Since there was a pending case she didn't need a judge to sign off on it.

"The subpoena is on its way. Great work, Eric. We've hit another home run."

CHAPTER THIRTY EIGHT

"Where are we at on Lucy's case?" Steve Windfield asked, looking at Megan across his desk.

Megan picked up her cup of coffee and took a sip. "I have some great news."

Windfield's eyes brightened. "Like what?"

Megan told him how she'd realized the police department would have a DNA sample for Tarkington from the mouth swab they did during booking.

Windfield grinned. "Excellent! When will we have the results of the DNA comparison?"

"I still haven't gotten the DNA reports from the police department. After they come I'll ask Martha Black"—Martha was a legal assistant in the prosecutor's sex crimes division—"to ship them to Logistics to do the comparison. Logistics told her that would take them at least a couple of weeks."

"Mattingly will throw a raging fit about admitting the DNA test taken by the jail."

Megan nodded. "I would too. But with the latest Supreme Court ruling he'll hit a brick wall." She repeated what she'd said to Eric about Old Man Tarkington laying the groundwork for his own grandson's conviction. Steve grinned at her and rubbed the side of his face.

Megan could see the wheels turning. He was thinking of all the ways Mattingly and Tarkington would try to block the DNA results from being admitted.

"I imagine they'll hire several experts to say the testing wasn't done correctly and it should be thrown out." Windfield tapped his pen on the desk.

"We'll be prepared. Defense attorneys try that all the time but it's hard to get the results blocked unless the testing agency is just a complete screw-up."

Windfield nodded, leaned back in his chair, and folded his hands behind his head. "I love it when a case comes together," he said with a big smile. "What else?"

Megan told him what Eric Covington had discovered when he went to the Towers. "I sent a subpoena to the apartment security guy and he's sending me the videos. I'm hoping to get them any day. We should be able to show Tarkington coming home and Lucy arriving and leaving, how she looked when she arrived and how she looked when she left. I saw some of their security video from a different day and the footage was clear enough to get a good look at the person coming into the building."

Windfield rubbed his hands together and grinned. "Mattingly and Tarkington will shit a brick." He leaned over the desk and shook Megan's hand. "Excellent work, counselor."

CHAPTER THIRTY NINE

Megan looked at her calendar. It had been almost two weeks since she had requested the information on Lucy's rape kit and Tarkington's DNA mouth swab from the police department. She knew they were busy at the department but it would only take a few moments to pull the kit and Tarkington's test results. She picked up the phone and punched in the chief of police's extension. That was one thing about being at the prosecutor's office—if you needed something it was usually only an extension number away.

"Police department," a voice bellowed. In the background she could hear the loud voices of inmates and police officers reverberating off cement floors and metal counters.

"This is Megan O'Reilly. A couple of weeks ago I made a request to have the rape kit test results on Lucy Hatfield pulled and sent to me along with a DNA swab test that was done on Defendant Craig Tarkington." Megan could hear the officer's walkie talking chatting away. "I was calling to ask the status of that request."

She waited while the officer radioed another division. She could hear a voice crackle through the static responding to the officer, but she couldn't understand what the person was saying.

"Yes, Ma'am. Thank you," the officer said. "Ms. O'Reilly, the lady I just spoke to said that you will need to talk to Chief Cutsinger about this. Do you want me to transfer you?"

Megan was at a complete loss. In all the years she had prosecuted cases she had never had to talk to the Chief himself about something like this. "Is there a problem?"

The officer didn't respond to her question. "I'll transfer you now."

She heard a click and a series of noises and then the phone started ringing on the other end. "Chief Cutsinger's office."

Megan paused and gathered her words. "Yes, this is Megan O'Reilly, I was just transferred from the jail to speak with the Chief about a rape kit and an inmate's DNA swab that I requested."

There was an awkward pause. "Is this regarding the Lucy Hatfield rape kit?" the lady on the other end asked.

Megan told her it was and what she needed.

"Hold please."

The line went silent.

"Hello Megan," a deep voice boomed in her ear. It was Chief Cutsinger himself.

"Sorry to bother you, Chief. I'm not sure why the department felt it was necessary to put me through to you. I know how busy you are." Megan went on to say why she was calling and what she needed. When she finished there was a pause—a pause she didn't like. She felt in her gut that something wasn't right. After what seemed like an eternity Chief Cutsinger spoke.

"Megan, I hate to tell you this." He let out a sigh of frustration.

Megan could feel her heart begin to beat faster.

"We've had a terrible accident here at the department with the rape kits. You'll be reading about it any day in the paper. It's awful and makes us all look like incompetent public servants." He paused. "I'm responsible as the Chief but I don't know how it happened."

"What's the problem?' Megan asked politely, trying to get him to cut to the chase.

The line was silent for several moments.

"The department accidentally destroyed quite a few rape kits. We had a lot of them that had been here forever and we needed the space. These kits were never even tested because the victims wouldn't cooperate with law enforcement."

"With all due respect, Chief, what does that have to do with Lucy Hatfield's rape kit and the DNA swab test? She has cooperated with law enforcement and has a pending criminal charge against the defendant."

The line was silent.

Megan's patience was growing thin. The nervous energy coursing through her didn't help any. "Chief?"

"When the old kits were destroyed some newer kits were accidentally destroyed as well."

Megan felt her stomach drop.

"Lucy Hatfield's rape kit was one of the ones accidentally destroyed."

Megan was stunned. This couldn't be right. What was going on here?

Chief Cutsinger said that it had simply been an accident and there was no other excuse he had to offer. "I can't believe it myself. We aren't the only department to have this happen recently," he said apologetically. "You'll be hearing about several other departments experiencing the same screw-ups—accidentally destroying new rape kits in the process of getting rid of old ones."

Megan could tell that he was genuinely upset. She had known Chief Cutsinger for years and he was always very professional. "I understand the kits were destroyed," she said. "But was Lucy's tested for DNA before it was destroyed? Do we at least have the test results?" Typically the police department didn't drag their heels when it came to testing.

Silence.

"I'm sorry, Megan. No. It wasn't tested. There's nothing to give you."

Megan leaned back in her chair and covered her eyes with her hands.

CHAPTER FORTY

Rape Kits Wrongfully Destroyed by D.C. Police Department, the headline screamed—front page, bold.

Megan was sick to her stomach. It had been less than 24 hours since her conversation with Chief Cutsinger and now, coincidentally, the media was all over the story. Megan read the Washington Post article again.

"Last week it was revealed that 25 law enforcement agencies in 14 states including the Washington D.C. Police Department destroyed rape kits in 400 cases before the statutes of limitations expired or when there was no time limit to prosecute.

The number is likely higher than 400. There are an estimated 17,000 law enforcement agencies in the country.

The destruction has occurred over the past two years and often followed flawed and incomplete investigations. Dozens of kits were trashed mere weeks or months after police took custody of the evidence, records showed. Many kits were also destroyed that were to be evidence in pending trials against criminal defendants accused of sexual assault.

Almost 80% were never tested for DNA evidence, a process that can identify a suspect or link that person to other crimes."

Megan threw the paper down on her desk. Her disappointment was almost unbearable.

"Unbelievable," she muttered. "Absolutely outrageous." She swiveled around in the chair and looked out the window at the D.C skyline. A blanket of gray fog covered the city and sheets of rain were pouring down. The weather fit her mood. Right now things looked pretty grim. She not only had no rape kit to back up the fact that Lucy had been sexually assaulted, she had lost the chance to nail Tarkington with a DNA comparison test using the DNA swab that had been taken when he was booked into the jail. It was inconceivable that everything had been destroyed —everything.

The rape kit getting destroyed was a devastating blow that made her insides feel raw. She was back to being left with Lucy's word versus Tarkington's. Lucy was a strong witness and presented herself well. But so did Tarkington, and he had the weight and resources of the firm and a Supreme Court justice grandfather behind him. Megan had suffered blows in the past when prosecuting cases, when witnesses disappeared or changed their testimony at the last minute, but this blow, the loss of the rape kit evidence, felt like the worst.

She called Lucy, told her what had happened and assured her that the case would still go forward.

We're screwed," Lucy finally said softly. "We've lost before we even got started."

Megan spent at least a half hour explaining to Lucy that all was not lost. They had suffered another blow but they still had her testimony and she was a very credible witness.

After what seemed like an eternity, Lucy came around. "We always overcome," she said and Megan agreed. What Megan didn't say was that this blow was by far the most devastating one and one that they might not overcome. The case of The People Versus Craig Tarkington now rested completely on Lucy's credibility.

Megan hung up and sat staring at the wall. When she'd called Windfield yesterday after her phone call with Chief Cutsinger, Windfield had been upset but said he felt she would still be able to prove the case somehow. She knew he was right. There had been many sexual assault cases successfully prosecuted on only the testimony of the victim, and something else was likely to present itself. Still, Megan wished she felt more confident about her ability to win Lucy's case.

She heard a knock and swiveled around to see Eric standing in the doorway. He'd called an hour ago after he saw the article in the paper and reminded her that despite the devastating loss of the rape kit, they still had the security video from Tarkington's apartment building.

"Did you get the email from the security officer about the video?" he said, sliding down into a chair.

That was another thing. Megan had gotten the email with the security footage about an hour ago. She'd only had time to glance at it but she saw enough to be disappointed in the quality. "They just sent me the outside footage," she told Eric. "It's not really clear at all—not like the footage you saw when you went over there. In the one they sent me you can see what looks like a woman coming into the building and leaving but I can't say one hundred percent that anyone would be able to identify the person as Lucy." Megan shook her head.

"But it shows the time and date, right?"

"Yes."

"We're putting this case together piece by piece, Megan. Let me see the security video they sent you." Eric leaned forward and placed his arms on the desk.

Megan tapped the keys on the computer and turned the screen around for Eric to see. She looked at him as he watched the video. She could tell by his expression he wasn't thrilled with what he was seeing either.

"Well, I think it's good enough. It establishes the date and time and I think the jury can tell it's a woman." Eric was in full cop mode. "On the way over to see you I called the guy who works security at the apartment building. He said he'll have the inside security video to you today. That's what could put the nails in Tarkington's coffin." Eric stood up. "Let me know when you get it. " He rapped his knuckles on the desk. "We may have had a little setback but the war ain't over yet."

CHAPTER FORTY ONE

Megan yawned and stretched. She'd been at the office since early in the morning and it was close to nine p.m. now. No matter how many times she went over Lucy's case, she couldn't think of anything else she could do to make it stronger. It was still down to the security video and Lucy's testimony.

Everyone at the prosecutor's office had gone home and the floor was eerily quiet. Eric had said she should have the inside security videos by this evening. She opened her email, leaned over and squinted at the list of new messages. There it was:

"Dear Ms. O'Reilly,

Please find attached the security videos you requested. Should you have any questions please feel free to contact me. Sincerely, James Calahan, Director of Security, The Lakeworth

Megan clicked on the attachment and waited for the videos to load. After a moment the screen came to life, showing a clear picture of a hallway and Tarkington's front door. She looked for the date and time the video was recorded and found it in the bottom left corner. The video footage had been narrowed down to show one hour before

Lucy said she'd arrived and one hour after Lucy said she'd left Tarkington's apartment.

Megan fast-forwarded the video until she saw Tarkington show up, coming home about a half hour before Lucy was set to arrive. The picture was crisp and clear, nothing like the outside security videos she'd seen. There was no doubt it was Tarkington on the screen. He was dressed in a blue polo shirt and jeans and was walking at a brisk clip. She would know that walk anywhere—full of confidence and determination. A green backpack was slung over his shoulder.

Megan felt a wave of relief wash over her. It was the first time she'd felt hope about winning the case since the blow of the rape kit being accidentally destroyed by the police department.

She watched as Tarkington unlocked his door and went inside. The video continued to play with nothing noteworthy happening in the hallway. She looked at the time in the lower corner of the video. Lucy should be coming at any moment. She felt excitement building in her and leaned in closer.

Then something strange happened: the screen began to jiggle and jump. Megan found the video stop button, pushed it, and then pressed play again. The video started again, continuing the stuttering. She saw patches of black and then snowy pictures of Tarkington's door. Her heart began to race and she felt her stomach tighten. She pressed stop again and then start again. The screen came back on. It was still snowy and the picture seemed to be cutting out and then returning briefly before it cut out again. As she was trying to fix it she saw something moving into the picture on the left side of the screen. It had to be a figure coming down the hall. Lucy.

Megan looked at the time on the screen. It was exactly when Lucy said she went to Tarkington's apartment. But the picture was so fuzzy Megan could only see a wave of movement on the screen. She looked down at the keyboard, trying to figure out what she could do to fix it. All of a sudden the screen went black.

CHAPTER FORTY TWO

Megan sat at the desk in her office. She'd spent an hour trying to bring the video back up after her computer screen went blank. No luck. She figured the security guy at The Lakeworth must have emailed her a faulty file. She'd tried several times to call the security office and only received the voicemail. She then she called the cell phone number for the security guy she and Eric had talked to, but every time she called number she got voicemail as well. She left messages at both numbers. Tired of waiting for someone to call back, she packed her stuff and headed to the car. She would swing by The Lakeworth, find security, and get another file sent to her of the video.

Megan walked up to the entrance of The Lakeworth and pressed a button by the front door. The intercom crackled to life.

"Security, can I help you?"

It was him—the guy she and Eric talked to. She felt irritated for a moment. Evidently he was at the office but just not returning calls.

"This is Megan O'Reilly. Can I come in and talk to you?"

The door buzzed and clicked.

Once Megan got inside she remembered Eric had said to take the elevator to the second floor and turn right. She hurried down the hallway until she came to a door that was half ajar, with a sign that said Security. She knocked.

"Come in," a scratchy voice called.

A man with dark hair, wearing a crisp white shirt with Security The Lakeworth emblazoned over the left breast pocket, was sitting at a desk in front of five large screens.

She extended her hand. "Thank you for seeing me."

The security guy motioned for her to have a seat.

"I know you're busy so I won't take much of your time." She reminded him who she was and why she needed the videos and explained what had happened when she tried to watch what he'd sent.

"I really need to see that footage. I figure the file must be bad."

The security guy pulled a pair of glasses from the center drawer of the desk and put them on, turned toward the computer on his desk, tapped some keys, and waited. From his change of expression Megan could tell something had come up on the screen. He leaned forward and squinted, then stabbed one key. Megan watched him roll his head from left to right and back as if reading something. She leaned back in the chair and waited.

"Give me one moment, Ms. O'Reilly," the security guy said, getting up from his chair. Before she could say anything he was out the door. When he came back he sat down, took a piece of paper out of his shirt pocket, and put it on the desk. He looked down at the paper and then back at the screen and typed in something. Megan watched him study the paper and then look back at the screen as if checking. After a few minutes he pushed the computer away. Megan felt her stomach tighten. She could tell he wasn't happy.

"I went down to check with our IT guy." He paused and raked a hand through his hair. "I thought what we had was a faulty file. It's happened before and all we do is resend it. We don't have that issue this time."

Megan saw his expression darken.

"We have a system failure."

Megan said nothing. She could feel the other shoe getting ready to drop.

"We don't have any footage of the floor you requested or even the grounds around the outside of the building for the period of time on the day you're wanting. We have no footage of anything. The system apparently crashed when we were downloading for a short period that night."

Megan felt a wave of nausea wash over her. "You have nothing?" she asked, stunned.

"No. I checked with IT to find out what they knew and if they had any video files for that date and time and they told me what had happened. I guess we had a security blackout for a few hours. I'm really sorry."

Megan sat for a couple of moments taking it all in. Finally she got up, shook the security guy's hand, put on her coat, and headed out the door.

CHAPTER FORTY THREE

Megan looked at the clock on her desk in her study. It was five a.m. Yesterday she had met with the security guy at The Lakeworth and had received the devastating news that there was no security video for the night of Lucy's rape.

She had spent the night sitting in her study going over every angle of Lucy's case. It seemed as if they could never get a break. Every time she felt that there was a piece of evidence that would help strengthen the case it turned out to be a dead end. She pushed herself away from the desk and stretched.

One thing was clear: She needed to have both Eric and Lucy over for coffee later that morning to talk. Something told her she needed to have them both come together so the three of them could brainstorm. Several times in the past, while she was working on a case, she'd called the victim and the whole prosecution team in for a meeting to go over the entire case. More often than not it was amazing how helpful that was in trial preparation. As she often did, she thought of Lisa Garrett and her stomach tightened. If she'd had a meeting like that during the preparation for Lisa's trial she probably wouldn't have made the mistake that cost them. She would have known that her main witness—the prosecution's main witness—had a perjury conviction several years earlier in another state. She'd been overly confident and lax in preparation and it had cost her dearly. She still woke up in the middle of the night sometimes thinking about Lisa and feeling like she'd failed her.

A few hours later Megan poured Eric and Lucy cups of coffee and sat down at the kitchen table with them. Without the rape kit results and the security video to confirm Lucy's story, the whole case was back to square one.

"It's hard to believe there was a freak system failure with the security cameras at Tarkington's apartment building at the exact moment you were arriving," Megan said looking at Lucy. She took a sip of hot coffee and set the cup back down. "It doesn't feel right to me. My gut tells me there's something else going on."

"Makes me wonder," Eric said. He reached for the Half and Half and poured a ribbon of it into his cup. "I called the security guy this morning and asked how long they've been having problems with the security system and if there's been any other system failures. He said they installed these security cameras two years ago and there's never been a single problem up till now."

"So the only time the cameras didn't work was when Lucy was about to arrive. Other than that the cameras have always been fine." Megan dropped a cube of sugar in her coffee and stirred.

Eric nodded. "The guy said the system rebooted four hours after the crash and it worked the rest of the night." He took a blueberry muffin from the basket on the table.

Megan leaned back in the chair and crossed her arms. "I want to know more about that system. I can't imagine they don't have a backup system or something."

"I know a guy who works for the company that designed and manufactured the system," Eric said. "I can check with him."

"Fantastic," Megan said. She wished she could think of additional ways to figure out what had gone wrong and whether there was something suspicious going on, but she couldn't. Still, this was better than nothing. She felt her mood brightening. She picked up the coffee pot and topped off her cup, took a deep breath and looked at her notes, searching for anything she might have missed.

"Lucy, when you were at Tarkington's that night, did you see or speak to anyone?

Megan studied Lucy's face. She had already asked Lucy this once before and she'd said no, but Megan had learned that sometimes people remembered things if you kept asking them the same questions.

"No…" Lucy paused and sat for a few moments thinking. "Well, yes. Yes. I did see someone."

Megan leaned in toward her.

"When I was leaving I was running so fast that I almost ran into a limousine parked in front of the building."

Megan and Eric looked at each other and then at Lucy.

"I know I startled the chauffeur and the guy who was getting out of the back seat."

"Did you stop and say anything to them?"

Lucy shook her head. "No. I was so upset I just wanted to get away from there. I didn't speak. But I remember thinking the guy who was getting out of the limo looked familiar."

"I'm surprised you didn't tell me this before." Megan took a sip of the steaming coffee.

"I just remembered. I was in such a state after Tarkington…" Lucy paused as if she couldn't bear to say what Tarkington had done to her.

"That's okay," Megan said. "But do you have any idea who he was?"

Eric picked up his pen.

"I want to say the guy was the main newscaster on channel 8." Lucy cast a glance at Megan and Eric. "The guy with salt and pepper hair who does the evening news."

"Bob Udell?" Eric asked.

"Yes, that's who he looked like."

"Did you see anyone else?" Megan asked

Lucy shook her head. "No."

Megan smiled at Eric. "Let's chat with Mr. Udell. Add that to your list."

"Will do." Eric made a note and flipped his spiral bound notebook shut.

CHAPTER FORTY FOUR

Megan set the bag of groceries down on the porch and inserted her key in the bottom lock and then the top one on her front door. She'd decided to go to the grocery store after Lucy and Eric left. The top lock was kind of sticky— she'd been meaning to call a locksmith to get it replaced but hadn't had time. As she twisted and turned the key she heard her landline ringing in the house. Even thought most people used only their cell she had kept her landline to use as an office phone and also to use with her home security system— the company had strongly advised her to keep the landline in case of a power failure.

She pulled and twisted the key back and forth. The phone continued to ring. Soon voicemail would kick in. She felt the lock slide. Finally. She twisted the knob and gave a push and the door opened. A pool of light flooded out onto the porch. She set the groceries down inside the door and hurried to the phone. It stopped ringing just as she reached out for it.

"Of course," she muttered. She looked at the clock. It was after ten p.m. Who would be calling at this hour? She couldn't imagine it would be a client. She went into the kitchen and put her groceries away, then went back into the living room, picked up the receiver and punched in the number. The recording told her she had one new message. She sat down in the chair beside the phone and crossed her legs.

"First message. The call is from a blocked number," the recording said.

There was a pause and a man's voice came through. "This message is for Megan O'Reilly. I know Craig Tarkington."

Megan's heart started pounding.

"Craig Tarkington is guilty. He told me what he did to her. Lucy's not the only woman he's raped and he'll probably do it again. I hope you can convince the jury of that." The caller hesitated as if considering whether to say more. Then the line went dead.

Megan stabbed at the key to replay the voicemail. She listened to it again, her heart beating so loudly she could hear it in her ears. She grabbed the phone and pressed star 69 to try to get the number of the last caller.

"The call is from a blocked number," the recording said. She grimaced and hung up. She pressed the *save message* button and then sat for a moment, her mind racing.

There was someone out there who knew Lucy had been raped by Craig Tarkington. But how could they find him? And why hadn't he identified himself? She grabbed her cell phone and punched in a number.

"Eric, it's Megan. Are you busy right now?"

"No. What's up?"

"How do I trace a blocked number that called my landline?"

There was a pause. "Trace a blocked number?"

"Yes. I need to know how to do that." She told Eric what had just happened and what the caller had said. She could feel his energy shift.

"You dialed star 69?"

"Yes. It didn't work."

"What time did he call?"

"A little over five minutes ago."

"Write the time down."

Megan grabbed a pen and paper.

"That's all the guy said?"

"Yes. I saved the message. How do we find out who the caller is?"

Megan could almost hear Eric's mind churning with thoughts.

"Pick up the phone right now and dial 1127."

"Hold on." Megan set down her cell phone down, grabbed the cordless landline phone, and punched in the number. She was so nervous she could barely breathe. The phone rang once and a recording came on. "This service is not available."

"It doesn't work." Megan repeated what the recording had said.

Eric let out a sigh of frustration. "Did the guy who left the message sound familiar?"

"No."

"Was there anything about him you picked up on? Did he sound young? Older?"

"Well. . ." Megan hesitated. "He sounded young. He didn't sound like an older guy."

"Who is your phone service with and what's the account number?"

Megan found a statement lying under some papers on her desk and gave Eric the information.

"Okay, I'll call the police and see if there's anything they can do to help us trace the call. They'll probably say they can't do anything unless it's a harassing or threatening phone call, but I'll see if I can pull some strings. And I'll start asking around about Tarkington's friends. Maybe this is someone he went to law school with. You should call your phone company right now and see if they can put a trace on your phone. It won't help for this call but if he calls again it will tell us the number and we can try and find him that way."

Megan said she would do that as soon as they hung up.

"Good. Let me see what I can find out."

CHAPTER FORTY FIVE

"I think it would have been easier to get into the Pentagon than to see Bob Udell," Eric said, sliding down into the chair across from Megan's desk. He rubbed his eyes and leaned back. "It took five voicemails before he got back to me."

Megan cast a glance at the clock on the wall. It was only eleven a.m. She'd come into the prosecutor's office at six that morning in an attempt to get something done on Lucy's case. It seemed like she had been there for days, getting little accomplished.

Every time she reviewed the file she felt downhearted. It seemed like all roads led to dead ends no matter how promising they had originally looked. The most productive part of the morning was Eric stopping in to report back on what he found in his investigations. It had been a week since she'd met with Lucy and Eric and received the mysterious phone message. Eric had been looking into Bob Udell and the security system for The Lakeworth. He had also been trying to get leads on Tarkington's friends.

"I finally called a friend who works at the TV station and told him I needed to talk to Udell," Eric said. "After that Udell called me back. He told me a big story about how he had been tied up working on a project." He told

Megan he'd explained to Udell why he was calling him and Udell denied being at The Lakeworth and seeing Lucy on the night of the rape. "He completely brushed it off and said he was out of town doing an interview that day. I could tell he was dying to get off the phone."

Megan leaned forward and rested her hands on the desk. "Why would he lie about being there? Do you think he knows more than he's saying?"

Eric paused and shrugged. "I don't know. I can't decide if he knows more than he's saying or he simply wanted to get rid of me. I had the feeling he has a pretty high opinion of himself and felt he had more important things to do."

Megan let out a sigh.

Eric leaned back in the chair. "I talked to the security guy again. For once there's good news. He said he looked into it and it appears that even though the inside security video system crashed, the outside system didn't. I talked to him about an hour ago and he said he would email me the video he does have for the night of the rape after we hung up. It should be here by now." Eric pulled a chair around behind Megan's desk and moved her laptop closer to him.

"Let me get my email pulled up," he said, pressing some keys while he studied the screen. He moved the cursor to where he wanted and then clicked. "Here it is." He pressed a button and the video started to play.

Megan leaned forward. She already didn't like what she was seeing. She was hoping for a clear, sharp, close-up picture, but all she could see was a grainy image. She tilted forward toward the screen. She could see a figure running out the front door of the building. The person had a coat on with what looked like the collar turned up. It could be Lucy.

"Look at the time." Eric stopped the video and pointed to the digital clock in the lower right hand corner of the picture. "That has to be Lucy."

Megan nodded. She pointed at the screen. There was a black limousine parked in front of the building. Megan reached out and pushed a button to restart the video. They watched again as the person emerging from the building—probably Lucy—rushed down the walk, looked up, apparently saw the limo, and stopped for a moment. Megan and Eric watched the chauffeur open the back door and let the passenger out. They both leaned in closer to the screen and then looked at each other. "It looks like it could be Bob Udell to me," Eric said.

Megan nodded. "Not the best picture but I'd say it could be him." The Bob Udell guy held out what looked like a briefcase and a coat and the chauffeur stepped in front of him, blocking Megan and Eric's view. They watched the figure they thought was Lucy hurry away along the sidewalk and out of view of the security camera.

The chauffeur and the passenger who looked like Bob Udell walked to the building entrance, the chauffeur remaining in perfect position to block any view of Udell the whole time.

The computer screen turned to snow.

Eric pushed his chair back. "I think you can tell the person leaving the building is a woman. And the time matches when Lucy says she left."

"I agree. Can I keep this? I want to study it." Megan looked at Eric. The security video wasn't what she was hoping for but it was better than nothing.

Eric pulled her laptop toward him and tapped a few keys. "I just emailed the file to you."

Megan rested her elbows on the desk and steepled her fingers. "I find it really strange that such a high end security system has a complete system failure at the exact times we need. What are the odds of that happening?"

"I agree." Eric shook his head. "The cop in me doesn't buy that it failed for no reason. If it had been down for the whole day—maybe—but not just a few hours and then back up again."

Megan looked at Eric. "My gut says that someone sabotaged the system. We need to look into this some more. Something's not right."

"Consider it done. One more thing. I checked on how we could get the number for the blocked caller."

"And?"

"I was right. According to the police department you'll need to report the call to your phone company and then file a police report saying the call was threatening or harassing. Once you do that the phone company will give the police the number and identity of the blocked caller. The company won't give it directly to you. After you make the report the police can give you the information"

Megan's expression darkened as she felt frustration ball up inside her. "The call wasn't threatening or harassing."

"The police were pretty adamant that unless it was threatening or harassing they couldn't do anything."

"I thought you were going to pull some strings?"

"My buddy who worked at the phone company retired a few weeks ago. When I called him at home he said he doesn't have any way to get the phone records. I'll keep digging to see if there's some other way to get the information, but I'm not optimistic."

Megan sighed, got up from her chair, turned, and looked out the window. "Now what," she said softly.

"I know. It appears to be another brick wall."

Megan turned around and looked Eric in the eye. Trial was rapidly approaching and they still had only Lucy's word against Tarkington's. "That's all we seem to have, Eric—one brick wall or dead end after another."

"It may seem that way, Megan, but we still have things to do. For one thing, there's a chance we might find the guy who left that message. I'm looking into it and tracking down who Tarkington runs with. Who are his friends? Where does he go to socialize? The person who left the message has to be someone who knows him pretty well."

Megan was silent, lost in thought. "I wonder what all Lucy knows about Tarkington? She was in the study group with him."

"I think it would be great to talk to her about that. We just need to keep digging to find that caller."

Megan agreed. "I'll give Lucy a call and set up a time for all of us to meet again."

Eric got up and headed for the door. "I've just started looking into this. You know how these cases go. You and I have gotten around brick walls in the past and we'll do it again. I'll be in touch."

CHAPTER FORTY SIX

The Ocean View was a high-end restaurant located on the south side of D.C. Megan had asked Lucy and Eric to meet her here for dinner because she knew it would be quiet on a Wednesday evening. The restaurant had great seafood and private dining rooms that could be reserved. Privacy was something Megan wanted.

It had been a couple of days since she and Eric had decided to meet with Lucy to find out what she knew about Tarkington and his friends. Now the three of them were seated in a private dining room toward the back of the restaurant. The room was elegant, with dark wood, soft lighting, and a crisp white tablecloth. A waiter took their drink orders as another waiter brought them a basket of warm bread.

Megan explained to Lucy that she and Eric wanted to talk to her about any background information she might have on Tarkington, as a starting point in their search for the caller who had left the message.

"I didn't run with Tarkington," Lucy said, taking a bite of the bread. "Plus, remember, we didn't go to law school together. I only knew him in the study group I attended when I was getting ready to take the bar again. And then when I was tutoring him, of course."

"Is there anybody he mentioned or anyone you noticed him being friendly with in the group?" Megan watched as the waiter set glasses of ice tea down in front of them.

Eric opened his notebook. "Can you tell us who some of his friends were?"

Lucy thought for a minute. "Bob Carlyle was someone he mentioned a few times during our tutoring sessions."

Eric scribbled down the name. "A fellow law student?"

Lucy nodded. "Once he mentioned that he and Bob played tennis at the country club every Saturday. I knew Bob a bit myself when I was in law school so it got my attention when Craig mentioned his name."

"Where's Bob now?" Megan asked.

"The last I knew, after he graduated he went to work as a corporate attorney for some big manufacturing company—a Fortune 500 one—in New York."

Eric made a note. "Do you have any more information on that company?"

"I think the company was named Mangas. That's all I know."

The waiter came over to the table, freshened their drinks, and took their orders.

"Who else?" Megan asked as she leaned back in her chair.

The waiter drifted into the room and placed a salad in front of each of them.

Lucy picked up her small silver cup of salad dressing and drizzled it over the greens. "Rick Montgomery. Rick was in our study group. He wasn't the best student and was always scrambling to learn everything during the study group meetings. I wondered why he went to law school. I got the feeling his family was loaded and he didn't have much get up and go. He seemed like a playboy. He and Tarkington were always talking about going to the Skyview Club."

Megan took her fork and stabbed a piece of lettuce. "Isn't that the private club in the Sentry building downtown?"

"That's the place where you have to have a private card for the elevator to go to the floor where the club is," Eric said.

Lucy nodded. "I think Tarkington played tennis with Bob Carlyle on Saturday morning and then partied with Rick on Saturday night. He mentioned stuff like that when we were making small talk during the tutoring."

"Did you notice anything unusual about his friendship with either of these two guys?" Eric drained the last of his iced tea.

"I didn't really know them. I just saw them as playboys who enjoyed spending the family money. "Lucy took her napkin and wiped her mouth. "I never got the impression Tarkington had a lot of close friends. As far as I could tell, Bob and Rick were the main ones."

Eric motioned toward the waiter to refill his glass. "I'll see if I can track down Rick."

"Do you know if Tarkington had any enemies?" Eric leaned forward and rested his arms on the table.

"It wouldn't surprise me," Lucy said laughing. "But I don't know who they are."

Megan noticed Lucy's expression change as if she'd remembered something.

"His best friend was Jack Temple. He talked about him a few times during our tutoring sessions."

"Jack was in law school with him?" Megan looked at Eric who was busy taking notes.

"No. He knew him from college. I think Craig mentioned Jack got an MBA and an accounting degree from Yale or somewhere. There were a few times when Tarkington mentioned during the study group that he had weekend party plans with Jack."

"Does Jack live around here?" Megan asked.

"Craig said Jack's family had a house in the Hamptons and that he and Jack went boating there."

Eric looked at Megan and then flipped back the page on his notepad. "Do you have any contact information for Jack?"

"No. But you can Google Jack Temple Hamptons."

Megan looked at Eric. "My gut tells me he's the caller. This could turn things around."

CHAPTER FORTY SEVEN

Megan watched as the luggage carousel laden with suitcases slowly snaked its way through the baggage pick-up area. People were perched and ready to grab their luggage as it came by. Like everyone else, she wanted to find her bag and get out of the airport. It was late on Sunday evening and she wanted to get home and get ready for another week.

She spotted her roller bag slowly inching its way toward her and grabbed it when it arrived, placed it on the floor, pulled out the extendable handle, and headed off toward the exit for the garage area.

"Garage 7," she said to the shuttle driver.

She leaned back in her seat and sighed. It had been a long weekend. At the last minute on Thursday she'd decided to fly to Pittsburgh and attend a seminar on prosecuting sexual assault cases. One of the prosecutors at the office had told her about this seminar and given her the brochure. She'd doubted whether she'd learn anything she didn't already know but had thought the seminar might give her an idea she hadn't already come up with about some fresh way to approach Lucy's case. Besides, every year she had to get six hours of continuing legal education to keep her license and she knew she could use a weekend away. The closer the trial date got the more stress she felt.

In the end she hadn't learned much from the seminar but the weekend away gave her renewed energy. One thing she did learn that weekend was that there was a lot of new case law coming down saying that juries wanted victims' testimony corroborated by other witnesses.

As the shuttle headed towards the airport parking lot she wondered if Eric had found anything on Tarkington's friend Jack Temple. Before she left for the weekend she had talked to Eric and had said he'd had no luck. He'd run an extensive background check on him and checked out all his addresses as well as his present, past, and most recent places of employment. He'd even flown to the Hamptons and talked to everyone who might have some information on him. Nothing.

The shuttle creaked to a stop at Garage 7. She grabbed her suitcase, tipped the driver, and headed to her car. She pulled out of the parking garage and eased onto the freeway. The night felt cold and the sky was black. Red taillights and white headlights dotted the horizon. Everyone was going somewhere.

It had been two weeks since the last meeting with Lucy and Eric. Time was going by fast and she feared the trial would be upon them and they would still have nothing to back up Lucy's story. Jack Temple had been the most promising discovery to date. Eric had talked to Bob Carlyle and Rick Montgomery, Tarkington's other two friends that Lucy had told them about, and neither of them had anything to offer that would be helpful in the trial. Which left Jack Temple as their biggest hope. There were still some outstanding questions about Bob Udell and a few other things, but Megan didn't have much hope that they would produce anything she could use to help Lucy.

She pressed the call button on the steering wheel and asked the car to call Eric. The phone rang several times before he answered. "I'm driving home from the airport and thought I'd check in and see if you've found out anything new." Megan turned up the speaker volume.

"Funny you should call," Eric said. "I was planning to get a hold of you tonight."

"Good news, I hope?"

The line was quiet.

"I have news but I'm not sure what to make of it all." Eric cleared his throat. "I talked to someone who's the groundskeeper at The Lakeworth. He told me that Bob Udell is at the apartments several times a week."

"Did you find out why?" Megan noticed that a light drizzle was beginning to fall and turned on her windshield wipers.

"Well, I asked around and finally found a friend of a friend who knows Udell and would talk to me. It appears that Mr. Udell has a boyfriend."

"I thought he was married."

"His wife thinks they are," Eric said with a chuckle. "Apparently Udell is having difficulty coming to grips with his sexuality and trying to hide the fact he's gay. You know how he's always in the media being pictured as the All American family guy."

"So he's just there seeing his boyfriend and doesn't want anyone to find out," Megan said, feeling disappointed even though she hadn't expected much from the Udell lead.

"From what my friend said, that pretty much sums it up."

Megan wondered briefly if it would be worth subpoenaing Udell and forcing him to testify in court. But it would be worse than nothing if he got on the stand and stuck to his story that he wasn't in front of the building that night.

Megan let out a sigh. "What about Temple?"

"I've searched for Jack Temple everywhere. I even have his social security number and can tell you when and where he got his last driver's license. There's not much I can't tell you about him."

"Then what's the problem? " Megan eased the car into the exit lane.

"He's disappeared."

"How can that be, Eric? For god's sake, he's from a high profile family and has a big-time job. He can't just disappear."

"I talked to his former neighbors, his friends, and the bartenders at places he used to frequent—you name it. Everyone says the same thing. One day he just seemed to disappear and no one has heard a word from him since. He left his job and home. Several of his friends were concerned about him and reported him as a missing person."

"What happened with that?"

"The police investigated and didn't find anything that made them think he was a missing person or a victim of foul play."

Megan felt her face get hot. She was so tired of taking one step forward and twenty steps back. "Is he dead?"

The line crackled. "I checked that out also. There's no death record for him anywhere in the U.S. The biggest brick wall I hit was his parents. I can't locate them anywhere either. One neighbor said a cousin lived in Altoona, Pennsylvania. I contacted him and he said he didn't know anything and hadn't talked to Jack in years. They weren't close at all."

"Eric, people just don't disappear into thin air." Megan tapped the steering wheel with her hand. Frustration was coursing through her.

"I agree. But it appears Mr. Temple has."

CHAPTER FORTY EIGHT

"All rise," the court bailiff said.

Megan looked out at the sea of faces in the galley. Reporters from all over the country were packed into the courtroom without an inch to spare. Word had gotten out that there was a final pretrial conference set for today. The purpose of the conference was to make sure everything was in place—all of the housekeeping, as Megan called the issues about to be addressed—so there would be no surprises during the trial itself.

The prosecutor's office had been fielding calls from national TV shows and big and small newspapers from all over the country, the entire press whipping itself and everyone else into a furor over accusations that the grandson of a conservative Supreme Court justice had raped someone. Windfield had instructed the whole prosecutor's office not to give any interviews and to have a standard reply of no comment to any questions the press asked.

Megan had arrived at the prosecutor's office at around six a.m. to avoid the reporters. Even at that time there were a couple of news trucks, their huge satellite dishes poking skyward, parked in front of the county building.

She managed to slip through the back door without being seen.

Now she watched Judge Crawford walk up to the bench and take his seat. The wave of people in the galley remained standing until the judge motioned for them to be seated.

The room fell silent.

"We are on the record. This is the case of The People versus Craig Tarkington," the court reporter called out, then rattled off a case number.

Judge Crawford slowly opened a thick file, picked up a pair of half glasses, flicked them open, and perched them on his nose. For several moments he sat quietly reading.

"Very well then," the judge said. "I note that this matter is set for our final pretrial conference today. Trial is set to start on September 30 which is a month away."

Megan looked across the room at Mattingly and Tarkington. Mattingly was writing on his legal pad and Tarkington sat quietly looking down at the table. Megan thought Tarkington looked more haggard than he did the last time she saw him, not long before his arrest. Living under the pressure of the charges and a pending trial had taken a toll.

Megan had talked to Lucy yesterday and told her that she didn't have to be in court today. Typically, this hearing was just for the court and the attorneys. It was unusual to see the press at a hearing like this, more evidence of the level of frenzy the media had created around the trial. Mattingly had probably chosen to have Tarkington there just to play to the press, Megan thought. There was no rule that said a defendant couldn't attend but many times they didn't.

"I want to make sure we're on track with this case and are ready to go to trial. The court will not entertain any continuances of this matter short of someone having a dire emergency." Judge Crawford looked at both Megan and Mattingly. She knew he meant every word of what he'd just said. He had a reputation of being a no nonsense judge who ran a tight ship and did not favor continuing a case. Megan had found that to be true when he presided over other trials she'd been involved with.

"Ms. O'Reilly, has the state provided all discovery to the defense?"

Mattingly jumped up from his seat. "No, Your Honor, she hasn't. I believe there is a video that she has not turned over."

Judge Crawford looked over the top of his glasses at Megan.

Megan stood up. "Your Honor, the video is being given to counsel today. The video in question is security footage from Mr. Tarkington's apartment building." Megan had brought it to Bremington Video Repair, a D.C. company that specialized in cleaning up videotape footage that was not as clear as the customer wanted. By video magic the business could sometimes make the picture clearer. Megan had just gotten the tape back two days before. She couldn't imagine how Mattingly had found out about it but somehow he had.

She had looked at the cleaned-up video and it appeared more likely now that the woman coming out of the building was Lucy. The footage did not determine one hundred percent that it was her, but it was clear enough to show that it appeared to be a woman exiting the building. This might corroborate her story about being there and leaving but didn't prove that Tarkington had raped her.

"Why has this tape not been given before now, Ms. O'Reilly? My discovery order was entered a couple of months ago and there has been more than ample time to turn this over." Judge Crawford rifled through the file and extracted a piece of paper. "I don't see it listed on your Notice of Compliance with Discovery that you filed with the court."

Megan felt her stomach tighten. "Your Honor, this videotape was originally not clear enough to be useful. We had it restored as much as possible by the firm of Bremington Video Repair. We just got it back recently and...."

The judge interrupted her. "How long ago?"

"Two days ago." Megan could see Judge Crawford was disgruntled.

"It took two days to turn this over? How long is it?"

"Only a few minutes, maybe five." Megan reached into her file and extracted a thumb drive. "I planned to give it to defense counsel today."

Judge Crawford motioned for her to give the thumb drive to Mattingly. "Let the record reflect that Ms. O'Reilly has given the video footage to Mr. Mattingly in open court this date."

The court reporter nodded.

Mattingly took the thumb drive, held it up, and studied it.

Megan could hear the reporters murmuring to each other.

"And what is on this?" Mattingly asked.

"It shows Lucy Hatfield leaving your client's apartment building on the night of the rape."

Mattingly shot a glance at Megan. "Your Honor, I object to counsel stating my client raped Ms. Hatfield. There has been no jury finding that a rape occurred."

Megan turned and looked at the judge. "The night of the alleged rape."

Mattingly continued staring at the thumb drive. "Judge, depending on what this video footage shows, it may cause the defense to need more time to investigate. This should have been turned over as soon as it was discovered." Mattingly shook his head and sat down.

Judge Crawford rubbed his face and adjusted his glasses. "Take a look at it, Mr. Mattingly, and if there's an issue, bring it before the court as soon as possible."

He looked at Megan. "Ms. O'Reilly, I see you have listed as witnesses the hospital personnel who took care of Ms. Hatfield the night of the alleged incident."

"Yes, sir."

"Typically the prosecutor lists expert witnesses. I don't see that you have listed any. Is that an oversight? I assume you have the rape kit results and the individuals who conducted the testing?"

Megan felt nauseous. Mattingly was staring a hole through her and she could feel the reporters waiting for her response.

"Judge, as the court may be aware, the District of Columbia police department has had a situation arise where rape kits were accidentally destroyed in hundreds of cases." She paused. "I was notified that Ms. Hatfield's rape kit was one of those destroyed."

A ripple of voices erupted in the courtroom and Judge Crawford cracked his gavel. "Silence!" He glared at the sea of faces in the galley.

"So you are not calling any experts to testify about the rape kit results."

"No sir. We will just be calling the doctors and hospital staff who examined Ms. Hatfield on that night. I have listed them in my discovery. Mr. Mattingly has already deposed them, some time ago."

Megan looked over at Mattingly. She could tell he was thrilled to learn why expert witnesses weren't on the witness list and why the rape kit results weren't among the discovery.

"No other witnesses? "

"I am also calling the security director of Mr. Tarkington's apartment building, The Lakeworth, who can authenticate the video. I will give Mr. Mattingly the gentleman's name and contact information today. "

Judge Crawford turned and looked at Mattingly.

Mattingly shot up from his chair. "Thank you, Your Honor. We have listed the prosecutor's witnesses on our witness list and will probably add the director of security at The Lakeworth. Mr. Tarkington may also testify." Mattingly paused and looked at the galley filled with reporters. "But as we know, the People have the burden to prove beyond a reasonable doubt that he is guilty of the charge they have lodged against him. Mr. Tarkington is innocent until proven guilty and does not have to testify."

Megan groaned inwardly. Already Mattingly was trying his case in the media.

"We are ready for trial," Mattingly said flashing a confident smile.

"Very good, counsel. I will confirm the trial date, September 30 at 9 a.m. Court is adjourned." Judge Crawford walked off the bench.

Megan looked across the room at Mattingly. He was whispering something to Tarkington. She watched as he turned, looked at her, and smiled. She had no doubt he believed he would win the case.

CHAPTER FORTY NINE

Megan looked across the room at the jury box. Seven women and five men had been selected as jurors after two days of questioning. She felt fairly confident that the people chosen would take their jobs as jurors seriously. That's all any lawyer could ask for. She'd learned over her years of trying cases that no one ever knew what a jury would do. She'd won cases she thought were losers and lost ones she felt were winners. Everyone who practiced law had the same experience. All a lawyer could do was present the best case they possibly could.

Megan sat quietly as the prosecution table and cast a glance around the courtroom. The moment everyone was waiting for had arrived. The judge was on the bench, the jury had been brought in and seated. The galley was packed with reporters and members of the public.

There was a soft murmuring of voices threading through the courtroom. Megan watched the court staff and the judge talking. No doubt taking care of some last minute details to make the trial run smoother. Tarkington, dressed in a blue suit, white shirt and dark red tie sat quietly looking down at the defense table. Mattingly was seated beside him busy arranging his file.

She leaned back and took a deep breath. It had been a long journey. Meeting Lucy that day in the coffee shop had taken her on a different path than what she believed she was walking on. Now she was back in a world she thought she had left behind at least ten years ago, the world of criminal litigation where she was a prosecutor. She had weathered the storm of questions and criticism and her own doubts and fears about taking this case. Many people, taking their cue from Craig Tarkington's attorney, had thought she was taking the case simply to attack the firm she had been fired from. But that couldn't have been farther from the truth. She went over the events of the last twelve months—how she had told the public at a press conference that she had chosen to accept this case because she had been the victim of a rape herself, how she had carried the regret about not going public to accuse her rapist and how she had been motivated by that regret to champion other victims of sexual assault until she lost the Lisa Garrett trial. Her honesty had seemed to subdue the barrage of questioning by the press and public.

She thought about how for all her and Eric's efforts they had hit one brick wall after another: the woman in New Mexico who'd refused to talk; another possible rape victim of Tarkington's who had been killed in a car crash; the rape kit that had been accidentally destroyed. And then there was the mystery caller. Eric had spent weeks trying to track down Jack Temple and had found nothing. Everyone Eric talked to who knew Jack said they hadn't seen him in months and that he had just disappeared.

Even his employer said he, out of the blue, gave notice and quit his job never to be heard from again. It seemed that a guy with a high profile family and a big-time job had just disappeared.

Now trial was starting and they still had nothing on Jack Temple, although Eric was continuing the search. The only evidence they had to support Lucy's case was a brief video from the security cameras at Tarkington's apartment building. They couldn't even use Lucy's claim that she had seen Bob Udell as she ran out of the building after the rape, since it seemed likely that Udell would deny he was there and that would make Lucy look like an idiot.

After several moments of instructing the jury on the day's events, the court reporter announced the case, when she finished the judge looked at Megan and told the jury that she would present her opening statement first

Megan stood and walked to the jury box. She stopped a respectful distance from the jurors and introduced herself. She then took her time outlining the prosecutor's case, looking at all the jurors one at a time, trying to make each one feel as if she was talking to him or her personally.

She told them how Lucy had met Craig Tarkington in a study group when she was preparing to take the bar exam and that Tarkington had hired her to tutor him because he was having difficulty and needed extra help preparing for the law school exam. Lucy had tutored him for about a month before the alleged rape happened. She described Lucy as a conscientious young woman, an upstanding citizen who was now a single mother struggling to support and care for a young daughter with a life-threatening illness, a daughter conceived on the night of the alleged rape, whose paternity had been established with Craig Tarkington being the father. She told them Lucy would testify and tell them in detail what had occurred on the night of the alleged rape.

When she sat down she felt good. She had kept her opening statement to twenty-five minutes, long enough to give the jurors a roadmap of what was to come but not so long as to bore them. She had seen lawyers lose a jury's attention by being too long winded.

Megan focused her attention back in the courtroom. Mattingly was about to give his opening statement. He started in typical defense lawyer style, stressing that by law the defense has to prove absolutely nothing and the prosecutor has to prove the case beyond a reasonable doubt. He went on to tell the jury about how Craig Tarkington was a successful and well-liked member of one of D.C.'s most successful law firms and was the grandson of a beloved, highly respected Supreme Court justice. He painted Tarkington as the innocent victim of a woman who used him for her own gain.

Megan made some notes on her legal pad while Mattingly rambled on. She looked at the jury. They were listening intently. Megan could tell that Mattingly was getting close to the end of his statement after what seemed like an eternity. She felt her stomach flutter with nervous energy. Mattingly thanked the jury for listening, walked back to the defense table, and sat down.

Judge Crawford turned and looked at Megan. "Ms. O'Reilly, please call your first witness."

Megan stood up.

"Your Honor, the People would call Lucy Hatfield."

The large wooden doors at the back of the courtroom opened and Lucy walked in. All heads turned toward her. Dressed in a blue blazer, white shirt, and blue skirt, she looked professional and conservative. Megan watched as she slowly walked down the aisle to the witness stand.

Judge Crawford peered at Lucy over the top of his half glasses. "Raise your right hand. Do you swear or affirm under the penalties of perjury that the testimony you are about to give is the truth?"

"I do," Lucy said.

"Please be seated." Judge Crawford motioned toward the witness chair.

Megan stood and approached Lucy. "Please state your name for the court and jury."

"Lucy Hatfield."

Megan led Lucy through a series of questions, the answers to which would give the jury a sense of who she was. She covered Lucy's educational background, her childhood in Arab, Alabama, and her daughter Lauren.

"How old is your daughter?" Megan asked.

"She'll be three in January."

"Does Lauren have any medical issues?"

"Yes. She has cystic fibrosis."

Megan nodded. "How is she doing?"

Lucy took a deep breath and smoothed her skirt. She looked at the jury and then back at Megan. "There have been some really tense moments but overall the doctors believe that her condition can be managed." A smile washed across Lucy's face.

Megan walked back to the prosecution table, paused, and looked at her legal pad.

"Who is Lauren's father?"

Lucy looked at Tarkington sitting next to Mattingly at the defense table.

"Craig Tarkington. She was conceived the night of the rape."

Mattingly bolted up from his chair. "Objection, Your Honor. There has been no finding that my client committed a rape. I move to strike Ms. Hatfield's statement and ask that the jury be admonished to disregard it."

Judge Crawford sustained Mattingly's objection and instructed the jury to disregard Lucy's previous statement.

Megan looked at Lucy. She could tell Lucy was rattled. Slowly, Megan walked closer to the witness stand.

"Have you legally pursued having Mr. Tarkington declared Lauren's father?"

Lucy nodded. "Yes. There was a DNA test and the court declared that he is Lauren's father."

"Does Mr. Tarkington visit and pay support?"

Mattingly was on his feet again. "Objection, Your Honor. It's irrelevant whether my client is paying support or sees the child."

"I will allow it. You may answer the question," Judge Crawford told Lucy.

"He doesn't visit. There's a support order but he isn't paying."

Megan inched closer to the witness stand. "Why isn't he paying support? If you know?"

"I understand he is appealing the court order." Lucy looked down at her lap and then back at Megan.

"Do you know why Mr. Tarkington isn't visiting Lauren?"

"He said he wants nothing to do with her."

Mattingly exploded out of the chair. "Objection, Your Honor! The witness is trying to prejudice the jury against my client!"

Judge Crawford ran his hand over his face. "Overruled, Mr. Mattingly. The witness's answer may stand."

Megan walked back to her table, sat down, and looked down at her notes. The room was silent except for the sound of a chair squeaking. Megan looked up at Lucy. "Tell the jury how you decided to go to law school."

Lucy explained it had always been something she was interested in and right after college she applied and was accepted at George Washington University Law School. Megan led her question by question through her law school experience up to the time she failed the bar exam.

"What did you do after you didn't pass the bar exam?"

Lucy sighed. "That was a devastating blow to me. After that I didn't know if I even wanted to be a lawyer. I gave it a lot of thought and finally decided that it was what I wanted to do." She paused and looked at the jury. "' I reapplied to take the exam in July 2016 and learned there were study groups that met regularly that helped people prepare for the test. I joined one in mid March and that's when I met Craig Tarkington.

"How long were you a part of the study group before Craig Tarkington asked you to tutor him privately?

Lucy sat for a moment thinking. "I'd say I had been in the group about two weeks."

"Did you have any contact with him outside of the study group before or after you started tutoring him privately?"

Lucy shook her head. "No."

"Did you ever date Mr. Tarkington?"

"No."

"Were you interested in dating him?"

"No," Lucy said emphatically. "There was nothing like that."

"How did it come about that you were hired to tutor him?"

"One day at the end of the group meeting Mr. Tarkington approached me and said he wanted to talk. He told me he was having trouble getting prepared for the bar exam even with the help of the group. He said that he could see I was really prepared to take the exam and seemed to know more than the other students. He said he really needed help and that he would pay me to tutor him one on one.

Lucy told the jury that she and Tarkington agreed to meet once a week at the law library where they could use one of the private study rooms. They agreed on a price Lucy would charge and decided to meet on Thursday evenings at seven p.m., and set the date for the first session.

"How did the initial sessions go?" Megan cast a glance at the jury. They were focused on every word Lucy was saying.

"They went fine."

"Mr. Tarkington did nothing inappropriate or anything that caused you concern?"

"Nothing."

"Did that ever change?" Megan walked closer to Lucy. She could feel Lucy's energy shifting.

"Yes," she said softly. Lucy looked at the jury and then back at Megan. "We had set a time to meet for our fourth session."

"What date would this have been?"

"April 20, 2016."

Lucy told the jury that she had been planning to meet Tarkington at seven p.m. at the law library like they always did. As she was getting ready to leave for the meeting, Tarkington called her and said he needed to push the session back to eight since he had some other things he needed to do before they met. He asked her if she would be okay meeting at his apartment to study instead of the law library.

"Did you find that strange?" Megan asked.

Lucy nodded. "Yes. Initially I did, since we always met at the law library. But Mr. Tarkington said a friend had to drop off some books he'd borrowed and his friend could only stop by that evening. The guy didn't want to leave the books with someone else or in the hallway."

Megan walked back to the prosecution table and sat down. "You agreed to meet Craig Tarkington at his apartment?"

"Yes." Lucy went on to explain to the jury that she arrived at Tarkington's apartment a few minutes before eight. He welcomed her inside and offered her a drink. They decided to study in the living room and Tarkington cleaned off the coffee table so they could place their books and study materials there. Lucy said that they studied for about an hour and then took a break.

"Tell the jury the layout of the living room and where you were seated in relationship to Mr. Tarkington."

Lucy explained that she was seated on the couch across from Tarkington. He was sitting in an overstuffed leather chair. Between them was a large coffee table.

"Did the guy show up who was returning Mr. Tarkington's books? Megan asked.

Lucy shook her head. "No. He never came."

Megan picked up her legal pad and slowly approached Lucy. "How long was your break after you studied for an hour?"

Lucy shifted in her chair. She said that after about twenty minutes she suggested to Tarkington they get back to work because it was getting late and they still had a lot to do.

"What happened next?"

"Mr. Tarkington seemed to ignore what I'd said and started making idle conversation." Lucy looked down at her lap and then back at Megan.

"What was he talking about?"

"He was making small talk about his family's law firm."

"Did anything happen that gave you some concern?"

Lucy nodded. "Yes." She told the jury that Tarkington came over to where she was seated on the couch and sat down next to her.

"What did you do when he did that?'

"I told him again that we needed to get back to work since I had to leave in about an hour."

"What did he say?" Megan could see emotion rising in Lucy.

"He just looked at me and…."

"And what?" Megan asked softly.

Lucy told the jury that Tarkington didn't say anything. After a moment he reached over and gently ran his hand down her cheek.

"What did you do when he did that?"

"I pushed his hand away and told him to stop."

"Did he?"

"No. He tried to run his hand down my face again. I pushed his hand away again." Lucy looked at the jury and then down at the floor. "I started to get up and he grabbed my arm and pulled me back down on the couch." Lucy told the jury that she pulled her arm away and yelled at Tarkington to stop. When she tried to stand up again he grabbed her by the back of the shirt and pulled her back down on the couch.

"The next thing I knew he was on top of me ripping open my shirt, running his hands up my legs, and trying to unbutton my jeans." Lucy stopped talking and sat for a moment collecting herself. "I yelled at him to stop and kneed him in the stomach."

"Did you get free?"

Lucy paused and took a deep breath. "No. After I kneed him he pushed me down on the couch even harder. He had both my arms above my head, holding me down, and was straddling me so I couldn't move. At one point he had his hand over my mouth so I couldn't scream." She paused. "I was struggling to breathe." Lucy said she continued to try to fight Tarkington off but she was no match for his strength.

Megan paused. Although Lucy was holding herself together, she could see the torrent of emotion threatening to boil over inside her.

"Did he say anything to you?'

"No. He just kept coming at me. No matter what I did I couldn't stop him."

Lucy described how Tarkington stood up and started to undo his pants. "I jumped up off the couch …."

"What happened next?"

"I didn't even get to head for the door. He grabbed me and threw me down on the floor. I landed on my back and hit my head. The next thing I knew he was on top of me. He ripped my shirt." Megan saw that Lucy was trembling. "He pulled off my pants. I screamed and told him to stop."

"Did he stop?"

"No. He raped me." Lucy hunched over and started to cry.

Megan glanced at the jury. They were all looking intently at Lucy.

For several moments the room was silent except for the sound of Lucy crying quietly.

Judge Crawford looked at the clock. "The court notes the time. We will close the record for today in this matter. We shall reconvene tomorrow at nine a.m." Judge Crawford cracked the gavel. "Court adjourned."

CHAPTER FIFTY

Two security guards helped Megan thread her way down the hall to the courtroom through the crush of reporters. She would never have made it through the courthouse's front doors without the guards' help. Outside, everywhere she looked there were television trucks and reporters, all broadcasting live to their TV stations. Microphones were being shoved in her face and reporters were yelling questions.

It was day two of the trial and Lucy was scheduled to be cross examined by Mattingly.

Lucy had been brought into the courthouse this morning through a private entrance at the back of the building that was mostly used by judges and wasn't accessible to the public.

"A question for Ms. O'Reilly," a reporter shouted now. Megan looked in the direction of the voice. As she did another reporter rushed toward her and shoved a microphone in her face. "How do you feel Ms. Hatfield came across to the jury yesterday?" The reporter bumped into her in his attempt to get closer and Megan tripped and started to fall. One of the security guards assigned to her grabbed her arm and steadied her and another guard pushed the reporter back. Megan continued along the hall, one of the guards gently negotiating her through the mass of people with his hand on the small of her back. The other guard positioned himself so that no reporter could get in Megan's face.

Once she was inside the courtroom she leaned against the wall, closed her eyes, and tried to regroup for the day to come. The second day of trial hadn't even started and chaos was already at an all time high. The courtroom was overflowing with reporters and other people. She'd heard from one of the security guards that several reporters had slept in their cars to be sure they were first in line for a seat in the galley.

She took one last deep breath, looked around, and saw Mattingly and Tarkington. Mattingly was busy flipping though his legal pad and talking to Tarkington. No doubt preparing for Lucy's cross examination. Megan went over to the prosecution table, set her briefcase down, snapped it open, and began removing Lucy's file. There were only a few blank pages left in her legal pad at the end of yesterday's trial notes, and she reached in her briefcase and took out a fresh pad. She had no doubt that she would be taking lots of notes during Mattingly's cross examination of Lucy.

"Good morning."

Megan looked up to see Lucy sitting down next to her. Her face was drawn and she looked exhausted. Megan knew that reliving the rape yesterday had taken a lot out of her. Today she would be going head to head with Mattingly. He would be coming at her from all angles. Megan had prepared Lucy and Lucy was ready—as ready as anyone could be. She was dressed in a black skirt and jacket and looked like a fellow lawyer. Today would be the one of the toughest days in Lucy's life. Megan prayed that she would be up to the challenge.

"All rise."

Judge Crawford entered the room and took his seat on the bench. He greeted the attorneys and asked if there were any preliminary matters the court needed to address before the jurors were brought in and the day's trial started. Megan and Mattingly told the court they were ready to commence.

Megan watched as the jurors filed in and took their seats. They made no eye contact with either her or Mattingly. Once they were seated the court made inquiry whether they had any questions and if they were ready to proceed. The jury foreman told the court they were ready.

"I believe we finished Ms. Hatfield's direct examination and we are now ready for Mr. Mattingly's cross examination." Judge Crawford nodded at Mattingly.

"The defense calls Lucy Hatfield to the stand," Mattingly said.

The room was silent as Lucy walked to the witness stand and sat down.

Judge Crawford looked at her. "Ms. Hatfield, you understand you are still under oath from yesterday."

"Yes, sir."

Megan had spent days preparing Lucy for this moment. She could feel her heart thumping in her chest.

Mattingly stood up. "State your name for the court please."

"Lucy Hatfield."

Mattingly began his cross examination by asking Lucy simple questions: What undergraduate school she had attended and how she came to choose George Washington University for her law studies. Slowly and methodically, he questioned her about her background. Megan could tell he was trying to get Lucy's defenses down. It always helped to try to get whoever you were cross examining to relax. It made putting the knife in so much easier.

"Tell the jury: Are you married?"

Lucy shook her head. "No."

"Never, or married and divorced?'

"Never married."

Mattingly looked down at his legal pad. "Who is Bob Relford?"

Megan saw surprise wash across Lucy's face. "He was a friend of mine."

Mattingly peered over the top of his glasses. "Was?"

"We were engaged for a short period of time and broke up."

"Mr. Relford was from a very wealthy family, wasn't he?" Mattingly cast a glance at the jury and back at Lucy.

Megan jumped up." I object, Your Honor. This question has nothing to do with the matter before the court."

Judge Crawford looked at Mattingly.

"Judge, it is relevant to Ms. Hatfield's character. If I may continue."

"Objection overruled. Continue, Mr. Mattingly."

"Isn't it a fact, Ms. Hatfield, that Mr. Relford dumped you because he said you were a gold digger and just wanted his money?"

Megan exploded out of her chair. "Objection, Your Honor! There is no basis for this question and I move to strike the answer and admonish the jury to disregard the question."

"I will allow the answer," Judge Crawford said.

Everyone in the room looked at Lucy.

"No, that is not correct," Lucy answered.

"Isn't it a fact that you sued Mr. Relford over some property—very nice property— you felt you should have been given when the relationship ended?"

Megan squirmed in her seat. This was the first she had heard of this, or even of Bob Relford. She had tried to anticipate everything Mattingly could use to discredit Lucy but it was impossible to uncover everything.

Lucy looked straight at Mattingly. "Yes I did. I co-owned the property."

"Your name was on the deed?"

Lucy's face reddened. "No, but I put money into it."

"The court found you didn't deserve anything and awarded you nothing, isn't that right, Ms. Hatfield?"

Lucy acknowledged that the court gave her nothing. She tried to explain it was because her name was not on the property deed but Mattingly cut her off.

"What about Dick Logan?" Mattingly peered at her over the top of his glasses. "He was a wealthy guy you dated, wasn't he?"

"He was a friend from college." Lucy leaned back in the chair.

"Didn't he break up with you for the same reasons? He felt t you were after his money? A smile appeared on Mattingly's face.

"No, that is not correct. I ended the relationship," Lucy said matter-of-factly.

Mattingly got up from his seat, picked up his legal pad, and walked to the witness stand. He stopped right in front of Lucy. "So if he would appear in this court and say otherwise he would be lying?"

Lucy paused for a moment. "He would be incorrect."

"So both these men are lying?"

"Both these men are incorrect."

Megan felt a small wave of relief wash over her. She knew that juries don't like it when witnesses call people liars and that Mattingly was hoping that was just what Lucy would do.

"How did you meet Craig Tarkington?"

"I met him in a study group when I was preparing to take the bar exam."

Mattingly took off his glasses and held them in his hand. "Mr. Tarkington is also from a very wealthy family, like your other gentleman friends, isn't he?"

"That's what I understand."

"You never dated him?"

Lucy shook her head and smiled. "No."

"You wanted to date him, didn't you?" Mattingly inched closer to her. Megan could tell he was trying to invade Lucy's space and intimidate her. Megan stood up. "Judge, I object to how close Mr. Mattingly is standing to Ms. Hatfield. He's attempting to intimidate her."

Judge Crawford looked at Mattingly.

"Sorry. That wasn't my intention." Mattingly stepped away from Lucy.

"Move on, counsel."

"Did you or did you not want to date Craig Tarkington?"

"In response to your question: No, I did not want to date Craig Tarkington."

"You didn't pursue him and offer to tutor him for free?"

"Certainly not."

Mattingly lowered his head a little, rubbed his chin, and then looked back at Lucy. "So if witnesses come in and testify that you were pursuing Craig Tarkington, they would be lying like Mr. Relford and Mr. Logan?"

Lucy sat up straight and leaned forward. "Mr. Mattingly, if anyone says that I was pursuing Craig Tarkington, they are incorrect."

Mattingly walked to the defense table, leaned over, and said something to Tarkington, then turned back and looked at Lucy.

"On the night of the alleged occurrence, it was your idea that you tutor Mr. Tarkington at his apartment, was it not?"

Lucy bristled. "No. It was not my idea."

Mattingly smiled. "Wasn't there a special program being held at the library and the study rooms were very limited that evening?"

Lucy shook her head. "No. There was a program but we wouldn't have had a problem getting a study room. Mr. Tarkington said he needed to work at his apartment because someone was dropping by some expensive law books and he didn't want them to be left in the hall."

"Ms. Hatfield, let's just cut to the chase. You've been pursuing a relationship with Mr. Tarkington for a long time, haven't you?" Mattingly placed his hands on his hips.

Megan saw anger flash in Lucy's eyes. "I have never pursued a relationship with him."

"You suggested that you tutor him at his apartment on other occasions before the night of the alleged incident, didn't you?"

Lucy locked eyes with Mattingly. "I have never suggested that."

"It was a well-known fact in the study group that you were infatuated with Mr. Tarkington and he wasn't interested. Wasn't it?'

Megan saw Lucy's anger deepen and blotches of red appeared on her neck. She knew that Mattingly was doing what every good defense attorney did: He was asking questions that would plant seeds in the jury's mind even if Lucy denied the allegation. He was pulling out all stops in this moment suggesting that Lucy wasn't who she said she was and had an agenda of using rich men for their money.

After doing years of trial work, Megan also knew that she had to be careful with her objections. Sometimes when a lawyer objected to a question the jury felt that a witness might have something to hide. It was always a delicate balancing act for the attorney. She decided not to object to Mattingly's current questions and let Lucy answer.

Mattingly switched directions. "You have sued Mr. Tarkington for money for the child you claim is his, haven't you, Ms. Hatfield?

"I've asked him to help support the child that was conceived because of the rape."

"Judge, this language is prejudicial. It has not been established that there was a rape. I ask that Ms. Hatfield's answer be stricken from the record and she be ordered to respond yes or no."

Judge Crawford looked at Lucy. "Ms. Hatfield, simply answer the question yes or no."

"Yes." Lucy's words were sharp and hard.

Megan could tell her nerves were frayed by Mattingly's constant badgering and she was ready to explode. The last thing they needed was for Lucy to lose her composure. Megan knew that Mattingly was hoping she would.

"It's always about money, isn't it, Ms. Hatfield," Mattingly growled.

Megan jumped up from her chair. "I object, Your Honor. Counsel is arguing with the witness," she said, stabbing her finger on the defense table. She was suddenly so angry she could feel herself trembling.

"Objection sustained," Judge Crawford said.

Mattingly paced back and forth in front of the witness stand with his hands clasped behind his back.

"Ms. Hatfield, tell the jury, who is Edward Thompson."

Megan looked at Lucy. She could see that Lucy was taken aback.

"He was a friend of mine." Lucy looked down briefly and back up at Mattingly.

"More like a lover? A married lover." Mattingly gazed at Lucy over the top of his half glasses.

"We had an affair," she said softly.

"He had an important job, didn't he?" Mattingly rubbed his chin. "Something like the head of the IT division for all the schools and licensing agencies in D.C."

Lucy nodded. "Yes. He helped run the computer system for the law school and the agency that administers the bar exam."

Mattingly walked over to the defense table, leaned against it, and crossed his arms.

"And why did this relationship end?"

Lucy shifted in her seat.

"His wife found out, didn't she?" A smiled appears on Mattingly's face.

"There were a variety of reasons. I don't know if she knew about us or not."

"Ms. Hatfield, you graduated from law school and sat for the bar exam in February 2013." Mattingly took off his glasses and held them in his hand.

"That's correct."

"And you failed the exam, correct?"

Lucy cleared her throat. "Yes."

Megan looked at the jury. They were locked on every word Lucy was saying.

"You took the exam again the next time it was offered, didn't you?"

"No."

"Why not?"

Lucy sat for a moment collecting her thoughts. "I didn't know if I wanted to be a lawyer."

Mattingly's expression changed. He walked up to the witness stand. "Ms. Hatfield, let me be sure I have this right. You've gone through law school and have taken the bar exam and failed. And *then* you wondered if you wanted to be a lawyer?"

Megan could see how uncomfortable Mattingly was making Lucy.

"I did an internship with a law firm for a year during my last year in law school. I got to see what the practice of law was really like. I wasn't sure when I sat for the bar the first time whether I even wanted to be a lawyer but I went ahead and took the test. When I failed I just decided to wait and give myself some time to decide whether being a lawyer was what I really wanted to do with my life."

"And you waited a few years before you decided to take the bar again?" Mattingly asked.

Lucy nodded.

"It was just two years ago.

Lucy said that she'd eventually decided that she would take the exam and try to get a job in business law. She had learned from the internship that she didn't like trial work.

"And this was the *only* reason you delayed retaking the bar exam? No other reasons?" Mattingly asked, moving his pen in the air accentuating his words. He turned and stared straight at her.

"Yes. That is the only reason."

Mattingly looked directly at Megan and a smile crawled across his face. "No further questions, Your Honor."

CHAPTER FIFTY ONE

Judge Crawford looked up at the clock on the wall. It was now nine sharp. He greeted the jury and told them what the day's agenda would be. "We are ready to proceed," he said nodding towards his court reporter.

"Ms. O'Reilly, when we stopped yesterday Mr. Mattingly had just finished his cross examination of Ms. Hatfield. Do you have any more questions of her before she is excused from the witness stand?"

"Yes, Your Honor. I do." Megan stood up and walked over to Lucy.

"Please tell the jury why you sued Bob Relford."

Lucy cleared her throat. "I put twenty thousand dollars toward the purchase price of a piece of property, a cabin in the woods that Bob and I were buying together. He said he would put my name on the deed. He never did."

"And Mr. Logan?"

"Our relationship ended because our lives were going in different directions. Plain and simple. It had nothing to do with money."

Megan cast a glance at the jury. Her lawyer instinct told her that her brief questioning had probably repaired any damage Mattingly had been able to do to Lucy's credibility on his cross examination. "I have no further questions for

Ms. Hatfield." She turned and walked back to the defense table.

Judge Crawford excused Lucy from the witness stand. "Next witness please."

Megan called Deputy Kyle Baker of the D.C. Metropolitan Police Department. He had been the one to take Lucy's statement at the hospital on the night of the incident.

Detective Baker told the jury that he had received a call from the Community hospital at around 11 p.m. on April 20, 2016, regarding a woman who was being treated in the ER. She had told the hospital staff that she was the victim of a rape and wanted to make a report to the authorities. The officer told the jury that when he arrived at the hospital he was taken to the room where the victim was being treated.

"Do you see that woman here in this courtroom?" Megan asked the witness.

"Yes." Detective Baker pointed at Lucy.

"How did Ms. Hatfield appear when you saw her in the hospital on April 20, 2016?"

"Shook. Very upset. I could tell she had been crying." The detective looked down at his notepad. "She had some scratches on her arm and bruising."

"Did you take any photos?"

"Yes,"

Megan retrieved a small stack of photos from the exhibit table and approached the witness. "Let me hand you what

I have marked as the People's exhibit A in six parts and ask you what these are."

The detective took the photos from Megan and looked through them. "These are the photos of the scratches and bruising I saw on Ms. Hatfield when I interviewed her at the hospital."

Megan took back the pictures and arranged them neatly in her hand. "Judge, I would ask for permission to show the photos to the jury. Mr. Mattingly has been provided a copy of these in our discovery material."

"Granted," Judge Crawford said.

Megan walked over and handed the photos to the jury foreman. She waited while each juror looked at them. Then she collected the photos and approached the court reporter. "I would move to enter the People's Exhibit A into the record."

Judge Crawford approved the request and directed the court reporter to show the pictures as entered as part of the record.

"Detective, to your knowledge did Ms. Hatfield submit to a rape kit test at the hospital?"

"Yes, the doctor and hospital staff had completed the exam by the time I arrived."

"Once a rape kit exam is completed, what ordinarily happens to the samples taken during the exam?"

The sound of squeaking leather could be heard as the detective shifted in his chair.

"The rape kit is sent to the D.C Metropolitan Police Department for processing and is held there until any trial that takes place."

Megan walked back to the prosecution table and sat down. "Does the D.C. police department have Ms. Hatfield's rape kit results?"

The detective shook his head. "No, ma'am." He paused and looked at the jury. "Her kit results were brought to the department. "He paused again. "However, Ms. Hatfield's kit was accidentally destroyed."

Megan let his words hang in the air. After a moment she turned around and looked the detective straight in the eye. "How could something like this happen," she asked incredulously.

The detective shook his head and a small red blotch appeared on his neck. He was silent for a few moments, then looked up and glanced at the jury, then back at Megan. He explained that a series of police departments along the East coast, including the D.C. police department, had accidentally destroyed several hundred rape kits in an effort to reduce a backlog of kits in storage. Some of the destroyed kits belonged to victims who were not cooperating with the police department in their investigations or were not wanting to pursue charges—others belonged to victims who needed the results for a trial.

"This whole mess was a combination of understaffing and poor communication. Unfortunately, Ms. Hatfield's rape kit testing samples were among those that got destroyed."

"So to be clear, Ms. Hatfield cooperated with the authorities and submitted to the rape kit exam but the results were destroyed—due to no fault of Ms. Hatfield's."

"That's correct, ma'am. It was the department's fault."

Megan looked at the detective. She could see that he was embarrassed to have to admit that the authorities had committed such a major screw-up. She glanced at the jury. They were looking at the detective with shocked disbelief.

"I have no further questions." Megan walked back to the prosecution table and sat down.

The judge invited Mattingly's cross examination.

"Thank you, Your Honor."

Mattingly leaned over, whispered something to Tarkington, and then stood up. "From looking at the photos, wouldn't you agree detective that these injuries could have happened in a variety of ways?"

There was a moment of silence.

"Yes sir."

"They appear to be scratches and a little bruising on someone's arm." Mattingly studied the photos. "I don't see any larger areas that look like a handprint, do you?"

"No sir. "

"And there is no DNA to connect these injuries to my client, is there?"

The officer looked down at his notepad and then up at Mattingly. "No sir. All DNA was destroyed before it could be tested."

"I have no further questions. Thank you."

Next Megan called Dr. Keith Winston, the doctor who was working in the ER the night Lucy came in. She asked him a series of questions establishing his educational and work backgrounds.

"Tell the jury, how did you meet Ms. Hatfield?"

Dr. Winston said that he had been on call the night Lucy came to the emergency room.

"Ms. Hatfield reported she had been the victim of a rape."

"Who was the alleged perpetrator?"

Dr. Winston looked down at his notes. "A Craig Tarkington."

"What did Ms. Hatfield tell you about what had happened that evening?"

Dr. Winston told the jury that Lucy reported she had been hired to tutor Craig Tarkington for his final law school exam. On the night of the incident she had been tutoring him at his apartment.

"Was she able to relay to you what had happened?"

The doctor nodded. He told the jury what Lucy had reported to him about the attack. It was exactly the same as her testimony.

"When you were talking to her, how did Ms. Hatfield appear to you?" Megan cast a quick glance at Tarkington. He was looking down at the table.

"When I came into the examination room I immediately noticed that her clothing was torn and she was very upset." Dr. Winston told the jury he initially conducted a basic evaluation of Lucy. He said her blood pressure was extremely high and she was shaking and crying.

"Was a rape kit completed?" Megan scribbled something on her legal pad.

"Yes, that's a typical procedure in these cases. The nurses stayed with Ms. Hatfield for around a half hour helping her calm down. After that I proceeded to conduct the rape kit exam."

"Please tell the jury what that involved."

Dr. Winston looked at the jury. "I conducted a full body scan for bruising and any external injury. I also checked to see if she had any internal injuries by palpating her abdomen. I could feel some swelling and ordered x rays. The x rays confirmed that she had sustained some internal bruising. I also did a vaginal examination and took samples of any fluids." The doctor paused. "It was obvious from my exam that she had had intercourse and there was some vaginal tearing."

"In examining Ms. Hatfield, did you notice anything about her that caused you concern or made you think she might be making a false report?"

"No."

"In your career, have you had women make false reports about being raped?"

"Yes, I have."

"Tell the jury what you have observed in women who are falsely reporting."

Dr. Winston looked at the jury. "Typically these women do not want to cooperate with law enforcement. They make a report at the hospital and delay making a formal report to the police or end up not making one at all. Ms. Hatfield was very cooperative and requested the police come to the hospital that night."

"During the course of your examination and speaking with Ms. Hatfield that night was there anything she said or did that made you suspicious she might not be telling the truth about what had occurred?"

Dr. Winston shook his head. "No. Nothing."

"Thank you, Doctor."

Judge Crawford looked at Mattingly. "Cross examination."

Mattingly got up from his chair and walked to the witness stand. He spent the next ten minutes asking the doctor questions about his background and education.

"Doctor, how long did it take you to examine Ms. Hatfield?" Mattingly crossed his arms.

"The whole examination took almost two hours."

"And were you present the whole time?"

"I stepped out a couple of times while the nurses were taking samples. "

"Doctor, how many rape kit exams have you done in your career?"

"Hundreds if not thousands."

Mattingly started to walk away, stopped, and turned to face the doctor. Bottom line, Doctor, Ms. Hatfield may have submitted to a rape kit exam but without the results there's nothing that proves conclusively that she was raped by Craig Tarkington. Do you agree?"

The doctor paused for a moment before answering. "Yes, that's correct."

CHAPTER FIFTY TWO

It was day three of the trial. The days had been long and arduous. So far Megan felt good about Lucy's case. It wasn't as airtight as she would have liked—a couple of corroborating witnesses would have made her feel better—but it had gone well. Lucy did a great job on the witness stand and her testimony was very credible.

Megan had been bombarded with questions from the media about how the police department accidentally destroying Lucy's rape kit affected the prosecution's case. Every time the press had a chance to get near Megan, a reporter shoved a microphone in her face and asked her to comment on that. "The rape kit is only one facet of the prosecution's case. Our case is very strong without it," she always said.

At the end of yesterday the Judge had asked the attorneys to be at the court early today to address a few questions. He requested that they arrive and be ready to go by eight a.m. instead of nine.

A mob of reporters was in the hallway outside the courtroom. Guards were positioned at the courtroom doors to keep the public out until court was in session. One of the guards told Megan that a crowd of reporters was already lining up in the hallway at four a.m., hoping to get prime seating for today's session. Rumor had it that the prosecution would be resting and the defense would be given the opportunity to present its case today.

Megan set her briefcase down on the prosecution table. She was alone in the courtroom except for three police officers standing guard by the entrance to the courtroom. The judge had ordered no one but the lawyers to be admitted until 8:45 a.m., As she was taking Lucy's file out of her briefcase she heard the doors to the courtroom creak open and turned around to see Mattingly walk in with Tarkington.

"Good morning, counselor," Mattingly said with a smile. Megan continued removing files from her briefcase. She glanced over at Tarkington. Today was his big day. Everyone was waiting to see if he would take the stand. Dressed in a gray pinstripe suit and white shirt and with his hair neatly trimmed he looked more like a banker than a criminal defendant. He was busy whispering something to Mattingly.

"All rise," the court bailiff said.

Megan stopped what she was doing and stood up as Judge Crawford entered the courtroom and took the bench. He picked up a pair of glasses and flicked them open.

"Counsel, I wanted to have this meeting to determine where we are in the trial. " He turned and peered over his glasses at Megan. "Ms. O'Reilly, from looking at your witness list it appears that the people should be resting their case today. Am I correct?"

"Yes, Judge. The People will rest."

The Judge turned to look at Mattingly.

"We are prepared to present our evidence today," he said.

"Will Mr. Tarkington be testifying?"

Mattingly stood up. "No, Your Honor. As we all know, Mr. Tarkington has no burden of proof. The People have to prove all elements of their case beyond a reasonable doubt."

Judge Crawford rested his chin on his hand and looked at Mattingly. "So you are not calling any witnesses and your client is not testifying. What does that leave?"

"We do have a witness, Your Honor." Mattingly placed his hands on his hips. "As the court knows, impeachment witnesses may not be determined until a witness has testified. After Ms. Hatfield took the stand it was determined that we have a witness who will impeach her testimony."

Megan felt her breath catch. Whatever witness he was about to call wasn't on the list he'd handed in to the court because he hadn't known whether he would need him or her. Megan knew Mattingly had set Lucy up— at the moment she wasn't sure how he had done it but she was about to learn. Evidently she had taken the bait and now Mattingly was going to use it.

"Judge, this is the first I've heard of this," Megan said, trying to block whatever was about to come.

Mattingly smiled. "Judge, we ask leave to call Gregory Turner."

"I object, Your Honor," Megan said as a matter of reflex. She had no clue who Turner was or what he would say. She needed to find Lucy and see what she knew. As the victim, Lucy only needed to be there when she was testifying.

Megan had suggested she sit in the courtroom with Carol McGuire, the victim's advocate assigned to her case, but it was still early and Lucy hadn't shown up yet. She was still probably down in the prosecutor's office.

Judge Crawford waived his hand dismissively. "Ms. O'Reilly, we all know that you can call an impeachment witness if the facts of the case merit it."

"I want the opportunity to talk to this gentleman then." Megan felt her nervous energy escalating. Something was wrong. Every cell in her body told her so.

"So, Mr. Mattingly, this will be your only witness?" the judge said.

"Yes, Your Honor. Based on the People's case we see no need for my client to testify or call other witnesses."

Megan felt a ball of anger explode inside her. She looked down at her notepad.

"When Mr. Turner arrives please allow Ms. O'Reilly to speak with him in the conference room," the judge told Mattingly. "If there's nothing else we need to address we'll recess for now and start promptly at nine."

Judge Crawford walked off the bench. At nine when the court session had officially started and the courtroom doors were officially opened, Megan saw a short, stocky man with a well-trimmed beard come into the courtroom. He was carrying a file under one arm and a raincoat draped over the other. Mattingly took his coat and spoke to him for a few minutes, motioned to Megan, and led the man toward the conference room.

Megan pulled out her cell phone and tried to call Lucy. Voicemail immediately kicked in. She shoved the phone back in her purse.

"Mr. Turner is back in the conference room if you would like to talk to him," Mattingly said, perching on the edge of the prosecution table.

"So what game is this, Mattingly," Megan said under her breath.

"No game." Mattingly raised both hands. "Ms. Hatfield lied." A smile crawled across his face.

Megan stared at him. She knew he was hoping to get a rise out of her.

"It seems that she wasn't telling the truth about why she took so long to take the bar exam. You know, she had to find herself and decide if law was really for her." Mattingly's voice dripped with sarcasm.

Megan looked him straight in the eye. She wasn't going to let him think he was rattling her even though her heart was thumping like a piston.

"Mr. Turner is the head of the licensing agency that runs the administration of the bar exam In D.C." Mattingly tapped his hand on the table. "The real reason she didn't take the bar exam after she failed the first time was that she was caught cheating. Her married boyfriend was the IT guy who worked for the testing agency and he gave her the answers to the test." Mattingly leaned forward and smiled.

Megan maintained her composure. She would die before she would let Mattingly see he had made any impact on her. But her insides were exploding.

Mattingly got up and motioned for her to follow him. Megan picked up her legal pad and pen and walked confidently toward the conference room.

She entered the conference room and took a seat at the end of the long walnut table in the center of the room. Mattingly and Turner sat done near her. She sat quietly while Turner explained in detail that Lucy had not been allowed to sit for the bar exam again because she had been caught cheating the first time she took it. He confirmed that the head of the IT department had given her the answers. This was the only reason she hadn't taken the bar again for a few years.

"This is a very serious offense that the law school and board of law examiners don't take lightly," Mr. Turner said. "There are many steps someone in Ms. Hatfield's position would have to complete before she would even be eligible to apply to take the bar exam again."

He went on to say that a student who has cheated on the bar can only sit for the bar again after they've taken and passed an ethics course recommended by the Disciplinary Commission for attorneys and law students. They also have to pass a grueling character and fitness interview with a panel selected by the Disciplinary Commission. It was a long hard process. She would also have to receive the approval of the ethics board before she could retake it.

When Mr. Turner finished telling Megan what had really happened with Lucy, Mattingly nodded at him and the two of them went back to the courtroom. Megan stayed behind for a moment. In just a matter of minutes the whole prosecution case had imploded. She could hear Mr. Turner's words in her head as clear as a bell and they made her nauseous.

Megan heard a tap on the door, looked up, and saw Lucy.

"Come in and shut the door." Megan was so angry she was shaking. Lucy sat down across the table from her.

"What's wrong?"

"Why in the hell didn't you tell me this?" Megan tossed her legal pad on the table. She was so mad she thought she might have a stroke. She could hear her heart pounding in her ears.

Lucy recoiled in her chair. "I don't know what you're talking about."

"The defense is calling a guy named Turner. He's the head of the licensing agency for the bar exam."

Megan could see the blood drain out of Lucy's face.

"He's here to testify that you lied to the court about why you didn't retake the bar exam sooner. "Megan shoved her chair back away from the table.

"It seems your married boyfriend was the head of IT and he gave you the answers." Megan shook her head in disgust. "Mattingly's going to use this to convince the jury that you're a liar and you lied about the rape too. Do you understand that? Our whole case is ruined." Megan looked at Lucy. She was ashen and tears were streaming down her face.

Megan stood up. "Your credibility is shot to hell. You *are* the case and now the jury will see you as a liar."

Lucy sat deathly still for a few moments.

"I'm sorry," Lucy said softly. "I don't know what to say."

Megan could see her eyes moisten.

"Maybe telling me the truth from the start would have been a good idea." Megan stopped pacing and looked at Lucy. "Did you think no one would ever find out?"

Lucy nodded. "I didn't see how they could. My records are confidential. I don't know how anyone could have found out."

"Well someone did find out and we are in a hell of a mess. We've probably lost the case."

Someone knocked on the conference room door. Megan turned around and saw the court reporter. "Judge is ready to start."

"Thank you," Megan said. She turned back to Lucy. She was still so angry she could hardly speak. "You're going to have to explain this to the jury." She grabbed her legal pad and pen and left the room with Lucy trailing behind.

"Judge, the defense would call Gregory Turner to the stand."

All heads turned as Mr. Turner got up from his seat in the galley and walked toward the witness stand.

"State your name for the court," Mattingly said.

"Gregory Turner."

"Tell the court what you do, Mr. Turner."

"I am the head of the agency that oversees the administering of the bar exam for law students who qualify to take it so that they may be licensed to practice law."

"Do you know Lucy Hatfield?"

"Yes."

"How do you know her?"

Megan felt her stomach start to churn as she listened too Turner answer Mattingly's questions. It was worse than she thought. Gregory Turner was a great witness. He was well spoken and credible.

"How is the bar exam given?" Mattingly asked him.

"The exam is administered by computer. The questions and answers are maintained by the state licensing agency." Mr. Turner pushed his glasses up the bridge of his nose.

Mattingly rubbed his chin and slowly paced in front of the witness box. "Ms. Hatfield told the jury that she had not taken the bar exam the next time it was offered, after she failed the first time, because she wasn't sure she wanted to be a lawyer. Is this statement correct, sir?"

Turner shook his head. "No. Definitely not. The reason she did not take the bar exam again the next time it was offered was that she was not eligible."

Mattingly stopped and looked at Turner. "Tell the jury why she was not eligible."

"She was caught cheating on the exam the first time she took it and the licensing agency wouldn't let her take it again until she successfully completed our ethics program and obtained permission from the licensing agency to sit for the exam again."

The courtroom erupted in murmuring and stirring and the judge banged his gavel demanding silence.

"Cheating on the bar is a very serious offense," Mr. Turner said. "Ms. Hatfield had to go through a very lengthy and serious process to see if she was even fit to take it again."

Mattingly stood for a few moments, letting Turner's words float in the air. "I have no other questions. Thank you, Mr. Turner."

"Cross examination, Ms. O'Reilly?"

"No, Your Honor."

"The defense rests Your Honor."

Megan felt sick. She looked at the jurors. Not one of them made eye contact with her. They were all either staring down at their laps or looking at the judge.

"Do you have any rebuttal witnesses, Ms. O'Reilly?" Judge Crawford asked.

Megan stood up. "Yes, Your Honor. The People would recall Lucy Hatfield." Megan could feel the tension in the air.

Lucy got up and slowly walked to the witness stand and sat down. She glanced at the jury. Megan noticed they still did not look back at her.

"You remember you're still under oath?" Megan said.

"Yes," Lucy said softly.

Megan stood, her hands clasped in front of her. "Do you know Gregory Turner?"

"I know of him but don't know him personally." Lucy looked down at her hands folded in her lap. "I know he's the head of the licensing agency which handles the bar exam."

"Who is Edward Thompson? "

Lucy shifted in her chair. "He was the head of the IT department for the agency that gives the bar exam."

"Were you having a romantic relationship with him?"

Lucy nodded. "Yes. For a while."

"Was he married?"

"Yes."

Megan recounted what Mr. Turner had told the jury about how Lucy had cheated on the bar exam with the help of Edward Thompson. "You told this jury that the reason you didn't take the bar exam for a few years was that you didn't know if you wanted to be a lawyer." Megan paused. "Was that a lie?" Megan was hoping that having Lucy admit what she'd done and explain why, showing genuine remorse would help her re-establish her credibility with the jury.

Lucy sat quietly for several moments. "Yes," she said softly.

Megan looked at the jurors. They all were staring at Lucy.

Megan moved closer to the witness stand. "Why did you lie about your reasons for waiting to retake the bar?"

The room was so quiet you could hear a pin drop.

"I don't know….. I was ashamed, I guess. An affair with a married man and cheating on the bar exam were huge mistakes. It's hard for me to admit them, even to myself."

"You didn't think anyone would ever find out?"

Lucy shook her head. "No. I didn't see how they would."

"Your married boyfriend was Edward Thompson, whom we heard Mr. Mattingly ask you about on direct examination?"

"Yes. He lost his job over this." Lucy raised her eyes and looked at the jury. "I'm sorry. I take full responsibility for what I've done. I tried to make things right and took all the required classes and passed all the interviews so I could sit for the bar exam again." She paused and let out a sad sigh. "All I can say is I am very sorry."

Megan walked back to the defense table and sat down. She looked directly at Lucy. "If you lied under oath about why you didn't take the bar exam after you failed, how do we know you're not lying now about Craig Tarkington raping you."

Lucy looked down at her lap and then at the jury. "All I can say is that I'm sorry I lied about cheating. I lied because I was ashamed of what I'd done. . I am telling the truth. Craig Tarkington raped me." She wiped away a small tear trickling down her face.

The courtroom was silent.

"No further questions, Your Honor."

Judge Crawford looked at the clock on the wall. "It's now after four p.m. on Friday afternoon. The court will stand in recess until Monday morning at nine a.m."

CHAPTER FIFTY THREE

Megan picked up the TV remote and pressed the button to change channels. There didn't seem to be much to watch on Saturday afternoon and she needed to find something interesting to take her mind off yesterday's court session. She looked at the clock; it was only one in the afternoon. She had been lying on the couch staring at the TV for two hours.

She turned off the TV, tossed the remote onto the coffee table, rolled over on her back and stared at the ceiling.

Yesterday had been the worst day she had ever had in court in her entire career—even worse than when she lost the Lisa Garrett trial. All the work she'd done to prepare Lucy's case had exploded in her face. After months of trial preparation, she'd thought she'd covered every possible angle to be sure there were no surprises—who knew that the biggest surprise would be Lucy's secret past. Lucy wasn't the one on trial, and Megan suddenly felt outrage that the whole trial had shifted from what a man's brutal assault on a woman, to what a woman had done some time in the past that affected her ability to be believed now about being assaulted. Mattingly had done what every good defense attorney does—he had planted a seed suggesting that the defendant was the real victim in the case, the victim of a liar.

She rubbed her eyes and let out a sigh. She felt as if someone had ripped her insides out. Lucy's case was lost—she knew it in her bones. She had little hope that putting Lucy back on the witness stand and having her confess and apologize would make any difference. Juries were a funny animal. Once you lost their confidence it was hard to get it back. Her gut told her Lucy had made a fatal error and one they most likely could not recover from.

Lucy's case would be going to the jury on the upcoming Monday. Megan wondered how long it would take the jurors to make a decision. She doubted it would take very long. In her mind she could hear the jury foreman announcing to the court "We the jury find the defendant Craig Tarkington not guilty." It made her nauseous. Tarkington being found innocent would be a huge blow not only for Lucy but for women everywhere who were victims of sexual assault. This case would be deemed by many to be another example of why many victims of sexual assault do not or even should not come forward. No matter how strong sexual assault cases appeared to be there was always something that seemed to make them derail and blow up, something that turned it into a trial of the victim instead of the perpetrator. Craig Tarkington, she feared, would more than likely be added to the list of men who have committed a sexual crime against a woman and walked free.

Megan reached for a throw draped on the back of the couch and pulled it over her. She turned on her side and closed her eyes.

Her phone started ringing and buzzing on the coffee table. She hoisted herself up on an elbow and glanced at the clock on the wall. She'd been asleep for a little over three hours. Slowly, she reached over and picked up the phone. *Eric Covington*, the screen read. She hadn't heard from Eric since the trial started. The last time they spoke he was pulling out all stops trying to find Tarkington's friend Jack Temple. So far, that had been one dead end after another.

She pushed herself up to a sitting position and pressed the Answer button.

Before she could even finish saying hello, Eric's voice came blasting through the phone.

"Megan, I found Temple!"

She sat for a second wondering if she'd heard right.

"Did you hear me?" Eric said excitedly.

"Yes…. but … I don't know where to begin. This is incredible. How…?" She ran her hand through her hair.

"He's definitely the guy who made the call to you about Tarkington." The line crackled, Eric's voice was cutting in and out. "Long story short. He's in the witness protection program."

Megan leaned back against the couch. "What?" That would explain how Temple had fallen off the face of the earth. "How…"

Eric interrupted her. "He's in Portland, Oregon, living under another name, David Wainscott. I'll tell you all about it when I get back later today. Right now I need to know how much time we have until the case goes to the jury."

Megan had so many questions she wanted to ask but she knew now wasn't the time. "Monday. It goes to the jury on Monday."

"This Monday? " Eric said, his voice filled with dismay.

"Yes."

"Shit. I don't know if we can get everything we need to do done by then and have him there for trial."

"Not to mention whether the judge will let him testify even if we can get a continuance." The phone connection was getting worse. "Where are you now?" She pressed the phone closer to her ear, straining to hear.

"I'm in Portland. I talked to Temple. He's willing to testify but he said he has to be subpoenaed. I also need to talk to his supervisor in the witness protection program. That's who I'm calling next."

Megan leaned forward and rested her elbows on her knees. She couldn't believe what she was hearing. Her heart was racing.

"We need some time, Megan. Monday is too soon to get this all done. We. . ."

The line went dead.

Quickly, Megan dialed Eric's number. Eric answered and started talking as if they had never been disconnected. "I don't think we can get Temple back there to testify and still meet all the requirements of the witness protection program before at least Wednesday. We need to continue the case until then. There will be certain requirements that will have to be met before the witness protection program will let him testify. I know that the courtroom will have to be secured and the public will not be allowed in the room during Temple's testimony. His testimony and his identification have to be confidential and that part of the court record will be sealed from public view."

"But Wednesday…" She felt her head beginning to ache. "The trial is basically over. I doubt the judge will let us reopen the evidence."

"Scan me a subpoena. Leave the place for the date blank so I can fill in when Temple will appear. I'll try to get him there sooner but I doubt it will happen before Wednesday."

Megan told him she would scan the subpoena as soon as they hung up.

"This is an incredible breakthrough," Eric said.

"Yes it is," Megan said softly. "I just hope it hasn't come too late."

CHAPTER FIFTY FOUR

It was Monday morning. Megan had spent the weekend researching the law about reopening evidence after the prosecutor had rested the case. She knew that the courts were loathed to reopen evidence unless there was a very compelling reason. The case law confirmed what she already knew—she had to present a compelling argument to the court that it was in the interests of justice and fairness for the case to be reopened and Jack Temple to be allowed to testify. Whatever she said, it was up to the court's discretion whether to allow the testimony or not.

Eric had flown back from Portland the day before and last night they'd met for dinner at The Blue Crab on the outskirts of D.C. Over dinner Eric had filled Megan in on how he located Jack Temple.

"As you know, I'd hit nothing but dead ends looking for him," he said. "He just seemed to have fallen off the planet. And then I got an idea. Maybe he was in the witness protection program. I know someone in that program who owes me a big favor. I can't tell you who or why they owe me. All I can say is that I asked him about Jack Temple. At first he wouldn't talk, but eventually, when I told him why I needed to find him, he admitted that he was in the program."

"Incredible." Megan said. "No wonder we couldn't find Jack."

"Yeah," Eric said. "The witness protection program relocated him to Portland about a year ago."

"Why is he in the witness protection program to begin with?" Megan picked up her glass of Perrier and took a sip.

"Apparently some of his high society friends introduced him to coke and he got hooked. He got in over his head."

"For some reason, I didn't get the impression that Temple was that kind of guy."

Eric wiped his mouth with his napkin. "You never know. The Witness Protection Program allowed me to meet him at an office outside Portland. He was straight with me. He told me he regretted getting mixed up with people he knew who liked to do cocaine. He said it took over his life for a while. Apparently some of his friends were buying from dealers involved in a big coke ring between the Florida keys and D.C." Eric took a bite of his hamburger.

"The friends told him they needed his help. There was a shipment coming in to D.C. and the regular guy who made the buy couldn't do it. Temple didn't want to do it but didn't want word to get out that he was into drugs and his so-called friends used that against him. And by that point he owed the dealer some money."

"I thought he was loaded."

Eric shrugged. "I did too but something must have happened. The guys he was involved with made it sound like it would be a simple drug buy. He wasn't really clear about exactly what happened but it sounded like they had him against the wall. Bottom line, he made the buy and the dealer he bought from was an undercover agent. And it was a substantial amount he bought. That's how he ended up in the witness protection program. He turned state's witness against the ring to avoid prosecution. The trial is coming up next spring. He could take down quite a few key people. From what he says, the public would be stunned to find out some of the big names who are this ring's customers."

"What made him contact me about Tarkington?"

Eric pushed his chair away from the table. "He's been tight with Tarkington for years. Apparently he knows Tarkington has had other issues with women. He didn't say who the women were or what happened. Tarkington told him he had sought counseling and was fine. One night a year or so after Tarkington told him he was on the straight and narrow, they were drinking on Temple's boat. Tarkington had drunk more than his fair share and started bragging that he had had sex with Lucy even though she didn't want to. He seemed to find it funny that Lucy had tried to fight him off. Temple said he told himself it was the alcohol in Tarkington talking. But when he heard about the criminal charges being filed against Tarkington, he said he knew he had to come forward, that what Lucy was alleging was exactly what Tarkington had told him."

"And so he didn't say who he was when he called because he can't come out of the woodwork right now."

"That's right." Eric nodded. "Being in the witness protection program makes life a little more difficult. Some things you just can't do like a normal person."

Megan looked Eric straight in the eyes. "Let's hope the judge will allow him to testify and do it in a closed courtroom. How do you think he'll hold up in court? Mattingly will try and eat him alive."

"He'll be fine. I've talked to him at length. He's solid."

Now, with the Monday morning court session starting in a few moments, Megan's stomach was in knots and she felt her head beginning to throb. She had been awake most of the night making a list of the points she wanted to argue to the court for allowing the testimony.

On Saturday she had emailed Judge Crawford's court reporter and asked her to let the judge know that she needed to start court on Monday addressing a new issue that had come up before the actual trial started. The reporter had emailed back and said the judge had been made aware and all parties should be in court at 8:00 to address the issue.

Judge Crawford took the bench now and instructed the bailiff to keep the jury out of the courtroom until further order. The galley was already filled to capacity with reporters. Judge Crawford folded his hands and rested them on the bench. "I understand, Ms. O'Reilly, you have something you would like to address with the court."

Megan stood. "Yes, Your Honor." She paused for a moment collecting her thoughts and then she glanced across the room at Mattingly. All of his attention was focused on her and what she was about to say.

"Recently, I received a voicemail message from a man who claimed to have evidence that would support the People's case that Craig Tarkington is guilty of raping

Lucy Hatfield. This person called me from a blocked phone number and did not leave any information we could use to contact him—no name, nothing. Eric Covington, our private investigator, determined who this person was and has been trying to locate him ever since I received the call and has had no luck until this past weekend. This witness is critical to this case. The witness..."

Mattingly exploded out of his chair. "Objection, our Honor! I know exactly where this is going," he said angrily, his face red. "This case is literally *minutes* from going to the jury for deliberation and the prosecutor wants to add a witness and I...."

Judge Crawford raised his hand and looked at Mattingly. "Continue, Ms. O'Reilly."

Mattingly flopped down in his chair, leaned back, and glowered.

"We have made a good faith effort to find this person and would have had him on our witness list way before now but we could not find any trace of him. We weren't even sure if he would be a witness until we located him and had a chance to speak to him."

Judge Crawford took off his glasses and laid them on the bench. "Ms. O'Reilly, in this day and age it's difficult not to find someone. You have a private investigator working for you and access to the internet and you are saying that you *still* had no idea where this person was or if he would even be a witness? This person just disappeared into thin air?" The judge waved his hand in the air.

"He's in the witness protection program Your Honor."

Judge Crawford looked directly at her. "That would make a difference." He pushed his glasses up the bridge of his nose. "Ms. O'Reilly, what exactly would this witness be testifying about?"

"He will testify that the defendant Craig Tarkington admitted to him that he raped Lucy Hatfield."

"Objection!" Mattingly said.

"Overruled." Judge Crawford nodded at Megan.

"We could not, in good faith, list him before now as a witness. Now that we have located him and he has confirmed that he was the caller and will testify for the People, we request leave of court to allow us to reopen our case and present his testimony."

"Is he available to testify today?" Judge Crawford asked.

Megan felt her stomach tighten. "No, Your Honor. We will need to have the witness protection program approve his testifying and certain safeguards will need to be in place for him to appear in court."

"How soon can he be here? We have a jury waiting to receive the case for deliberation and they believe they will be receiving it today. The jurors have been here for several days and I imagine they are ready to wrap this case up and go back to their normal lives."

Megan could tell Judge Crawford was not happy. She shifted her weight to the other leg. "The soonest our witness could be here is Wednesday."

Megan looked across the room at Mattingly. He shook his head and threw his pen down on the defense table.

Tarkington, his hands folded in his lap, looked down at the floor.

"*Wednesday.*" Judge Crawford let out a sigh.

Megan picked up her legal pad and flipped back a couple of pages. "I have researched the law on this issue and it states that the court has discretion to reopen the evidence if, under the totality of the facts, it appears that to reopen the evidence will serve the interests of justice. I can have our private investigator appear by phone and give testimony right now about all the efforts that have been made to locate this person before now, if the court would like."

Judge Crawford shook his head. "We are all familiar with Mr. Covington and his work. He leaves no stone unturned." He turned and looked at Mattingly. "Mr. Mattingly."

Mattingly abruptly pushed his chair back and stood up. "Thank you, Your Honor. Ms. O'Reilly can't try this case by ambush. As the court knows, there comes a time when the evidence is closed. Ms. O'Reilly and myself both only get one bite of the apple. This case has been pending for some time and now that it is getting ready to go to the jury she wants to reopen it." He shook his head. "I have not been made aware of any other witness until just now. We strenuously object to the evidence being reopened. Ms. O'Reilly's time to present her case is up and I do not see any compelling reason to reopen the evidence."

Judge Crawford rubbed his face and looked at Megan. "You believe that this person can be here by Wednesday?"

"Yes, Your Honor."

The courtroom was so silent you could hear a pin drop.

Judge Crawford leaned over and whispered something to his court reporter. She quickly tapped the computer keys, studied the screen for a few moments, then leaned over and whispered something to him. Judge Crawford rubbed his face and sat thinking. After a few moments he rocked forward and placed his hands on the bench.

"I understand each party's position. The evidence is closed. However, I also understand the need for justice to be served and what the case law says about this type of situation. What I am prepared to do is continue this matter for a week. We will reconvene next Monday morning. This will give Ms. O'Reilly time to have the witness brought here and the defense time to investigate this person and depose him if they so choose.

"Since this is involving a person in the witness protection program, the court will be closing the courtroom to the public on Monday and issuing a gag order so that no one involved in this case may discuss this witness or divulge any information including his name to anyone. The records of his identity and testimony will be sealed from the public." He paused and looked around the room. "Should anyone violate this order they will be subject to contempt and sanctions by this court." The judge turned and looked at Megan. She could see from his stern expression that he was not happy.

"Ms. O'Reilly, please make arrangements for Mr. Mattingly to interview this witness and complete whatever discovery he deems necessary."

"Yes, sir."

"Court adjourned."

Megan cut a glance at Mattingly. He was busy talking to Tarkington. She could see a large vein protruding on Mattingly's forehead. Tarkington was looking down at his lap, shaking his head.

"Ms. O'Reilly," someone shouted. She turned around and saw a crush of reporters rushing toward her yelling questions. Two security guards formed a shield so the reporters couldn't get to her and two other guards grabbed her briefcase and hurried her toward the judge's private exit.

CHAPTER FIFTY FIVE

Jack Temple and four Federal Marshalls arrived in D.C. on a private jet at five a.m. on Wednesday. A white SUV with tinted windows was sitting on the tarmac in the pitch black of early morning, there to meet the plane. Megan was waiting in the SUV along with a Federal Marshall.

No one would have suspected that the five men exiting the plane, all wearing jeans, polo shirts, and baseball hats, were Federal Marshalls accompanying a key witness from the witness protection program. Megan somehow knew that the one who was shorter and younger looking than the others, with dark-rimmed glasses and close-cropped dark graying hair, was Jack Temple. She watched him cross the tarmac and approach the SUV. Once he was inside, she extended her hand and introduced her. She noticed that his handshake was firm and he looked her directly in the eye. She liked that. "I need to talk to you at length but not here."

He nodded, they settled back in the seat, and the driver slowly inched toward the exit and pulled onto the highway headed toward downtown D.C.

Arrangements had been made for Temple and his four Marshalls to stay at the Astor Hotel not far from the courthouse. The hotel was ten stories and offered every available amenity a guest could want. The witness protection program had reserved all the rooms on the top floor and requested that public access to that floor be denied while Temple was staying there. The fire exits on the tenth floor were locked from the hotel floor side so that no one on the outside could gain access to the floor and only the occupants staying there could open the doors in case of an emergency. The hotel had programmed the elevator not to go past the ninth floor unless a computer code was entered. Only certain hotel employees and the witness protection program Marshalls had the code. Not even Megan had it. She would be meeting with Temple at an as yet undisclosed-to-her location later today.

The hotel had made arrangements for Temple and the federal marshals to come into the hotel through a private entrance located in the underground parking garage. When the SUV pulled up in front of the entrance, Megan shook Jack Temple's hand and reminded him that his schedule for the next several days would be meetings with her and Eric and a deposition with Mattingly. Jack Temple thanked her and got out of the SUV with his four accompanying Marshalls.

CHAPTER FIFTY SIX

At five a.m. on the following Monday, Jack Temple arrived at the courthouse in the back of a delivery truck with the words The Office Supply Box painted on the side. Even at five in the morning there were reporters camped out in front of the courthouse, and all precautions were being taken to assure none of the press or even the public got a glimpse of him.

The delivery truck inched its way down the ramp to the underground parking garage at the courthouse and stopped in front of the entrance to the building. Five Federal Marshalls stood waiting at the entrance. The witness protection program had taken over security for the courthouse for the day and had strategically stationed a battalion of marshals throughout the building.

The offices on the fourth floor where the courtroom was located were closed for the day and the floor had been vacated until further notice. Federal marshals were stationed at each staircase on the floor and at the elevator. The elevator had been programmed not to stop at the fourth floor without a special code being entered.

All the security cameras in the garage, basement, and elevator and on the entire fourth floor had been disabled so there would be no video footage showing Temple.

Jack himself had a beard that he had probably grown since becoming involved in the witness protection program and was wearing a baseball cap and a pair of dark-rimmed glasses.

Inside the courthouse he was escorted by four agents to a private conference area behind the courtroom which was used exclusively by attorneys to speak confidentially with their clients. In the center of the room was a large walnut conference table with six chairs. The room had a bathroom, refrigerator, and microwave. It had no windows. This room would be where he stayed at all times until Megan called him to the stand, with two agents stationed outside the door and two other agents positioned at each end of the hallway. Once his testimony was completed he would be taken by the marshals to the airport and to their private plane and flown back to Oregon.

When Megan arrived at eight a.m. she was greeted by a crush of reporters and TV trucks encircling the courthouse square. With the help of security she threaded her way through the crowd of reporters who were shouting questions and shoving microphones in her face. The security guards pushed the reporters back and blocked the cameras with their hands. They got Megan in the building and onto the elevator as quickly as they could.

At nine o'clock sharp Judge Crawford entered the courtroom and took his seat on the bench. Federal marshals were standing guard at all the courtroom doors. The press, much to their dismay, had been barred from the courtroom and relegated to the main floor of the courthouse.

Megan cast a glance across the room at Mattingly. On the defense table in front of him was a stack of papers and files. Since he had deposed Temple on Tuesday he had filed a flurry of pleadings and briefs objecting to Temple's testimony and asking the court to block him from testifying. Megan had responded to each one citing case law as to why Jack Temple's testimony should be allowed. Today, Judge Crawford would make a final ruling.

Megan had also talked at length to Jack. She had spent hours with him going over his testimony and alerting him to what she anticipated Mattingly would ask him. She'd told him Mattingly would do his best to try to make it look like he had made some secret deal with the authorities to testify against Tarkington, in order to get a reduced sentence himself.

Judge Crawford opened his glasses and perched them on his nose. "Counsel, I have read all the briefs and pleadings filed regarding the issue of Mr. Temple testifying today and I am well versed in this area of the law." He paused and looked at Mattingly and then at Megan. Megan felt the tension rising in her.

"Every case has to be judged on its particular set of facts." The judge paused and looked again at both Megan and Mattingly. "In this case it does appear that the People made every attempt to locate the witness to no avail until he was found in the witness protection program. Although I understand defense counsel's basis for objection, I find that the People made a good faith effort to locate this witness. It just wasn't possible due to Mr. Temple being part of the witness protection program. In light of this, I am denying the defense request to block this witness from testifying and find that it would serve the interests of justice to allow his testimony."

Megan breathed a sigh of relief.

Mattingly shot up from his chair. His face was bright red. "Judge, we ask leave to take an interlocutory appeal from this ruling and request that the trial not go forward pending a ruling from the court of appeals."

Judge Crawford peered over his glasses at Mattingly. "Denied, counsel. You may take the issue up by the regular means of appealing a case if your client is found guilty,"

"But Judge, I...."

"Have a seat, Mr. Mattingly. The court has ruled."

Judge Crawford cast a glance at his bailiff and instructed him to bring in the jury. He welcomed the jurors once they were seated, explained the agenda for the day, and told them that it would be different because a witness was part of the witness protection program. He explained that they were sworn to keep all information regarding the witness confidential and that should anyone divulge anything regarding this person they could be held in contempt of court and sanctioned. When he finished instructing the jurors he turned and looked at Megan. "Ms. O'Reilly."

Megan stood. "Thank you, Your Honor. The People call Jack Temple."

The private door at the back of the courtroom opened and Jack Temple walked into the courtroom. Dressed in a white oxford-cloth shirt, striped tie, and black dress pants, he looked conservative and professional. Eric and Megan had seen pictures of him on the

internet when they were still searching for him. In old pictures he had longish blond hair, a beard and mustache, and no glasses. In the more recent photos he had been clean shaven. Now he had on those dark-rimmed glasses and had short dark graying hair and a beard. Megan suspected that his appearance had been altered by the witness protection program. He walked to the witness stand and turned to face the judge.

"Raise your right hand. Do you swear and affirm under the penalties of perjury that the testimony you are about to give is the truth and nothing but the truth?"

"I do."

"Please be seated."

Megan stood. "State your name for the court, please."

"Jack Temple."

Megan looked over at Tarkington. He showed no sign of anxiety that one of his closest and oldest friends was about to help convict him. Instead he was busy writing notes while Mattingly opened a file that probably contained Jack Temple's deposition. Megan knew they had both studied every word of Temple's deposition and were hoping he would say something today that didn't match his original statement. Mattingly was like all defense attorneys; they look for a molehill and make a huge mountain out of it. A mountain they hope will discredit the witness.

For the next twenty minutes she had Temple testify about who he was, his educational background, his family, and his career. She gave him ample time to answer her questions and did her best to make him feel comfortable—as comfortable as he could be testifying in a court of law against a former good friend.

"Mr. Temple, are you a member of the witness protection program?"

Temple shifted a little in his chair. "Yes, I am."

Megan asked him a series of questions about how the witness protection program worked.

"Tell the jury, Mr. Temple, how it came about that you are part of this program." Megan cast a glance at the jury. They were hanging on Jack Temple's every word.

Temple cleared his throat. "I got involved in cocaine." He paused. "I made some very bad choices."

Megan had him explain how he got involved with friends who did cocaine and then how he got hooked himself. "I spent a lot of money on it and was in debt to a dealer."

Megan walked back over to the defense table and sat down. "Tell the jury what happened."

"I was told by the dealer that I needed to buy a substantial amount of cocaine from a trafficking ring—to work off some of my debt." Temple adjusted his glasses, looked down at the floor and then at Megan.

"Did you do that?"

Temple nodded. "Yes."

"What happened next?"

"I made the buy for them and it turned out the guy I bought from was an undercover police officer." He told the jury that he had been charged with several felonies. Due to the amount of the drug he'd bought they were high-level felonies that could put him in prison for a long time.

"The original plea agreement I was offered would have given me thirty years in prison."

"What did you do once you realized how serious your situation was?" Megan leaned against the edge of the prosecution table.

Temple told the jury that he had asked his attorney to speak with the prosecutor handling his case about what, if anything, he could do to get his prison time reduced.

"The prosecutor said that if I helped to bring down the drug ring and get some of the dealers put in prison it would help my case. The police had been trying to find out who all was involved and had hit a brick wall."

"So you were asked to turn state's evidence and be an informant."

"Yes."

"Is the criminal case against you resolved?"

Temple shook his head. "No. I'm awaiting trial. My own trial date is not until next year. The case where I'm testifying against the cocaine dealers is set for trial in a few months."

Megan had him explain how large the ring was and the danger he was in by testifying against its members and how his safety was being guarded by the witness protection program.

"Is being here today putting you in a potentially dangerous situation?"

"Yes." Jack ran a hand through his hair and let out a sigh.

Megan looked down at her notes. "Tell the jury, do you know Craig Tarkington?"

"Yes. We've been friends for a long time."

Megan had Temple explain about how and when he first met Tarkington and describe their relationship.

"We've been friends since we were kids," Temple said. "We grew up next door to each other. In the last ten years we've spent many weekends boating and hanging out."

Megan watched him shift in his chair and look briefly down at the floor. She could see that he was uncomfortable.

"I would imagine that since Mr. Tarkington is a long-time friend of yours, testifying against him is hard for you."

Temple nodded. "Yes, it is. Very hard. It's something I wish I didn't have to do."

Megan walked around behind the prosecution table and sat down. She looked down at her notepad and flipped a few pages.

"Why are you testifying?"

"I need to."

Megan noticed how Mattingly was completely focused on Temple.

"Do you mean that your testimony in this case will help you in your own criminal matter?"

Temple shook his head. "No. I don't mean that. I feel I need to come forward to help stop Craig's behavior. "

Temple went on to tell the jury that over the last three years he had been hearing about situations involving Craig Tarkington and women that weren't good.

"He would be very aggressive with them and didn't like to be told no." Temple said he personally knew a couple of women who told him Tarkington had forced himself on them.

"He forced them to have sex with him?" Megan said.

"Objection, Your Honor," Mattingly said angrily. "I object to any allegations made by some unidentified women. If these women exist then they need to be here and be put under oath and testify."

"Ms. O'Reilly?" Judge Crawford looked at Megan.

"The basis of this testimony is what Mr. Temple learned about the defendant Craig Tarkington's sexual proclivities. It is not hearsay. It is used to explain why Mr. Temple has decided to come forward and testify. It is not offered as evidence of the truth of the allegations."

"Objection overruled," Judge Crawford said. "Continue."

"These women you know said Craig Tarkington forced them to have sex with him?"

Temple nodded. "Yes. They told me Craig sexually assaulted them."

Megan looked at Tarkington. He was staring a hole through Temple.

"Did these women ever file charges against him?"

"No. Craig told me he resolved it with them."

Megan crossed her arms. "Resolved it?"

"My understanding is that there was some type of agreement worked out and Craig paid them some money and it all went away. From what he told me it was all done informally. No suit was ever filed."

"How many women are we talking about?"

"Two. I think there might be other women Craig…" Temple paused as if searching for the right word… "assaulted too. But I only knew two of them."

"Objection," Mattingly shouted.

"Overruled. You may continue, Ms. O'Reilly."

"How long ago was this?" Megan pulled out another her legal pad and scribbled a quick something.

"The first one was probably five years ago. Then a year later a different woman told me something had happened to her." Temple told the jury that as part of the private settlement with these women Tarkington agreed to go into counseling.

"Did he go to a therapist?"

"He said he did but I really don't know."

Temple stated that after these incidents things seemed to smooth out and he didn't see or hear about any other behavior out of Tarkington that caused him concern—not until sometime in the summer of 2015.

"What happened then?"

Temple looked across the room at Tarkington then back at Megan.

"Craig came to my house in the Hamptons for the weekend. We planned to go boating, cook out, and relax. On Saturday night we decided to go into town to The Cove for dinner. We saw some people we knew there and decided to stay until the band started playing around nine o'clock. We ran into a couple of women we knew and bought them drinks."

Temple paused.

"About midnight the woman I was dancing with left with a group of her friends to go to a party. She invited me to come along but I was dog tired and didn't go."

"Where was Craig when this occurred?"

Temple shrugged. "I didn't see him so I sent him a text and told him I was going back to the house and would leave the door unlocked so he could get in. The house was only a ten- minute walk from the bar."

"Did Mr. Tarkington text you back?"

"Yes. He said he'd be fine and would see me later."

Temple testified that when he got home he took a shower and was heading to bed when he remembered he forgot to turn off the sound system on the boat. He said he pulled on a T-shirt and some shorts and tennis shoes and headed down to the boat slip which was just beyond his backyard.

"When I got close I could see there was a light on in the living room area and I heard music. Inside the boat I noticed an empty wine bottle on the coffee table and two glasses that weren't there when we left for dinner. I turned off the light and headed back toward the stateroom. All of a sudden I heard what sounded like a woman crying out for help. As I hurried toward the sound I heard another voice. It was Craig's. He was yelling...."

Temple paused.

"Yelling what?" Megan asked.

"Yelling at someone to shut up."

"What did you do next?"

"I ran to the room where the noise was coming from and pushed open the door."

Megan could see that recalling the incident was upsetting him. Good for the jury to see that, she thought.

Small beads of perspiration were forming on Temple's forehead. He glanced at Tarkington and then down at the floor.

"When I opened the door I saw Craig on the bed straddling a woman—she had no clothes on and was screaming for him to stop and trying to fight him off. He had one arm pressing down on her upper chest."

Temple stopped.

Mattingly was on his feet. "Objection, Your Honor! This testimony does not pertain to the case at hand."

"Overruled," the judge said.

"Was Craig Tarkington clothed when you entered the stateroom?"

"He had his shirt on but his pants were off."

"What did you do?"

"I yelled at him, grabbed him by the collar, and pulled him off the woman."

Temple said that as soon as he pulled Tarkington off the woman she jumped up and grabbed her clothes. She was the young woman he had seen Tarkington talking to at The

Cove. He remembered her because she looked too young to be in a bar. She was sobbing. Before Temple could say anything to her she ran out the door and off the boat.

"I turned around and looked at Craig. He just stared at me and said she was a little tease. I was furious. I grabbed him by the shirt and hauled off and punched him in the face."

Megan saw Tarkington look away from Temple and down at the floor.

"What did you do after that?"

"I told him to get his shit, excuse my language, and get out. He wasn't welcome on my boat or in my home."

Temple said Tarkington tried to tell him that what he'd seen wasn't what it looked like. "But it was obvious to me what was going on. He was forcing himself on this young woman. No doubt about it."

Temple told the jury that after this happened he had no contact with Tarkington until he ran into him in the Hamptons about six months after this had happened.

"He was there seeing his parents and we were both at the same party. He apologized about the incident on the boat and said he was back in counseling. We talked for a while and he kept saying he was sorry."

"Did you mend the fence and become friends again?"

"Sort of. I didn't know what to think. I didn't want to believe he was a guy who attacked women but…" His voice trailed off.

"What made you come forward now?"

Temple let out a sigh. "About two and a half years ago, not long before I was arrested, Craig and I were out drinking one night. I had gone to D.C on business and we met for dinner. We were at the Back Room Bar having drinks and talking. "He asked me how I was. At that time things were going badly for me. The drug dealer was after me to pay back the money I owed him and my girlfriend had broken up with me because of everything that was going on with me. I didn't want to go into all that with Craig, so I just told him I was miserable about the whole break up ordeal. We weren't drunk, just talking."

"Did Mr. Tarkington say anything to you that caused you concern then?"

Megan noticed Judge Crawford looking up at the clock. It was almost three p.m.

Temple nodded. "Yes. He told me about meeting a woman who ended up tutoring him for the bar exam. He said that he met with her several times and really liked her. I remember he said her name was Lucy. Smart and pretty. He seemed to think she liked him too. He didn't say what made him feel that way." Temple shifted in his chair. "He said they made plans to meet at his apartment to do a tutoring session. When she arrived they started working and after a while they decided to take a break. Craig said that he came over and sat down right beside her with their legs touching."

"What did Lucy do?"

"He said she ignored him."

Temple went on to say that Tarkington told him he kept trying different things, leaning over really close and touching her leg. Finally, she told him to stop and got up off the couch. Craig said that he pulled her back down and tried to kiss her. She pushed him away. He tried to kiss her again and she got up and headed for the door."

"Tarkington told you she said no. You're sure of that."

"Very sure. He seemed to find the whole thing amusing. I told him he couldn't treat women that way. He laughed at me and said no one could touch him because of his family and their money. I hadn't really seen that side of him before even though I knew he had assaulted other women. Before he had acted contrite when we talked about it and I believed he was."

Megan glanced at the jury and looked back at Temple.

"He said that she was just a tease and he taught her a lesson," Temple looked down at the floor.

Megan said nothing several seconds. "By lesson, did he mean he forced her to have sex?"

"Objection!" Mattingly yelled. "The witness is assuming Mr. Tarkington's intention."

The judge stared at Mattingly for a moment. "Sustained. Please restate your question, Ms. O'Reilly."

"Did Mr. Tarkington tell you he forced Lucy Hatfield to have sex with him?"

"Yes." Temple was silent for a few moments, collecting his thoughts. "He told me that she screamed and fought him off. He said she was stronger than he thought she would be—but no match for him. He went on a tirade telling me how she was like other women: They lead you on and then say no."

"What was your response when he told you all that?"

"I felt sick. I thought he had gotten help but obviously he either hadn't or it wasn't working. I just wanted to get away from him."

Megan walked up to the witness stand. "Why didn't you make a police report?"

Temple paused. "At the time I was being threatened by bad people and wasn't sure if I would even survive if I got the police involved. I wanted no where near any cops or to be on radar with them. I guess I was so caught up in my own problems I made myself stop thinking about what Craig had done."

"What made you come forward now?"

"I saw news about the trial in the paper and on TV. I knew the allegations were true. What the victim said was what Craig had told me. I realized how wrong it was to do nothing and let him get away with another assault against a woman."

"Are you getting any breaks on the sentence in your own criminal matter for testifying against Mr. Tarkington?"

"No, I'm not. I'm doing this because I don't want any other women to be sexually assaulted by him."

"No further questions, Your Honor." Megan walked back to the prosecution table and sat down. She cast a glance at Tarkington. He was ashen. Mattingly was staring straight ahead looking stoic. Megan knew he was trying to act as if the lacerating testimony he had just heard hadn't hurt his client.

"Ladies and gentlemen of the jury, this will conclude today's testimony. We will resume trial tomorrow morning at 9 a.m. Court adjourned." Judge Crawford cracked the gavel.

CHAPTER FIFTY SEVEN

The next morning Megan took a seat in the nearly empty courtroom. Promptly at nine, Jack Temple was escorted into the room by his guards and took a seat in the witness stand.

Today was Mattingly's day to try and take apart Temple's testimony and destroy his credibility in front of the jury. Megan has spent most of the night going over in her head all the questions she anticipated Mattingly would ask Temple on cross examination and how to respond on her redirect if Mattingly managed to draw any blood

"You may proceed, Mr. Mattingly," Judge Crawford said.

Brockton Mattingly walked up to the witness stand, stood right in front of Jack Temple, and placed both hands on his hips. "How many years did you say you could be facing in your criminal matter?"

"Thirty," Temple said softly.

"Thirty years? That's a long time isn't it, Mr. Temple." Mattingly rubbed his chin. "How old are you?"

"Thirty-one."

"So you would lose quite a chunk of your life if you are convicted."

Temple nodded. "Yes, sir. I would."

"From your testimony, it sounds like you're risking your life by testifying against the drug ring dealers."

"That's correct."

"I assume that you're willing to do just about anything right now to save you from serving thirty years in prison."

"Anything that is legal, sir."

Mattingly smiled. "Would you agree with me that Mr. Tarkington's case is a very high profile one?"

"It appears so." Temple leaned back in the chair.

"You're telling this jury that you're getting no breaks in your criminal matter from testifying against Mr. Tarkington."

"That's correct."

"You are doing this simply to help right a wrong, so to speak."

"Yes."

Mattingly walked back and stood in front of the defense table. "Your testimony is that Mr. Tarkington has told you that he committed what you believe to be a reprehensible offense against Ms. Hatfield."

"Yes sir."

Mattingly took Temple through his testimony about the incidents he described involving Tarkington and the other women, asking Temple a seemingly never ending series of questions about the other incidents.

"You feel those women were harmed as well, is that correct?"

"Yes sir, I do."

"And these alleged incidents occurred over a period of time, starting several years ago?"

"Yes, sir."

Mattingly made a sweeping motion with his arms toward the jurors. "You're telling this jury that you stood by while the other offenses that you say occurred happened, and did nothing. You didn't go to the authorities or make a police report? Did you do that, Mr. Temple?"

Temple leaned back in his chair, crossed his arms and shook his head. "No, I didn't."

"Were you in trouble with the authorities over this criminal matter when these other offenses allegedly occurred?"

"No."

Mattingly cut a glance at the jury. "So you did *nothing* to help these other women who you claim were victims of Mr. Tarkington. But now you want to come forward for Lucy Hatfield. Do you know Lucy Hatfield?"

"No sir, I don't."

Mattingly sat down at the defense table. "Would you agree with me that the People would have a feather in their cap if they could convict Mr. Tarkington?"

Megan jumped up. "Objection, Your Honor. It is irrelevant what the People

want or don't want regarding the defendant."

"Objection sustained." Judge Crawford let out a small sigh. "Next question, Mr. Mattingly."

"So this is the only time you've decided to come forward and do something to report Mr. Tarkington. Now, when you're facing thirty years in prison."

"That's correct."

"And you're telling the jury that you're getting no break from the authorities for testifying against Mr. Tarkington."

"That's what I am saying."

Mattingly shoved himself away from the table and tipped the chair back.

"You claim you walked in on Mr. Tarkington and a woman on your boat."

"Yes. A young woman."

"You don't know what was going on in the room before you opened the door and saw them, do you, Mr. Temple?"

"No."

"Would it surprise you to know that when Mr. Tarkington came back from the bathroom he caught this woman rifling through his wallet trying to steal money from him?"

"All I know is what I saw and it didn't look like it had anything to do with the young girl going through his wallet."

"But you agree, there could have been something else going on before you walked in."

"I'd be really surprised. I know what I saw. Mr. Tarkington had his pants off." Temple crossed his arms.

"Bottom line, Mr. Temple, you claim you were so concerned about these other alleged victims but you only became concerned enough to come forward and try and help another alleged victim—Ms. Hatfield-- when you got in trouble. Now you are all on board to try and pin a false allegation against Mr. Tarkington to save your own hide."

Megan bounded up from the chair. "Objection, Your Honor. The question is argumentative and counsel is testifying."

"Objection sustained. Move on, Mr. Mattingly."

Mattingly cast a disbelieving glance at Temple. "No further questions, Your Honor."

Judge Crawford looked at Megan. "Any other witnesses for the People?"

"No, Your Honor. The People rest."

Judge Crawford glanced at the clock. "Very well then. Counsel, be prepared for your final arguments. The court will adjourn until tomorrow morning at 9 a.m."

Megan watched the jurors walk out of the courtroom slowly, heads down, no expression on their faces.

CHAPTER FIFTY EIGHT

Megan set her briefcase down by the desk in her office, kicked off her shoes, and flopped down in her chair. It was over. Well, almost over. Closing arguments had begun at 9:30 a.m. and had taken over two hours for both sides to complete. The judge had said that lunch would be brought to the jury and that they would be given time to eat before they started deliberation. She cast a glance at the clock. It was a little after noon. She wondered how long it would take the jury to render a verdict.

She leaned back in her chair and stretched. She was bone tired from the stress and strain of the trial. In the courtroom she had to be aware of what was going on at every moment, listening to every word a witness said, observing the jury, keeping ahead of the defense and their next move, especially with a seasoned trial lawyer like Mattingly who knew every angle of how to try a case and put his client in the best light.

She heard a tap on the door. "Come in."

Eric entered the room with a large pizza box. Lucy followed him carrying a six pack of Pepsi. "Lunch is served," Eric said, placing the box on Megan's desk and opening it. The room filled with the aroma of pizza. Lucy put the Pepsi down next to the pizza and sat in one of the chairs in front of Megan's desk.

"I'm starving. Breakfast wore off before I even started my closing argument," Megan said with a laugh. She twirled her chair around, opened the credenza behind the desk, and pulled out some paper plates, knives, and forks.

Eric cut the pizza, scooped out a big piece, put it on a paper plate, and slid it over to Megan. He gave Lucy a piece and cut himself one. For several moments the room was silent as they sat eating.

"How do you feel the trial went?" Eric took a napkin and wiped his mouth.

"I think it went great." Megan rapped her knuckles on top of the desk. "Knock wood."

She looked at Lucy. She had only taken a couple of bites of pizza.

"Are you ok?"

Lucy said nothing for several seconds. "I'm just worried. You never know. Look at all the women who've tried to come forward and make men accountable for sexually assaulting them and gotten nowhere." She shrugged. "And I made the huge mistake of lying about cheating the first time I took the bar exam and made myself look like a liar in front of the jury."

"The fact that you owned up to your mistake probably impressed the jury; it usually does. Hopefully we repaired the damage."

Lucy said nothing.

Megan picked up her can of Pepsi and opened it. She knew Lucy was right. Truth be told, she was also concerned about how much damage Lucy's lie had done to the People's case. She had done everything she could to rehabilitate Lucy's credibility in front of the jury and now all they could do was wait and see if it had worked.

"I think you covered every base you could and did an excellent job presenting the case," Eric said.

Megan thanked him. Since the charges had been filed she had gone over Lucy's case in her mind hundreds of times. She had no clue what she could have done to present it any better than she had

Lucy nodded. "You did a great job, Megan."

"I think the jury tracked with your closing argument and were really interested," Eric said.

Megan knew from her years of practicing law that you had to keep the jury's attention and make sure you didn't lose it or confuse them. She had started her closing argument by reminding the jurors that Lucy tutored Tarkington various times at the library and he had never made any advances toward her then.

"Lucy Hatfield's life changed the night she agreed to meet the defendant at his apartment for a tutoring session," Megan had said, then deliberately paused.

After that she'd recounted to the jury Lucy's testimony about Tarkington's brutal attack, how Lucy had done everything in her power to fight him off but wasn't strong enough. She reminded them of how Lucy had completed a rape kit test and been very cooperative with the authorities. She went over the testimony of the ER doctor who treated Lucy on the night of the rape, how he had found vaginal tearing when Lucy came to the hospital on the night in question, how he did not believe Lucy was lying about what had occurred and that he considered what he had observed during his examination to be consistent with her allegations.

The jurors were completely focused on Megan during her entire closing argument.

She knew the weakest part of the case was the fact that Lucy had lied about why she had delayed taking the bar exam. When she came to that part of her closing argument she walked up to the jury box, placed her hands on the railing, and looked each juror directly in the eyes. She told them in no uncertain terms that Lucy had done something wrong—very wrong—in not telling the truth about why she delayed taking the bar exam.

"You heard Lucy take full responsibility for not telling you the truth. " She paused. "She came clean to everyone here even though she knew she could be charged with perjury. She made a mistake and owned that she did. But Lucy is not on trial here. Lucy is the victim, not the perpetrator, and the charge being weighed here is rape, not lying, something far more serious."

Megan lowered her eyes and paused, then looked at the jurors again. "Jack Temple risked his safety to come to this courtroom and testify against Craig Tarkington, his childhood friend." She reminded the jury of what Jack

Temple had said about the Tarkington assaulting other women and emphasized that Temple wasn't promised any breaks in his criminal case for testifying in Lucy's matter—that the only reason he came forward was that he knew Craig Tarkington had to be stopped.

At the end of her closing argument she sat down, feeling good about what she'd said and fairly confident about their chances of getting a guilty verdict.

Mattingly, in typical defense lawyer mode had spent his time during closing argument emphasizing that the People had the complete burden of proof to convince the jury that Craig Tarkington was guilty of the charges beyond a reasonable doubt and reminding the jury of what a high standard of proof that was.

"The People cannot present any objective evidence that a rape occurred that night," Mattingly told the jury. "There is no evidence backed by science to prove that these allegations are correct. Nothing." He opened his arms and shrugged.

He went on to say that the only thing the People had to rely on was the testimony of Lucy Hatfield—a liar. Mattingly hammered the issue of the importance of credibility in a witness. He acknowledged that Lucy admitted she lied and took responsibility.

"But it took the defense impeaching her testimony to get her to acknowledge the truth. She had no intention of telling anyone what really happened with her law school exam until she was pushed against the wall with nowhere else to go. Lucy Hatfield's credibility is the foundation of the People's case. Her testimony can destroy my client's life. You, as the jury, have to decide whether this time she is telling the truth or she's lying again."

Megan could still feel how Mattingly's words hung in the air. Just thinking about what he'd said made her nauseous now. It was true, whether the People won all boiled down to whether the jury believed Lucy.

Her phone rang now, jolting her back to the moment. "Hello."

Eric and Lucy stared at her as she sat listening and said nothing for a few moments. Then she thanked the caller and hung up.

She looked at Eric and Lucy. "The jury has reached a verdict." Megan glanced at the clock. The jury had been out four hours.

There wasn't a single empty seat in the courtroom. The reporters who hadn't arrived early enough to get a seat were standing against the walls lining the galley. This was the moment everyone had been waiting for. The courtroom was electric with anticipation.

"All rise," the bailiff said.

A wave of motion could be felt as everyone in the courtroom stood. Chairs squeaked and benches creaked. Megan watched the jurors file into the jury box and take their seats. They made no eye contact with her or Mattingly.

"I understand that the jury has rendered a verdict," Judge Crawford said. "Is that correct, Mr. Foreman?"

Megan watched as juror number nine stood and looked at Judge Crawford. Megan had suspected from the start that this man would be elected foreman. He was tall and had a commanding presence. During jury selection she had gotten the distinct impression from his answers and demeanor that he was a leader.

"Yes, Your Honor, "the jury foreman said now. He gave the jury ballot to the bailiff who passed it to the judge.

"The audience and the prosecution may be seated. Mr. Tarkington and Mr. Mattingly please remain standing, "the judge said.

Megan looked around. There were eight security guards strategically placed at different points around the courtroom.

"Order shall be maintained as the court reads the verdict," Judge Crawford said, peering over the top of his glasses at the crowd. Carefully, the judge opened the sealed envelope and took out a piece of paper. He unfolded it and read its contents.

Megan cut a glance at Tarkington. He looked white as a sheet. Mattingly was standing with his hands folded in front of him.

Judge Crawford, still holding the jury ballot, turned and looked at Craig Tarkington. "The jury finds the defendant Craig Tarkington guilty of the rape of Lucy Hatfield."

A cacophony of voices broke out in the courtroom. Some people were cheering; others were angry and yelling.

Judge Crawford slammed the gavel down. "Order!"

Megan watched as the guards rushed up to the people who were yelling and tried to quiet them. One lady continued to cheer despite the guards' attempt to settle her down and was ushered out of the courtroom.

Judge Crawford banged the gavel several more times. "Guards, remove anyone else who continues to disrupt this court!" he growled.

Megan looked at Tarkington. He had his head down and his hands on the table, almost as if he was bracing himself. Mattingly was resting one hand on his back, saying something into his ear. Tarkington shook his head in response.

Megan looked for Lucy in the galley. She was seated next to Carol McGuire, the victim's advocate. Tears were streaming down her face. She looked at Megan and mouthed, "Thank you."

Once order was restored Judge Crawford continued. "Mr. Tarkington, you are hereby remanded to the county jail pending your sentencing hearing which is now set for November 10."

"Your Honor!" Mattingly said. "My client is no flight risk and there is no need for him to be remanded to the jail pending sentencing."

Judge Crawford turned to Mattingly. "Your client has great assets that he could use if he chose to flee the jurisdiction. This is the court's policy. Court adjourned." Before Judge Crawford was even off the bench a crush of reporters began running out of the courtroom, reporting the verdict on their cell phones.

EPILOGUE

It was a beautiful summer day with not a cloud in the sky. Megan stood on the sidewalk feeling the warm breeze wash over her.

She studied the front of the house. With the help of a realtor and a good contractor, the old Victorian house had been renovated into a beautiful office building. In April, six months after the Tarkington trial was over, she had begun looking for office space. She had spent ten years working in an office in a brand-new building with a spectacular view of the D.C. skyline, and now she wanted something different— something real.

After a few weeks of searching, the realtor had shown her this house on the outskirts of D.C. The area was part of an old neighborhood with historic homes that dated back to the early 1900s. She had always loved the look of older houses with their large porches and beautiful woodwork. When she saw this house she fell in love. And with twelve spacious rooms, it would work perfectly as a law office.

She smiled as she looked at the names etched on the big front window. O'Reilly and Hatfield Attorneys at Law. She unlocked the front door and walked into the large lobby, with its high ceiling and beautiful woodwork. Today it was decorated with five large vases holding freshly cut flowers. The vases were strategically place around the room. A drink table bearing an assortment of sparkling water, soft drinks, and wine stood against one wall and next to that was a table with an array of appetizers. In a little while the office would be filled with people celebrating the opening of the new firm.

Megan made her way back to her own office, sat down behind the desk, and thought back over the past year. It had been a long haul since she and two other senior lawyers, Kate Williams and Christie Charles, and two experienced paralegals, Lisa Remy and Jill Sandefur, had been let go from their jobs at Tarkington, Wagner, Krieg and DeVoe.

Once the jury returned a guilty verdict against Tarkington, the media went wild and had a field day. The Tarkington name was bantered about from newspaper to scandal sheet. Megan felt confident that the Tarkington family had never known such embarrassment. They had always prided themselves on the reputation they'd built, both in society and in the high echelons of the law. The rape conviction had taken a wrecking ball to everything they had worked to achieve. Megan didn't know what they were doing to try to recover but she was sure they were doing some type of damage control that probably included Supreme Justice Tarkington.

The court had given Tarkington ten years in prison, five years over the minimum sentence. The sentencing hearing had been a media circus, with reporters from all over the country employing all types of tactics in an effort to get the best seats in the galley. Extra security had been hired and placed inside and outside the courtroom. After the sentence was handed down and the court was adjourned the media scrambled to take photos of Tarkington being led away in chains and shackles. Megan couldn't get out of her mind how haggard he looked. Without his expensive suits and perfect haircuts he looked like any other criminal defendant.

After he had been taken out of the courtroom, Lucy, who was sitting in the galley, had run up to Megan and hugged her. Megan was thrilled for the victory, not just for Lucy but for every other woman out there who had been sexually assaulted by a man.

The lawsuit Megan and the other women had filed against the firm for age discrimination was set for trial four months after Tarkington's criminal trial ended. Not long after Tarkington's conviction and sentencing and in the heat of the media frenzy, Megan had received a call from Justice Tarkington. He'd wanted to set up a meeting with her and the Tarkington family attorney to discuss the pending discrimination lawsuit. Megan wasn't totally surprised when he called. Justice Tarkington was a shrewd man and a politician to the bone. He knew the importance of damage control. The Tarkington family couldn't take much more bad publicity.

Megan, Christie, Kate, Lisa, and Jill met with Justice Tarkington along with the firm's attorney and managing partner. After several hours, an agreement was reached that all the women would receive back pay from the date they had been let go. They would also receive the pay they would have earned until the age they would have been eligible to retire—including all bonuses and full retirement. This offer was all subject to the women entering a confidentiality agreement not to disclose anything—including that they had been offered a settlement or accepted one. The court records would be sealed from the public so no one would ever know what had happened. The settlement agreement was signed by all the women and made part of the court record.

Megan leaned back in the chair and sat listening to the silence. She thought about the moment she'd met Lucy in the coffee shop and about how much admiration she had for her. Lucy had been attacked by Craig Tarkington, a man from a powerful and politically connected family, and had shown the strength to come forward and ask the law to make him accountable—something she, Megan, had not had the courage to do herself years ago. Lucy had stood tall and faced the media scrutiny and the character assassination by Brockton Mattingly, Tarkington's attorney. Lucy had made a mistake in not telling the truth to the jury about why she hadn't taken the bar exam sooner and had almost paid a huge price for it, but fortunately the jury accepted her apology and believed that she was telling the truth about Tarkington.

Lucy's life had turned around even more now that Lauren was medically stable. Thanks to the wonderful doctors at Children's National, Lauren was living a life like any other four-and-a-half-year-old girl.

Lucy had taken the bar exam last July and passed with flying colors. Soon after that Megan had made a decision. She asked Lucy out for lunch and invited her to join her, Kate Williams and Christie Charles in a new law practice Megan was forming. Lucy had been so happy she had tears in her eyes and accepted without a moments hesitation.

Tarkington was serving his sentence at a prison in upstate New York. The facility housed all level of prisoners, from those with first-time offenses to seasoned career criminals. Megan had heard that he had been segregated from the general prison population due to threats by other inmates.

Right after the verdict came in, Mattingly had been on TV announcing that he would immediately be filing an appeal for his client. Megan had watched one of his interviews. He was full of righteous indignation, but she knew he was mostly putting on a show for the media.

Megan looked at her phone. It was a quarter to twelve. She heard the front door open and people start to come in. The quiet office began filling up with the sound of talk and laughter. She walked out to the lobby.

"There she is!" Lucy said. She was standing at the food table setting down a fruit bowl. She smiled happily at Megan.

Megan smiled back and began walking around the room greeting the guests. It seemed like there was an endless flow of people streaming in through the front door. Since all the publicity around the Tarkington conviction, she had become a champion of women's causes. From the looks of the people in the lobby, she had garnered the attention of all the major players in the women's organizations in D.C.

"Megan!" someone called. She turned around and saw Eric threading his way through the crowd. Eric had just come back from vacation in the Caribbean and had a great suntan. He looked better and more rested than she had seen him in years. At the sight of him her heart beat a little faster. She had driven him to the airport for his flight to Barbados, and as they were standing at the curb beside his suitcase, there was a moment when they looked at each other silently and she'd thought that he was going to kiss her. Then the moment passed. As she watched him disappear through the sliding glass doors into the airport, she wasn't sure, but she thought she might be feeling disappointed he hadn't kissed her.

He came up to her and hugged her. "What a turn-out," he said.

"Isn't it wonderful?" She looked across the room and saw Lucy serving guests drinks and appetizers. Lauren was by her side helping. Megan couldn't believe how much Lauren had grown. She was no longer a little girl confined to a hospital bed. She was a happy playful child with a presence that lit up the room.

"It's about time," Eric said looking at the antique grandfather clock in the corner of the room. Megan had gotten the clock a couple of months ago at an auction in New York. It had cost a small fortune but she didn't care—she had always loved grandfather clocks.

She walked to the center of the lobby and motioned for Lucy, Christie, Lisa, Kate, and Jill to join her.

"If I may have everyone's attention," Megan said, raising her voice over the laughter and conversation. She waited for the noise to subside. "I would like to thank everyone for coming here today to help us celebrate a very special occasion."

A ripple of applause flowed through the room.

"What is the saying? Enjoy the journey? Well, it has been quite a journey. If you had told me four years ago that I would have been trying a high profile criminal case and after that opening my own law firm, I would have laughed. I had no intention of doing either one—that is, until I met a woman named Lucy Hatfield." Megan paused and looked at Lucy, then looked toward the back of the room and saw news reporters with their cameras perched on their shoulders filming her as she spoke.

"Today we are here to celebrate the opening of a new law office. A law office dedicated to serving the needs and protecting the rights of women. O'Reilly and Hatfield's sole focus is providing high quality representation for women from all walks of life—and in all areas of the law. Megan looked at Lucy. "It has been an honor to serve as the prosecutor in your case and to join with you as a partner in this law firm."

Lucy walked forward smiling, her face radiating happiness and hugged Megan. After several moments Megan pulled back, looked at Lucy and grinned. The air was electric with emotion.

Manufactured by Amazon.ca
Bolton, ON